CW01432723

BOTTICELLI'S INFERNO

By Stefano Impellitteri

To those who
open their eyes every morning
and start fighting

Thank you!

The bathroom door is ajar,
the rhythmic ticking of a drop breaks the silence.
Twilight and surreal calm.
The bathtub, filled with water and blood, is a black mirror.
Beneath the surface, Elisabetta's hair floats like mist.

Eli, why did you do it? Where did I go wrong?
What was your true hell?
Your Inferno.

Part
I
PARADISE

1.1

Florence, March 2023

Lorenzo stepped through the doors of the police station, his bag knocking against the frame. Damn. He hoped nothing had broken. He really needed to be more careful with his drawing gear.

The officer in the glass booth glanced over the top of the *Corriere Fiorentino*. He smiled and nodded toward the chairs in the lobby. "Good morning, Berti."

"Good morning." Lorenzo sat down, resting the bag on his lap. He opened it—everything was fine. The graphics tablet was intact—a lucky break, considering it had cost as much as a Cubist painting.

He'd bought it dreaming of masterpieces. Instead…

But he'd made his peace with it. Drawing wasn't just about drawing lines—it was about making them speak. Except when it came to composite sketches, where every face had to be neutral, stripped of emotion. Maddening work— empty eyes and shallow portraits dredged from the blurred memories of unlucky victims.

But that was the job. Art didn't pay the bills.

Not his art, anyway.

Beyond the glass entrance, an ambulance pulled up, lights flashing. The officer looked up and stepped out of the booth.

"Here they are." He folded the paper and dropped it on the coffee table. On the front page, a photo showed a sculptor beside a statue of the Virgin Mary, tears of blood on its cheeks—yet another scam dressed up as a miracle.

Superstition—cheap tricks for free publicity. Faith and art had always shared a bond, and there was something spiritual in that union. But blood flowing from stone? That wasn't God's work.

Maybe they'd called him in to sketch a con artist. Or maybe just another drunk brawler caught in an alley without cameras.

Two paramedics opened the rear doors of the ambulance and helped down a young girl with curly hair pulled back. She leaned on them, unsteady. Mascara streaked under her eyes, blending with the bruises on her battered face. Sixteen, maybe. A kid. Poor thing—she was in bad shape.

The officer unlocked the electronic door, sighing as he bit his lip. "Mr. Berti, do a good job. That girl—Martina—is my daughter's age. Let's hope she remembers the details of that bastard's face."

That bastard... Lorenzo nodded. It was never easy to coax images from someone who had been through a traumatic event. Violence came in many forms—but one in particular was the hardest to face.

He tucked the graphics tablet under his arm, hoping it was just a robbery. "What did they do to her?"

The officer shook his head, eyes down. "Rape."

Oh God—of all things.

He froze, his heart heavy.

The girl entered, supported by the paramedics. She limped, each step drawing a small whimper. She kept her gaze low. "I'm not crazy—I'm telling you it wasn't a man," she whimpered, shoulders hunched as if she were cold.

The paramedic gently stroked her hand. "You're right. Only an animal would do something like that."

"That's not what I mean." She tried to pull away, but staggered. "I mean it wasn't… human. It was something else."

Poor kid—still in shock. She passed close by, and for an instant Lorenzo caught her green eyes, bright with tears between the bruises.

His throat tightened.

He looked away, clutching his graphics tablet.

The officer led her through the first door and, with a nod, motioned Lorenzo inside. "Berti, with this girl, do your best."

Of course—his best.

It was going to be torture for them both.

From the room came sobs. Lorenzo started to rise, but his legs wouldn't move. Those cries gripped his chest, and he knew they wouldn't stop soon. Worse, he would have to turn her sobs into a portrait, forcing her to relive, again and again, the memory of the eyes of the man who had violated her.

Then the nose. The ears. The sneer.

The details.

It had to be done. He drew in a breath. "Martina, right?"

The officer confirmed with a nod. Lorenzo stood and stepped into the office. The smooth linoleum floor caught the glare of the neon lights. The air smelled of stale coffee and the faint disinfectant clinging to her wounds from the hospital. She sat hunched at the desk, elbows planted on its surface. Her curly hair was messy, damp with sweat, gathered in a loose bun. Eyes downcast.

15

Lorenzo wanted to leave. Asking her about the violence she'd endured felt like violating himself, too. But that bastard had to be found.

He walked around the desk, pulled a chair closer, and forced his voice to stay calm. "Hi, Martina. May I?"

She didn't look up. "It won't do any good. I swear to you, it wasn't human..." A nervous twitch made her lip quiver.

She was clearly in shock; this would be a difficult session. She needed reassurance. "My pencil can draw anything. If it wasn't human, together we'll figure out what it was."

She stayed frozen, giving no sign she was ready to talk. She needed another push. Lorenzo bent down until his eyes were level with hers. When she finally met his gaze, he softened his voice to a whisper, drawing her in. "I'm on your side."

He stayed there, watching her.

The girl nodded.

Good. A first connection. He sat down. No handshake — no contact. Right now, she had to hate men. "My name's Lorenzo. I'm going to ask you a few questions. Don't worry if you can't answer — I'll help you."

He went through the procedure in his head: first, *create a safe environment. Lighting — adequate.* Temperature — comfortable. No weapons in sight.

Avoid distractions: remove images of faces that might influence memory. No photographs on the walls — good. But a policeman was leaning in from the doorway. "Could you leave us alone?"

The officer stepped back. Silence settled in, heavy, broken only by the girl's ragged breathing. *Isolation and reassurance —* avoid influences, let her know it was normal to recall only fragments. "We'll get to your attacker's face little by little. I'll ask questions to help me draw his face. We'll catch him."

The girl slapped the table. "Who—what are you going to catch? I told you it wasn't a man—will you believe me?" She rubbed her hand, then clasped both together, twisting her fingers for comfort. A wooden bead bracelet slipped down her sleeve and, trembling, she began to thumb the beads—a rosary, complete with a crucifix.

That agitation had to be addressed or they'd get nowhere. He couldn't contradict her—*only use open-ended questions.* Lorenzo picked up his stylus. "What made you think it wasn't human?"

"It laughed." Another twitch pulled at her mouth.

"And why did that make you think it wasn't—"

"It laughed without taking a breath. Without stopping to breathe while it was abusing me. It just kept laughing, without a pause, the whole time. As if it didn't need air. It wasn't a man."

Raped without ever escaping the sound of her attacker's laughter—the thought alone was revolting. In moments like that, perception could be distorted; more likely, the endless laughter was a trick of trauma. "Did you notice anything else?"

"Plenty." She slid the rosary off her wrist and gripped it in both hands. "It laughed and talked at the same time, like there were two people inside it. Its voice was doubled, metallic. And its eyes... Saint Jerome, help me!" Sob after sob shook her. She clutched the beads and her lips moved in a spasmodic prayer, fingering them one by one.

Unfortunately for her, she'd just given him something he couldn't ignore. "You mentioned the eyes." He switched on the graphics tablet and, with a tap of the stylus, opened the folder of reference stock images. He turned the screen toward her.

"Were they elongated or deep-set? Do you see anything here that comes close?"

He waited, patient.

This called for delicacy—the kind you need when you know you're treading on fragile ground. *No suggestive hints*: use neutral words, build questions from the witness's own language. If only she would give him something to work with.

She shook her head. "I... I don't know. The light kept me from seeing their shape."

During the assault, she must have been blinded by a light source. "From the chandelier?"

"No. From the attacker himself. They lit up, with white flashes." She didn't blink, a thin veil of madness in her gaze. "And he was always talking to the cat."

"A cat?"

"Yes. A black cat." Another spasm jerked her mouth.

Lorenzo kept his face stiff to hide his skepticism; the bond of trust had to hold. Understandable—the poor girl wasn't lucid. Her tics said more than her words: at this rate, they'd get nowhere.

He set the tablet aside. This was one of those cases where rushing a composite sketch would be less than ideal.

They knocked on the open door. A bespectacled man with a shoulder bag waved in greeting. "Have you already started? Sorry I'm late. I'm a technician with the RIS forensic unit; I've been assigned to help produce the composite."

And who was this—some new sketch artist? He was wrecking everything. "We were already at work. I'm Lorenzo Berti, and this assignment was supposed to be mine."

"And... how's it going?" The man glanced at the still-blank graphics tablet. He grimaced, stepped inside, and pulled a laptop from his bag. "I need to test an artificial intelligence program. It'll generate the image in a few minutes."

A shiver of irritation ran down Lorenzo's spine. Artificial intelligence again—were they trying to replace him even in forensic sketching? He opened his mouth to protest, but caught the girl's eyes, which flicked uneasily between the two of them.

If there was a victim here, it was her.

Starting an argument now would have been tactless—it wasn't the time. And besides, his own drawing was going nowhere. He gave Martina a faint smile and stood. "This technician knows what he's doing. Let's see what happens, all right?"

She nodded, lips pressed tight. "Could you first contact one of my brothers in faith? I'm drawing close to a Christian order devoted to Girolamo Savonarola, and I feel the need to confess."

The man addressed her directly. "We'll contact them soon." He hadn't even introduced himself—to her or to Lorenzo. He took the chair and typed something on the keyboard. "I've already pasted in my colleagues' report. Just answer the questions that pop up."

On the dark-toned screen, a cursor blinked beneath the words: *When you're ready, we'll begin.*

Given her state of mind, the program wouldn't get anything useful. Lorenzo crossed his arms and let a half-smile tug at his lips; he wanted to see how it would handle a wanted man whom the victim claimed was possessed by the devil.

The technician rotated the laptop toward the girl and stood. "Shall we grab a coffee?"

"But…" Lorenzo's eyes narrowed. "We're leaving her alone?"

"Of course—the AI will handle everything." He leaned in, lowering his voice. "After what she's been through, she'll find it easier to talk about such delicate matters with a machine." He headed down the hall with a police officer toward the coffee machine.

Such an impersonal approach was unacceptable. Lorenzo let them file past and walked the other way, toward the water dispenser by the entrance. Artificial intelligence. The world was moving too fast for him. He slid a plastic cup free, set it under the spout, and let a thread of water run. The water cooler gurgled with bubbles inside.

From the room came no more whimpering—just the rapid clatter of keys. Unbelievable. He was on the verge of being replaced by a machine… He sipped from the cup and returned to the waiting area.

On the coffee table lay a flyer showing Botticelli's *Venus* recast as an influencer taking a selfie—hijacked for an ad campaign. Who had thought to cheapen one of the Renaissance's greatest treasures in such a trite way? Probably a marketing intern, egged on by AI.

From Martina's room came a cry. "Saint Jerome, help me! It's him! It's his face!"

Lorenzo crushed the flyer in his hand and leapt to his feet. He ran toward the office. From the opposite direction, the technician was hurrying too, a tiny cup of coffee in hand, dark drops spattering the floor behind him. They entered.

The laptop screen faced the doorway, as if the girl had turned it so she wouldn't have to look at it. The man's face was rendered with startling clarity, almost photographic. His sharp features were chiseled. His eyes, elongated at the outer corners, gleamed with a malevolent intensity. Thick, arched brows gave him a stern look, while the line of an aquiline nose divided his hollow cheeks symmetrically.

Martina wept with her hands over her face, the rosary pressed to her forehead, rocking as she prayed. The reconstruction was flawless, with no detail left to chance—more lifelike and vivid than any human artist could produce, and completed in minutes.

The technician pointed at the screen. "Your man." There was a trace of satisfaction in his voice.

Lorenzo swallowed his dismay; even he couldn't help but admire the work the AI had done, a face so real it seemed as if the portrait might breathe. The fact that they had a composite was excellent news. But proof that his profession had become obsolete—that was anything but encouraging.

In his palm he still clutched the crumpled flyer with Botticelli's heretical photomontage. There was only one place he could hope to find a little peace: before the original *Venus*. His job was on borrowed time, and, like a retiree whiling away the hours watching roadwork, it was time to surrender to melancholy—at the Uffizi Gallery.

Uffizi Gallery

The advantage of being an artist in Florence, the City of the Lily, was having the world's greatest masterpieces only steps away. If beauty truly lies in the eye of the beholder, then

Florence itself becomes both brush and canvas, inviting the gaze to linger.

Lorenzo looked again down the long corridor. Every step through the Uffizi was a step into the history of art. The Botticelli collection had a line that spilled out onto the street; it was moving quickly, which was never a good sign. How much did visitors miss when they spared only a fleeting glance at such priceless works?

Often, Lorenzo had gone into a museum just to admire a single painting. It was like walking into a library — you don't read every book. You choose one.

He stopped before the most extraordinary room in the entire Uffizi: the Tribuna, Francesco I de' Medici's dream shaped in stone, marble, and light. A red cord barred the entrance, and rightly so. Even the floor was a masterpiece — an intricate sunburst of precious stones and multicolored marble. The octagonal structure symbolized the union between the earthly and the divine — assuming the divine truly existed.

His mind drifted back to Martina's words, to her faith and her terror at having been raped by a demon who laughed without ever taking a breath and spoke to hellish cats. Lorenzo was a skeptic by nature, yet he couldn't deny that something mystical dwelled in the human spirit. Art itself would be meaningless without it.

The marble's veins drew intricate patterns under the soft light, conjuring shapes and associations. Unease stirred in him again, still raw from his encounter with the girl. Two dark specks on a tile seemed like eyes, a face taking shape around them — eerily like the one the AI had generated. Lorenzo swallowed, a knot of fear tightening in his stomach. He needed to calm himself.

But the morning's account kept circling in his mind. The sharp-featured face from the composite sketch seemed to watch him from every corner of the room. Something was building inside—an unfamiliar anxiety, the feeling of falling into an unexplored abyss. Then came other faces, unfamiliar, and finally a cascade of hair like Elisabetta's. His Elisabetta, the one he had lost.

A roar, a sudden chill, and a deep, inhuman laugh rose in his head, like an echo made of countless voices. He wasn't breathing. What was happening to him?

He forced himself to breathe and turned: a German tourist had stumbled, his group's laughter booming up to the high ceilings.

No. He had to calm down. He was letting his imagination run away with him.

Time to freshen up and steady himself.

He walked on, past the line for the Botticelli collection. A young woman in an elegant skirt suit—the skirt a pencil cut—was speaking with a gallery attendant. Her alarmed voice came fast, edged with a French accent. Something about her tugged at him. Lorenzo stopped, staring.

The black hair with bluish glints, the poised stance, the intensity of her gaze… Again. She reminded him of Elisabetta.

Not in appearance so much as in presence—that intangible resemblance you can't quite capture with your eyes, yet feel all the same.

She raised her voice again. "I'm telling you, he was escorted to the office by one of his colleagues, dressed like you. He couldn't have just vanished!" Her full lips pulled back from white teeth she was gnashing in anger. Bluish capillaries showed through her pale skin.

Her skin seemed almost transparent—translucent—just like Elisabetta's when he found her.

Dead. In a tub brimming with water and blood.

A laugh welled up from deep inside; Lorenzo shook his head and raked his fingers through his hair. He needed to wash his face, pull himself together.

He moved down the corridor, turned the corner, leaving behind the line and the furious girl still arguing with the staff. A bathroom—he had to find a bathroom.

Down the stairs, he spotted a sign with an arrow. The queue was so long it blocked the view of the restroom door. Across the way, a wing of the corridor was cordoned off with red tape—maintenance, maybe. A bald usher stepped out of a room; as the door closed on its automatic arm, it revealed a restroom inside. The bald man smiled, slipped into the restricted area, and vanished around the corner.

On one side, the endless queue. On the other, a staff restroom. His breathing was shallow, anxiety rising. He had to get a grip—he'd use the staff bathroom.

He ducked under the red tape. Someone shouted something in German, but he ignored it and stepped inside. The place was empty. A wave of dizziness hit him. He hurried to the sink, turned on the tap, splashed cold water over his face. Better.

He turned off the tap, but the sound of dripping continued. Behind him came a breathy voice—air and soft whimpers.

In the mirror's reflection, a toilet stall door was slowly opening. The sounds came from there—not from inside his head.

He turned, let his fingers brush the cool surface of the door, and pushed it gently. A man lay sprawled in a twisted position on the toilet, head tipped back. Each ragged breath lifted his chest unevenly, as though every gulp of air was a battle. A dark red stain spread across his shirt.

"Help!" Lorenzo lunged toward him, straightened his head, grabbed a wad of toilet paper, and pressed it against the blooming red spot. "Help!"

The man jerked. "*Inferno*. Hell!" A flicker of clarity lit his eyes.

It really was hell today. "Easy, now —"

A spasm. "*Inferno. The door is Mars. The light within the eyes,* Botticelli. *The solution is the light... in the eyes.*" His voice faded into breath. His eyes rolled back, showing only the whites.

Lorenzo stared at him, trying to make sense of the fevered words. The door burst open. An usher rushed in, calling into his walkie-talkie. Behind him, the French girl saw the scene and screamed.

The bald man who had left that bathroom — he had to be the killer. Lorenzo had seen his face. Unless they suspected him first: after all, he'd been with the victim… and he was the only one with the man's blood on him.

1.2

The police had turned the bathroom into a maze of yellow tape and numbered tent cards. Investigators moved around the scene—and the body—in a kind of choreographed dance, snapping photos from every angle.

In the hallway, Lorenzo pinched the bloodstained fabric of his shirt and peeled it from his skin. That metallic scent pulled him back to his first encounter with violent death. It wasn't the first time he'd seen a bloodied corpse, and certainly not the most harrowing.

He had found Elisabetta—dead by her own hand—in the bathtub, back in their university days, less than a year after they had moved in together. He forced the pain of those sad memories back down, but he wasn't the only one carrying grief in that corridor.

A short distance away, seated on the floor and surrounded by paramedics, the young woman in the tailored suit—the same one who had just argued with the gallery attendant—was sipping a glass of water. Lorenzo couldn't guess her connection to the victim: her reaction to the body had been too cool for a lover, yet too raw for a purely professional tie.

"Mr. Berti." The inspector beckoned him over, then turned to the woman. "You as well, Miss Dupont—if you're feeling better."

She rose with effort, her sheath dress clinging to long, slender legs, and stepped closer. A faint scent of cinnamon lifted from her hair.

The inspector nodded toward the stain on Lorenzo's shirt. "Mr. Berti, about your situation…" He looked up at his face and paused, frowning. "Haven't we met?"

"Probably. I'm a forensic illustrator—I often work with law enforcement to reconstruct crime scenes."

"Ah, that explains it. All the better, since, for obvious reasons, you'll have to remain available as a witness." Again, his chin tipped toward the stain.

Lorenzo's first instinct was to cover it. Anxiety tightened in his gut. "You're not saying I'm a suspect, are you?"

"For now, no. A German tourist saw someone dressed as a gallery attendant leave the bathroom before you went in. He's sure no one else came out until security arrived. At present, we haven't found the weapon that killed the victim. If you didn't leave, the real assailant must have taken it."

"And you need a witness?" Lorenzo pointed toward one of the many security cameras. "Don't you already have footage?"

The inspector sighed. "Deleted. All of it."

"What?!" the woman burst out, her French accent breaking through. "This is the Uffizi! How could anyone get into the control room and erase the recordings?"

"They didn't get in. They did it remotely—logged in and wiped the past twenty-four hours. Whoever it was, they're powerful and organized. Help us understand, Miss Dupont."

She said nothing. The faint crinkle of evidence bags filled the silence—a hair, a fiber, a swab soaked in some bodily fluid…

Lorenzo glanced at her. She was watching him, uncertain. After all, he was wearing the victim's blood, and his alibi rested solely on an unnamed witness. He needed to make a connection—just as he did in his work.

He extended his hand. "I haven't yet offered my condolences for your loss. My name is Lorenzo. I have no idea what's going on, but I'll cooperate fully."

Her gaze shifted from his hand to the blood, then to his eyes. She sighed and took it. "Adrienne Dupont. I am… I was Mr. Manfredi's secretary—he was an antique art dealer." She turned to the inspector. "And as I've already said, if you want answers, you'll need to find his notebook."

The inspector patted his jacket and pulled out a pen. "Tell me again what happened."

"The bald man in a gallery attendant's uniform promised Mr. Manfredi a private meeting with the Uffizi's director, and they left together. Left on my own, I chatted briefly with the rest of the staff. They kept insisting they had no bald colleagues, and I lost my temper with them."

True—Lorenzo had seen her arguing. "But what was Manfredi supposed to discuss with the director of the Uffizi?"

"My boss wanted to show him some notes. Recently, he'd been extremely nervous, on edge. He claimed to have found clues about certain missing works—material he refused to share, even with me."

"What works?" The inspector flipped open his notepad, pen poised.

Adrienne's gaze flicked between them, her reluctance plain. "The missing works from Botticelli's *Inferno*."

The victim's last words came back to Lorenzo, pounding through his head in spasms, carried on a thin breath. "He mentioned Botticelli to me, too!"

"What?" Adrienne's eyes widened. "What did he tell you?"

"It was something like... *Inferno. The door is Mars. Botticelli — the solution is the light within the eyes.*" Lorenzo dredged through his old university memories of art history, but nothing came. "You mentioned the missing works. As far as I know, Botticelli's *Abyss of Hell* isn't missing — the map of Dante's *Inferno* is in the Vatican Museums."

Adrienne nodded. "It's not just a work of art. It's something... greater. They didn't realize until 1882 that it was actually the cover for an entire illustrated edition of the *Divine Comedy*, commissioned by the Medici. Some of those drawings have never been found."

It was fascinating — a fusion of art, culture, and mysticism. The inspector kept writing without looking up. "How many are missing?"

"Ten drawings. The last two, it seems, Botticelli never had time to draw. But the real mystery concerns six of the *Inferno drawings* that vanished. Manfredi believed they'd been deliberately made to disappear."

"Made to disappear?" The inspector stopped taking notes. "Why would anyone make six works vanish? Money? The black market?"

Adrienne shook her head. "No. Something else. But to find out, we need Manfredi's notes — and I have no idea where they are."

"He must have said something..."

"Only that he suspected a sect of fanatics who believed those drawings were dangerous to humanity. I never took it seriously—I thought they were just the ramblings of a man obsessed with ancient mysteries. Until now." She fixed her gaze on the empty aluminum coffin near the bathroom. Once the forensics team was finished, it would hold her boss's body.

Hell, the Vatican, fanatical sects… Lorenzo's head was spinning again. He felt the urge to splash water on his face. It felt like coming full circle—this wasn't even the first time he'd run into religious fanaticism. He'd faced it before, with Elisabetta.

She'd been the one to ask him to save her from her parents—rigid zealots who had forced her into an unhappy life. Her cloistered upbringing had left her with a deep sense of inadequacy. In a kind of bitter reversal, once free of their control she'd been drawn to the opposite extreme: the occult and Satanism. Until her suicide.

Lorenzo rubbed his eyes and peeled his damp shirt away from his chest. The sleeve tugged at his shoulder. A pale yellow, resin-like crust stained the fabric where the victim had grabbed him.

He'd seen that dried gelatin before. "Adrienne, before coming to the Uffizi, did you visit any kind of lab?"

She tilted her head, puzzled. "Yes. We went to the museum's restoration labs, the ones near the Boboli Gardens. Why?"

Lorenzo pointed at his sleeve. "This is dammar resin. It's used for finishing and restoring drawings—comes in pebble-like lumps, melts with heat. Manfredi must have transferred it to me when he grabbed me during his last convulsions. Check his hand for residue—it's likely he dipped his notes into one of those resin buckets."

The inspector clicked his pen twice and walked over to the corpse. He spoke quietly to a colleague in protective gear, then looked back and nodded. They had a lead.

"You again?" The bespectacled AI technician was heading toward them, giving Lorenzo a sidelong look. "This time I'm sure they called me just for the composite sketch." He held up his laptop case.

A sour prickle of irritation stung Lorenzo, but there was also a flicker of satisfaction. "I'm the one who saw the suspect—I'll draw the portrait myself. No machine needed."

The inspector stepped between them. "And once you've changed, I'd like you to join Miss Dupont and me at the labs. I have a few questions—and in this case, a forensic artist could be very useful."

❦

In the back seat of the unmarked service car, Lorenzo watched Adrienne's reflection in the window. Her presence seemed to fill the entire interior.

She shifted slightly, smoothing the fabric of her sheath dress, which clung like a second skin. Elisabetta used to do that too—his former girlfriend had loved wearing daring clothes, especially after breaking free from the suffocating grip of her parents.

Yet, even in their new life together, she'd never found happiness. Wild mood swings—now anger, now euphoria. An obsession with horror and the occult... Lorenzo drew a slow breath, as if searching for air. It felt like yesterday. The fact that she'd taken her own life right after leaving her family had made him the target of unfounded accusations. And now, it was happening again.

"*Vous êtes compétiteurs?*" Adrienne's French accent pulled him back into the car, which the inspector was driving.

"What?"

"You and that bespectacled guy with the laptop. You were exchanging sarcastic remarks. Are you competitors?"

"More or less. I'm a portrait artist; he uses AI programs. Think of it as David versus Goliath, just for comparison's sake."

"I understand." She took out her phone and opened an app. "I've tried exploring this technology. It's very practical, but it will never match human sensitivity. We have a spiritual dimension—an essence that transcends any device's computing power. Do you want to ask it something?" She smiled, looking livelier.

Or maybe she was faking it, proving a painful truth: it's easier to pretend you're fine than to explain why you're not. Lorenzo swallowed the bitterness in his mouth; that was what had cost him Elisabetta. She hadn't been happy and had hidden it. That was why she'd killed herself.

Adrienne poised her fingers over the screen. "Can't think of anything to ask?"

"Try asking for the key to happiness."

She wrinkled her nose. "Nothing too demanding, I see." She typed it in, and the screen returned an answer: *The key to happiness is a complex and subjective concept; there is no universal answer that works for everyone.*

Adrienne shrugged. "See? I doubt AI will ever rival a Botticelli."

"Or hide secrets in drawings that could put humanity at risk," he added with a trace of sarcasm. The more he thought about that story, the less believable it seemed. Could someone really have a reason to make those drawings of Inferno disappear?

The car rolled to a stop, and the inspector cut the engine. Lorenzo stepped out; the cooling metal ticked faintly in the sun. Ahead, the entrance to the Boboli Gardens gleamed white. A second vehicle, this one marked with the colors of the State Police, pulled up alongside them.

Adrienne got out too. "This way." She headed toward a building to the left, just outside the park.

They followed. A light breeze carried the sweet scent of spring blossoms. Soon they reached a building with ornate cornices, symmetrical windows, and a colonnaded portico — the Palazzina delle Cacce Superiori. Adrienne led them inside; two private security men raised their hands to block the way, but the inspector's badge sent any objection packing. They made their way down to the basement laboratories.

A soft light filtered through the tall windows. The air was thick with the scent of wax, dyes, and the sharp tang of solvents. Metal beams and pipes crisscrossed the ceiling; wooden tables were strewn with papers and ancient fabrics, while tripods supported masterpieces under the meticulous care of restorers. They froze mid-brushstroke or mid-spatula, watching the newcomers with quiet curiosity.

"Good morning, I'm Inspector Minopoli. I need to see where you keep…" He glanced over at Lorenzo.

"The dammar resin barrels, please."

A grizzled man rose from his stool and pointed with a ruling pen toward some open buckets in a corner. Inside, the amber-yellow pebbles gave off a scent of wood and citrus. One bucket seemed fuller than the others—if the diary was inside, it would be like plunging something into water and watching the level rise.

The image of Elisabetta in a vermilion bath of blood flashed through Lorenzo's mind. His vision blurred; all he could see was her corpse, laughing. The laugh came from inside him, breathless, inhuman, spreading through his mind like a grin that couldn't be contained. His ears rang.

"Congratulations, Berti. It was right in there!"

Adrienne stood holding a leather-bound notebook; several resin buckets had been shifted. It was as if he'd been gone—absent—for several seconds.

The young woman opened the notebook and began to read.

La Storia come un romanzo Dal 1481 a oggi, ricostruito il cammino dei dipinti

Caccia alle dieci tavole scomparse della *Divina Commedia* di

Botticelli

La vicenda dei fogli di pergamena su cui il pittore ritrasse l'opera di Dante è degna di un film: 85 approdarono a Berlino, sette in Vaticano, ma alcune si persero per strada. Dove potrebbero essere?

Daniela Cavini

At the conclusion of the celebrations for the Dante year, on November 16, 2021, the Italian Embassy in London displayed for the first time a decorated copy of the first edition of the *Commedia*, printed in 1481 in Florence, with 20 engravings based on drawings by Sandro Botticelli. Of Botticelli's original drawings for *The Divine Comedy*, eight works from the *Inferno* have never been found.

1.3

In the laboratory, everyone froze. Lorenzo stared at Adrienne, the diary clutched in her black-painted hands. She was reading with feverish intensity, hunting for answers. She flipped through one, two, three pages — then stopped.

The inspector leaned toward her. "Miss, hand that to me. This material has been seized as evidence. We'll have it analy —"

"Wait." With a sudden burst of defiance, the young woman looked up, her brow furrowed. "I want to understand what happened to Mr. Manfredi — and whether I'm in danger too." She bent over the notes again, tapping a line with her finger. "Look: *The door is Mars, the solution is the light within the eyes.* Isn't that what he told you?"

"Yes." Lorenzo knew he'd never forget those moments for as long as he lived. "Does it explain anything?"

"No. But there's more. *Canto 1: A symbol on a blue background, with a red sewn band. It bears a golden lion with its head turned and a silver sword in its mouth, decorated with gold details and topped by three stars.*"

The inspector craned his neck to see the page. "Is there a drawing?"

"No drawing—but the coat of arms is tied to the first Canto of the *Inferno*. The one with the three beasts—the three animals that block the way to salvation."

"And what are these three animals?"

"One is the 'lonza,' a feline—maybe a lynx, maybe a leopard—that stands for lust. Then the lion for pride, and the she-wolf for greed."

"Got it." The inspector snatched the diary from Adrienne's hands. "In any case, I told you this is evidence. It's going to forensics."

It was a rude, heavy-handed move—unexplained and unprofessional. Lorenzo stepped closer. "I believe Miss Adrienne is the most qualified person to decipher her employer's notes. And she has every right to see them."

"No—not when her boss kept them hidden from her." The inspector flipped through a few pages. "So, recap: Mr. Manfredi is an art dealer who believed he had clues about Botticelli's missing *Inferno* drawings—or rather, the ones that had been made to disappear—because he thought they contained a secret that could endanger humanity." He looked up from the notes, raising his brows in disbelief. "Do those sound like the thoughts of a rational man to you?"

Skepticism was the immediate response, but in the back of Lorenzo's mind still echoed an inhuman laugh that needed no oxygen. Adrienne folded her arms. "The fact remains, the disappearance of those drawings is documented. And the unifying theme of the missing works is the *Inferno*, which lends itself to... a broader view. Less skeptical."

The inspector grimaced. "Maybe so. But instead of believing far-fetched theories, I prefer to rely on new technology." He pulled out his phone, unlocked it, and opened the same AI app he'd used earlier to ask about the key to happiness.

Of course—the inspector used that technology too. Just what we needed. He activated the microphone and brought the device to his mouth, clearing his throat. "Act as an art history expert and tell me about Botticelli's *Inferno* works."

On the screen, a swirling blot appeared, morphing—the loading indicator. It stopped, and a female voice began to read as text scrolled: "One hundred Dante illustrations on parchment were commissioned from Sandro Botticelli between 1480 and 1495 by Lorenzo di Pierfrancesco de' Medici, called *il Popolano*, second cousin of Lorenzo the Magnificent. For the same patron, Botticelli created two of his most famous works: *Pallas and the Centaur* and *Primavera*, both now housed in the Uffizi. The known *Divine Comedy* drawings number ninety-two. The only completed one is the introduction to the *Inferno* Cantos—*The Map of Hell*."

Adrienne turned to the inspector, hands on her hips. "Exactly. Only one of the hundred drawings was completed: the map of Hell. And only eight are missing from the entire collection—the first Cantos of the *Inferno*. And my boss—who claimed he'd found clues about these supposedly dangerous works—was murdered."

Her face hardened, her French accent heavier than usual. "Listen, Inspector, drop the condescending tone. I didn't put much faith in my boss's theories either—but look how he ended up."

The policeman made a face and tapped the microphone icon again. "Where are these works kept?"

Again, the distorted shapes swirled on the screen as it processed. "Botticelli's *Map of Hell* is housed in the Vatican Museum, along with Cantos I, IX, X, XII, XIII, XV, and XVI of the *Divine Comedy*. Eight *Inferno* works are missing: II–III–IV–V–VI–VII, XI, XIV. The other eighty-five works are kept at the Kupferstichkabinett Museum in Berlin."

The inspector chuckled. "Strange — the Vatican has the cover and Canto I; then there's a gap where the missing drawings should be, and after that they've got the rest of the *Inferno*. I'd say those pieces fetched a tidy sum for the Holy See — probably sold on the black market. Or maybe they revealed inconvenient truths. But nothing mystical." He went back to flipping through Manfredi's notebook with a sadistic, sneering look.

He seemed a different man from the professional image he'd projected at the Uffizi — as if the subject itself had tainted him. He held up a page. "Miss, it says here: *Ask Walter Oyster*. Who is that?"

"I don't know."

"Sure…" The agent's acidic tone was openly disrespectful. "I think you're lying. Weren't you the victim's secretary? Surely you arranged and tracked Mr. Manfredi's appointments. You're hiding something, aren't you?"

Lorenzo bit back a curse. There was a way to deal with people, and the one the policeman had chosen wasn't it. He moved close enough to brush Adrienne's shoulder, making sure she could feel his presence. "Your attitude is far from professional. First you rip the diary from her hands for your experts, then you ask her to cooperate and start accusing her. If she says she doesn't know this person, there's no point pressing. Ask your friend — since he knows everything." He nodded toward the smartphone.

The inspector snickered, lifted the phone, and tapped the microphone again. "Search for Walter Oyster in connection with art, history, Sandro Botticelli, the *Inferno*, the Vatican, and the *Divine Comedy*."

The swirling blot danced again on the screen, twisting as if to reassure them it was working. "I found several Walter Oysters, but none related to the listed topics."

Served him right. The inspector gritted his teeth, switched off the screen, and shoved the phone into his pocket. "We'll head to the station, I'll ask you a few last questions, and you'll sign the report. Then I'll driv—"

Adrienne took Lorenzo's arm. "Then we'll leave—you won't need to drive us anywhere. I know someone who'll help me get back to the hotel." She looked at him: her black irises sparkled with determination, but only on the surface. Beneath lay unease and fear—eyes like Elisabetta's. On her finger she wore a wedding ring.

"I'll be happy to escort you."

***

"Wait!" Adrienne caught Lorenzo by the arm, halting him halfway up the hotel's staircase. She was being far too familiar. Her gaze was fixed on the Florence Cathedral, rising against the evening sky.

The sun washed the heavens in warm shades, from vibrant orange to pale pink, framing the Cattedrale di Santa Maria del Fiore in an almost divine aura. The white marble of its façade seemed to burn in the light of the setting sun.

Yet that splendor was only a shell; inside, it was even more breathtaking. What other monument could boast

Brunelleschi's majestic dome and shelter works by Vasari, Zuccari…

Adrienne sighed. "'C'est magnifique!' Magnificent."

It was.

And so was she, standing there, lost in admiration for Florence.

Lorenzo pulled himself back to reality. "Since you work in art, I imagine this isn't your first time in Florence."

"Third time." She lingered a moment longer, then her awestruck expression clouded. "Thank you for standing up for me — with the inspector."

Warmth melted in Lorenzo's chest. "Think nothing of it. If anything, I wish I'd done more."

"Then have a drink with me. Here, in the hotel bar." She cast a wary glance up and down the street. "I don't feel safe."

He didn't either; things were getting out of hand. Besides, he still wasn't comfortable around women — not since Elisabetta. Not yet. And there was the wedding ring on Adrienne's finger.

But leaving her alone after what had happened didn't feel right. "All right, I'll stay a while. But you really shouldn't worry; the police know your hotel. And we're very close to the city center."

"The police…" Her face darkened further, helped along by the last ray of sunlight vanishing behind Brunelleschi's dome. "I don't trust them. Always quick to blame the Vatican — and money. I can assure you the Vatican has nothing to do with this."

The weight she placed on those words suggested she knew more than she was saying. But Lorenzo didn't feel like pressing.

They stepped inside, leaving behind the final glimmers of sunset. Hanging lamps cast a warm glow; the polished marble floor mirrored the gleam of dark wood furnishings. Adrienne led the way to the bar with practiced ease—she had clearly been here before.

On the counter lay an assortment of snacks: small green olives glistening under pinpoints of light, thin slices of cured meats, and neat cubes of cheese. A young man in black livery greeted them. "Welcome. What can I get you?"

Adrienne perched gracefully on a tall stool, crossing her legs in her fitted dress. "I'll have a Spritz, thank you."

"Make that two." Lorenzo forced himself not to glance at her legs—how he would have loved to sketch them. Awkwardly, he climbed onto his stool, fixing his attention on the one thing that could distract him: the strange day that refused to end. "You really have no idea who that Walter Oyster is in your boss's diary?"

She hesitated, then speared an olive with a toothpick, brought it to her lips, and slid it off. "I told you the truth— Manfredi didn't tell me everything."

The evasive tone left no doubt: she was hiding something. But why? Didn't she trust him, or was her conscience not entirely clear?

The bartender set their drinks on the counter. Adrienne took hers and sipped. A droplet clung to her lower lip, catching the light in a brilliant spark. If he could have painted that mouth on panel, that droplet would have been the focal point.

Lorenzo shook his head—he was staring too much. He downed half his glass in one gulp; he needed to calm himself. What was happening to him?

She tapped her glass with a black-painted nail. "Which is more beautiful — sunrise or sunset?"

"What?"

"I was thinking about the view earlier. They're both at the same height on the horizon, yet they're not the same. You're a painter; I wondered which you prefer. You must have contemplated it dozens of times."

He recalled countless sunsets that had amazed him with their colors, and a few sunrises. "Maybe sunsets are more beautiful, but I couldn't say why."

She nodded and sipped again. "I prefer sunset too; there must be a reason. It feels more… spiritual." She pulled out her phone. "Let's see what it says." She typed in the question. Testing that machine's answers intrigued him too — and worried him.

The loading screen wavered as it processed the query, then displayed: *"Sunset is perceived as more beautiful for two reasons: in the morning, you are more sensitive to light, so you notice fewer nuances. In the evening, the air is dirtier and more polluted, which filters the sun's red and orange reflections more effectively."*

Interesting. Lorenzo drank again, his head beginning to spin. "So basically, sunsets are more beautiful because there's more pollution."

She laughed. "Then it's true — imperfections create beauty."

That line made everything around him swirl, until he had to grip the counter to steady himself. He drew a deep breath and blinked. No — it wasn't just those three words; it was also Adrienne's smile. Too much like Elisabetta's… far too much.

Reality and memory blurred, Elisabetta's white teeth and slender lips flooding him with joy. He missed her.

Adrienne drank again and sighed. "Sunset offers itself to the world every day and, every day, it still captivates."

Like Elisabetta's smile—always surprising him, even a second apart. He had lost it because he hadn't seen the pain it masked. With Adrienne, that smile was before him again. And what if hers hid something too?

"Are you all right?"

"Yes." Lorenzo set down the glass, leaving a finger's depth of golden nectar inside. "Maybe... I'd better go."

He reached for his wallet, but she stopped him with a firm grip. "Let me. I'm the one who invited you. I just need one last favor."

The last. Then he would go home and forget this woman. And that absurd business about Hell and Botticelli. "Only if it's quick—I'm getting very tired."

"No, not for today. For tomorrow. I was wondering— does the Uffizi have a library with information on the artists it displays? I want to do some research on Botticelli's *Inferno*."

"Well, yes. There's the archive that—"

"Perfect." She rummaged in her bag and pulled out a sheet of paper, folded in half. She opened it to reveal a sketch of a coat of arms. "Remember when the inspector yanked the diary from my hands? I accidentally ended up with this page about the three beasts from Canto I. I need to find out what my boss knew and why he was killed. To do that, I have to uncover what Botticelli hid in those works. Would you come with me to the archive?"

Again, she was far too familiar.

And again, she smiled at him.

Awakening memories that dragged him to hell but tasted of paradise. He glanced at the wedding ring on her finger and nodded. "I'll be here at nine."

1.4

Domenico

The sun had set some time ago. Inside the parked Audi A8, Domenico sank into the leather seat—soft, so comfortable it was nauseating, fit only for those willing to be corrupted by pleasure. Could the Great Girolamo not have given him a more modest car? Something that wouldn't make him feel soiled, complicit in the shameless opulence to which the world had surrendered.

He had to adapt. With a sigh, Domenico tilted the rearview mirror until the hotel's staircase came into view. Manfredi's secretary had gone inside, accompanied by the illustrator who had seen his face. They'd been in there a while.

And here he was outside, keeping watch. His bald head made him easily recognizable. He tugged his hat lower, leaned forward over the steering wheel, brushed his fingers against the burl-inlaid controls—then quickly pulled back. Disgusting. Everything in this car made him sick to the touch. And the blue glow of the concealed LEDs was worse still, as though he were drowning in pure extravagance, trapped in a cabin corrupted by the devil himself.

He rubbed his hands together. Dark flecks of blood marked the sleeve of his jacket—the blood of the sinful art dealer he had killed.

That demon, servant of dark forces, had met the end he deserved. Whether he had served Satan or the treacherous Vatican no longer mattered; his corrupted soul had sealed his fate.

Manfredi had shown no remorse, not even at the edge of death. Nothing had made him reveal what he'd learned about Hell, and he hadn't even carried his diary. Satan was doing everything he could to prevent the Apocalypse, but he would never stop the faith of the Keepers of the Flame. Saint Jerome was with them.

Something stirred in the mirror: the illustrator was coming down the hotel steps, alone. He slipped through the pedestrians toward a waiting taxi. He'd been upstairs for over an hour—no doubt clinging to that woman in lustful embrace.

Domenico turned the key, the engine rumbling to life. He picked up his phone and made the call. "Maestro, he's just left. Should I follow him?"

"No. Leave. You need rest; I have tasks for you tomorrow. Go to the villa in the center, near the hotel."

That one? May the Saint forgive him. Of all places, that palace? He pressed the accelerator, the sedan leaping forward. "Maestro, can't I go to the shack in the industrial district instead?"

"No. You must remain in that area. We already know the movements of the secretary and her friend—you'll catch up to them. The bug you planted in the hotel bar was providential."

So, the adulteress had gone back to binge at the hotel bar, enslaved by alcohol and pleasure. *Recidivus, perseverare diabolicum*—the recurring vice marks its master. "I saw her order a drink before she even checked in. What awaits me tomorrow, Great Girolamo?"

"For now, just keep an eye on them. They'll be heading to the Uffizi archives."

Domenico slowed for a stop sign, then continued toward the villa. "And what are they after? Do they have the art dealer's diary?"

"The diary is in police custody; it will take time for me to get my hands on it. The inspector used his smartphone to run searches with artificial intelligence. We're inside his phone — we have the transcripts. He was looking for information on someone named Walter Oyster. For now, we don't know who he is."

"And the secretary doesn't know either?"

"No. She ran some strange searches — asked something about sunset and happiness. But we're monitoring her phone; sooner or later, we'll find something. Rest. Tomorrow your faith must be strong."

Easy for him to say. How was he supposed to rest surrounded by the villa's luxury and splendor? "Maestro, may I atone before bed? I've been overcome by vanity and pride all day." A twinge of shame tightened his throat. "At the Uffizi, there were moments I looked at those paintings with desire. I feel corrupted."

The Maestro was silent. His holy breath rasped over the microphone in three breaths. "Very well. But only one pass for penance. Tomorrow you must be at full strength — you cannot bleed. Remember, we do this for the Apocalypse. The fifth seal must be broken."

"Of course. I understand. Thank you, Maestro."

The call ended just as he reached the villa's massive wrought-iron gates. Metal leaves, bound in curling tendrils, gave the palace a baroque and sumptuous air. Leaning over the passenger seat, Domenico opened the jute sack and rummaged through the keys, the clink of dozens of rings breaking the night air.

The villa's silver remote surfaced in his hand. He pressed the button, and the gates swung open under the pulse of the signal light.

He drove up the spotlight-lined driveway, parked, and stepped out with the sack in hand. The garden, lush with begonias and nasturtiums, reeked of vanity. The entrance, shaded by a portico of Corinthian columns, was nothing but a tempting path to soft beds and comfort — the devil's lures. But Domenico had been to this brotherhood property before. He knew how to keep damnation at bay.

He skirted the building toward the pool in back, its surface hidden under a blue tarp. Passing it, he continued to the tool shed, large enough to house the chlorine pumps. Cold, damp, and cramped — just to prove to the Saint he would not bow to corruption. Girolamo Savonarola was his martyr, as he was to all the Keepers of the Flame — custodians of his fiery sermons against the Holy See, sermons that had sparked the divine Bonfire of the Vanities in his time. When the Church chose its master, the flames themselves had embraced the Saint.

Domenico flung open the shed door, met at once by a dense wave of chlorine fumes. Sickles, shovels, and buckets loomed before him; from the pump came a low, steady hum. He couldn't wait to shed those elegant clothes.

He set down the bag and drew the bloodstained switchblade from his jacket — impure blood, Manfredi's. He would clean it later. Emptying his pockets, he found the crumpled Uffizi flyer he had picked up to pose as a gallery attendant. It was creased beyond repair, the printed image of Botticelli's *Adoration of the Magi* warped and wrinkled. Yet the painting's vivid colors and poised figures still seemed almost angelic in their beauty.

2 Corinthians 11:14: *Satan himself masquerades as an angel of light.*

Domenico studied the image. The flyer claimed Botticelli had given the Magi the faces of prominent political figures — among them the Grand Duke of Tuscany and the Medici. It was political propaganda.

Only one figure in the scene met the viewer's gaze: Botticelli himself, in self-portrait, positioned beside the Saints and staring out with pride and defiance. Such arrogance — turning his eyes from Christ! No wonder Botticelli had betrayed Savonarola, selling his soul to the devil and embedding infernal clues in a work dedicated to the Evil One.

The Keepers of the Flame had to recover the works the Vatican had made vanish, and at last unleash the Apocalypse. But first — his atonement.

Domenico stripped, naked as the worm he was, and prostrated himself in tribute to the Saint. A rough plank, still scented with fresh resin, leaned against the rusted pump. Light, but it would serve. He took it, along with nails and a hammer.

He drove in forty-five nails, letting the sharp points jut from the other side — one for each day of Savonarola's imprisonment and torture, from April 8, 1498, to May 23, the day of his execution for heresy.

And to think the Saint had foretold it all, four years before it came to pass: *The wicked will come to the sanctuary, break down its doors with axes, and set it ablaze. They will arrest the righteous and burn them in the city's main square. What the fire has not consumed, what the wind has not scattered, they will cast into the water.*

And so it came to pass.

On April 8, they stormed the convent and set fire to the door. On the day of the hanging, the square was packed. On the scaffold stood Friar Girolamo Savonarola, barefoot and clad in only a shirt, with Friar Domenico and Friar Silvestro at his side.

The crowd murmured, then hurled insults and mockery. Young hooligans had hammered nails into the boards of the scaffold, forcing the condemned to walk barefoot over them. Children crouched beneath the walkway, stabbing at their feet with sharpened sticks as they passed. Yet the Saints already seemed elsewhere—Friar Domenico whispered a hymn, and Girolamo crossed it in silence.

The executioner slipped the rope around his neck and shoved him into the void. As the body swung, chains held it upright in the flames. The executioner lit the pyre. *"Now's the time for miracles,"* the faithless jeered. The flames leapt upward, but a gust of wind drove them back from the three condemned. *"A miracle! A miracle!"* voices cried, and many fled.

But the Saint was to be a martyr, and soon the flames straightened, wrapping around them. Children pelted the bodies with stones as they turned to ash. Women tried to gather some of it, but soldiers drove them away. To keep the ashes from becoming relics, the Signoria ordered the remains of the pyre thrown into the Arno.

Domenico looked down at the plank bristling with nails. It was nothing compared to Savonarola's Passion, but enough to atone for the day's sins. He positioned it with the points upward, prayed, begged the Saint's forgiveness, and set his first foot down.

The wicked will come to the sanctuary, break down its doors with axes, and set it ablaze. The purifying spikes pierced his heel, and the peace of pain rose through his leg. He deserved it — slave to desire.

A second step, and the whole sole of his foot was filled with saving agony. *They will arrest the righteous and burn them in the city's main square.*

A nail longer and crueler than the rest scraped bone; Domenico stumbled, stepping down with the other foot outside the path. The metal lodged deep in his flesh lifted the entire plank before it came free with a dull *clack*.

He rose to his feet.

Great Girolamo had commanded that the path of redemption be walked only once, to avoid losing too much blood and weakening himself — but it had to be done properly.

He began again. The floor was speckled with red drops. *They will arrest the righteous and burn them in the city's main square.*

Tomorrow he would follow the two sinners — the secretary and the draftsman. One way or another, he would uncover the secrets of the infernal works and unleash the holy Apocalypse. He lowered his leg and focused on the pain of salvation. *What the fire has not consumed, what the wind has not scattered, they will cast into the water.*

In the painting *Adoration of the Magi* by Sandro Botticelli, the depicted figures are members of the Florentine aristocracy of the time. This painting transforms the Gospel theme of the homage of the three Magi to Jesus into a representation of prominent figures of Florentine society of that period.

The character who looks
directly at the viewer
is Botticelli's self-portrait.

1.5

Lorenzo stepped over the threshold of the office and held the door open for Adrienne—a courteous gesture intended to make her feel safe. The purplish shadows under her eyes were as deep as the heavy makeup framing them, a sure sign of a sleepless night.

The antechamber to the archive was a bare, cavernous space, its walls clad in decorative pine paneling. Lorenzo approached the counter. A secretary looked up from a stack of documents and offered a professional, detached smile. "Good morning. How may I help you?"

It fell to him to take the lead. "We'd like to access the archive. We're researching the life and works of Sandro Botticelli."

"Of course." The woman extended a well-manicured hand, her nails painted a vivid red. "May I have your identification, please?"

He handed his over; Adrienne passed hers as well. From beneath the cuff of her blouse peeked the tattoo of a rose's thorny stem. He hadn't thought she was the type to get tattoos.

The receptionist kept their documents and gestured toward a row of chairs against the wall. "Please wait there."

They sat. A television mounted on the opposite wall was tuned to Sky TG24, the sound muted. On the screen, two policemen were gripping a man by the shoulders—a man whose face looked disturbingly familiar. Lorenzo squinted, and recognition struck like a slap. It was Martina's rapist.

Beside the video feed, an AI-generated composite sketch appeared. A chill crept up his neck: the drawing was identical to the suspect. You couldn't tell which was real and which was the sketch; every line and shadow perfectly mirrored the man they'd arrested.

His heartbeat quickened, agitation rising. Lorenzo tore his gaze from the screen. This was it—his profession would vanish. A knot of unease swelled in his chest. He tried to steady himself by tracing the grain of the wood paneling with his eyes. The knots in the pine looked like eyes, watching him. The surrounding striations seemed to shape themselves into faces, emerging from the wood's texture. They were staring.

At him.

Familiar faces: the rapist from the news clip, and the bald killer from the Uffizi. They seemed to be laughing—though the sound wasn't coming from them. It was in his head. The air around him thickened, pressing down and stealing his breath.

"Did you see something funny?" Adrienne was watching him, her expression worried.

"What?" Lorenzo jolted, sucking in a breath. "I don't understand."

"You were laughing. Looking around and laughing. Nonstop."

Had he actually done that?

His heart pounded like a drum in his chest. "No, nothing. Everything's fine." My God, nothing was fine. But better to change the subject. "I noticed the tattoo on your wrist. A rose?"

She pulled down her sleeve, covering her hand to the knuckles, a faint blush in her cheeks. "Memories of youth."

"You speak of youth in the past tense? You shouldn't."

She laughed. "That's your fault, for keeping your distance. Let your guard down; I don't know anyone else in Florence I feel I can trust."

A shiver ran through him; with his eyes closed, he could almost have believed Elisabetta was beside him. He nodded, hiding the turmoil inside behind a strained smile. "I just have trouble with strangers."

"I don't have much to tell. I love classical music, but I'm not opposed to rock. I work in the art world; paintings aren't my greatest passion, but I adore sculpture and working with clay."

"Clay."

"Yes." Lightness returned to Adrienne's gaze. She switched the leg she had crossed and folded her arms over her stomach. "I'm a pragmatic, tactile person. For me, art should be touched, not merely imagined. That's why a Bernini moves me more than a Botticelli."

Every remark she made carried a sensual charge—a desire to touch, to hold. Lorenzo felt a flicker of excitement, remembering how Elisabetta had made love—fiercely, as if it were combat. Adrienne seemed different, and better. She radiated a calm Eli had never possessed, perhaps because it simply wasn't in her nature.

"Sir, ma'am…" The receptionist, now standing, gestured toward a heavy reinforced door that had just clicked open. "You may go in."

They passed through the entrance and descended two flights of stairs into the basement. A vast room with an almost four-meter-high ceiling opened before them. Along the upper perimeter, fixed skylights with grates offered fleeting glimpses of the legs of passersby on the sidewalk outside.

A massive desk occupied the anteroom, facing a wall of glass, beyond which stretched a sea of shelves crammed with ancient volumes. The air was dry, steeped in that distinctive scent of aged paper with a faint trace of furniture wax.

A man in white cotton gloves moved carefully among the shelves, cradling three enormous tomes against his chest. He stepped through the opening, sealed the glass wall behind him, and laid the books on the desk. "Botticelli, right?"

They nodded in unison. The archivist handed them cloth gloves with the practiced gesture of someone who had done it a thousand times. She moved to the corner of the little room, where an unobtrusive armchair stood, so she could keep an eye on them without intruding. She sat and took out her phone.

Alright. They were here. Now what?

Lorenzo took the first book from the pile and opened it. "What exactly are we looking for?"

Adrienne leafed through the one beneath it. "Let's start with a general scan—see if the coat of arms from Manfredi's notes shows up, the one tied to the first canto illustration." Her deep black eyes swept the pages.

"For example," she went on. "This is interesting. His full name was Alessandro di Mariano di Vanni Filipepi, called Botticelli—maybe because he was short and chubby. Basically, he was body-shamed." She let out a quick laugh. "He had a nasty temper, like most artists. If noise interrupted his work, he'd throw stones at rooftops."

A nasty temper, like all artists. Lorenzo lacked that spark of passion—maybe that was why he'd never made it. He pointed to a passage in his book. "Here it talks about the *Divine Comedy*: in a document dated Florence, 1540, it records that Lorenzo di Pierfrancesco de' Medici commissioned a lavish manuscript of the *Divine Comedy*, with the scribe Niccolò Mangona writing the text and Sandro Botticelli producing the illustrations—one for each canto, plus the first, showing a cutaway of Hell."

Adrienne leaned closer, so near he could feel her body heat. Her sweet cinnamon scent overpowered every other smell. She kept reading. "Except for *The Infernal Abyss*, the illustrations were painted on the inner, smooth side of the parchment, while the text went on the outer, more porous side—the grain side. The illustration for the eighteenth canto of *Inferno* was painted in tempera."

Her gloved finger traced down the lines as the text shifted to the Venuses in his paintings.

Then Adrienne stopped. "What's this—*The Portraits of the Infamous*?"

The name nagged at Lorenzo, though he couldn't say why. He didn't know those works by Botticelli, so he read aloud: "The Pazzi Conspiracy was a failed coup attempt against the Medici. In 1478, an attack during mass in Florence Cathedral resulted in the killing of Giuliano and the wounding of Lorenzo de' Medici. The conspiracy's failure led to mass executions, the exile of the Pazzis, and the confiscation of their property."

Adrienne picked up from there. "On commission from the Medici, Botticelli painted portraits of those who had been hanged, thus immortalizing the vile traitors—*The Portraits of the Infamous*. These were removed in 1494, after the Medici were driven out of Florence, and no trace of them remains. They disappeared. Today, all that survives from that period is the portrait of Giuliano de' Medici, which…" She kept reading, but to Lorenzo her voice had turned into a muffled murmur.

The Portraits of the Infamous.

Exactly what he did with his composite sketches.

His mind froze, his temples throbbing. It was as if he and Botticelli had made the same compromises: being paid to capture the faces of despicable people, as a form of punishment. But it punished the artists too, forcing them to use their skill on criminals and cowards.

And they did it for money.

Selling their art that way made them more immoral than someone who sold their body.

"You see?" Adrienne shook him. "Those portraits are gone. Just like the *Inferno* works Manfredi claimed to have found. There might be a connection that—" She froze, staring upward.

What had she seen to unsettle her so badly? Lorenzo followed her gaze to the ceiling. Pressed against the skylight glass was the face of the Uffizi killer—the bald man—features flattened, hands cupped to block the glare so he could peer inside.

Was it another vision? He squinted.

The bald man straightened and limped away, as if injured.

Yet at the Uffizi he hadn't limped. It had to be a vision—but Adrienne's trembling grip on his arm said otherwise.

Her face had gone pale. "You… you saw him? That was him—the fake gallery assistant?"

It hadn't been a vision.

They were being followed.Lorenzo grabbed his phone. "Let's call the inspec—"

"No!" She caught his arm.

For a moment they stayed like that, in contact, until Adrienne let go. "Listen, I don't trust this. And… I didn't tell the police everything." A hint of remorse softened her voice and her gaze.

So he'd been right, then. What was the truth? Asking her meant taking on a huge commitment, but he couldn't stop himself. "What didn't you tell them?"

She waited a moment, then sighed. "You know Walter Oyster, the expert in Manfredi's notes? You can't find him because Oyster isn't a surname—it's a nickname."

"A nickname?"

"Yes. The Oyster is a Rolex model, self-winding. Manfredi used it as a nickname for Walter Obermann—it's the watch he wears. If we want to talk to him, his office is in Turin."

The Portrait of Giuliano de' Medici was commissioned by Lorenzo the Magnificent, his brother who survived the attack, to commemorate his death on April 26, 1478, during the Pazzi Conspiracy in Florence. Botticelli painted the image based on a marble bust made from the deceased's death mask. The portraits of the infamous conspirators of the 1478 Pazzi Conspiracy disappeared at the beginning of the 16th century. It is unknown whether they were destroyed, lost, or simply hidden.

1.6

Lorenzo stopped short at the forecourt of the University of Turin. The modern building challenged the classical lines of the old academic buildings with its sleek, rounded forms — a harmonious fusion of glass and steel. "So, this Walter Oyster Obermann works here?"

Adrienne nodded and looked around, wary and watchful. She was searching for any hint, any sign that might reveal a tail. Lorenzo swept the scene in turn. The university's façade, dominated by broad glass panes, opened onto a lush, green courtyard. There was no trace of the fake gallery assistant.

Students and professors hurried along the paths. On a low wall, a young couple kissed; then the girl opened a book, turned, and curled up, resting her back against the boy's chest. Her lips moved — she was reading to him. A cool breeze stirred a few leaves, and the two drew closer still. They were a beautiful sight.

Adrienne kept scanning for possible pursuers; she hadn't lingered on the romantic scene. "Looks clear," she said. She'd been upfront from the start about being a practical woman.

The noise swelled — an onrush of journalists with microphones and cameras burst into the garden and vanished through the university entrance, drawn by who knew what.

"Come on, let's go." Adrienne caught his hand and pulled him toward the building.

By the hand, not the arm.

Taking someone by the hand was a very intimate gesture.

Small, slender fingers, skin soft and warm. He could picture those hands shaping wet clay—her grip was firm, a promise she'd mold the material with gentle resolve. And caress with the same intensity.

But on her ring finger gleamed a gold wedding band.

She steered him to a side entrance of the university, avoiding the one the journalists had used. Inside, wide, bright corridors bustled with people. There must have been some special event.

The tide of students moved forward, eyes fixed on their phones, fingers darting over touchscreens. Two distracted boys collided with Lorenzo, shoving him against a door. An A4 sheet reading *No entry* came loose from the wood.

The boys gave him sheepish smiles. "Sorry, we didn't mean it."

Lorenzo waved it off and picked up the fallen sign, reattaching it with the strip of tape. "I wonder why everyone's so distracted and excited."

Adrienne chuckled. "Exactly—everyone glued to social media, did you see? It reminds me of those portraits."

She meant *The Portraits of the Infamous*. "What do they have to do with social media?"

"These days we've got social media for public shaming. Back then, they had paintings. That was the point of them, wasn't it?"

Right. Lorenzo kept his thoughts to himself, though the comparison sent his mind spinning toward his work. Adrienne went on. "If those portraits were meant for that and then vanished, who knows what the missing drawings of the *Inferno* were for."

Manfredi had found out—and it had cost him his life. Lorenzo's gaze roamed again, searching for pursuers. In the middle of that human crush it was impossible to pick out suspects; they could be anyone—or no one.

"This way." Adrienne took his hand again; caught in that touch, Lorenzo couldn't keep his eyes open.

He was a grown man, not a boy! He had to pull himself together. Ever since he'd been with this woman, it felt as if he were reliving the fever of adolescence, chasing after Elisabetta. Years spent courting her, until she begged him to take her away from that family.

And to her final surrender, in the bathtub.

Behind closed eyes, he could see the details of the day he'd found her. Beneath the water's surface, it wasn't Elisabetta's face anymore—it was Adrienne's. Black hair drifting in suspension. Lorenzo slipped his hand from her grasp and stopped in the corridor.

"What's wrong?" Adrienne covered her neck, startled.

"N-nothing." Stay calm, he told himself. "I just tripped. Are you sure you know where we're going in all this chaos?"

"Yes, we're here. The office is…" She glanced toward a door where two workers were taking down a sign. A new plaque lay on the floor: *Research and Study of the Phenomenon of Artificial Intelligence.*

Lorenzo froze. Here too? That technology was a train everyone seemed eager to get on—except him.

"Excuse me!" A man with an air of authority, a university badge on his jacket, and a folder under his arm pushed through the commotion. "If you're journalists, Barbero will be giving his lecture in the main hall, on the other side."

That explained the commotion. Lorenzo wasn't much of a history enthusiast, but everyone knew Alessandro Barbero. "No, we're not journalists—we're looking for Walter…" He turned to Adrienne.

"Walter Obermann," she finished. "He used to work in this office—at least until a couple of months ago."

The man studied them, weighing the truth of their words. Then his tense brow eased. "Walter Obermann," he repeated, tapping his chin. "I'm afraid you won't find him here. He's in Berlin, at the Kupferstichkabinett—the Museum of Prints and Drawings. Left a few weeks back."

The news hit them hard—they had come all this way for nothing. They exchanged a look; Adrienne's shoulders sagged.

The man sighed. "So, are you looking for information on the *Divine Comedy*?"

Lorenzo gave a start. "And how do you know that?"

"Well, Professor Obermann is an expert. He deals with religion and faith, all the way down to Satanic cults. But what really makes him famous in academic circles is his specialization in Dante's life."

Adrienne shot him a knowing look—they were on the right track. She pulled out her phone and opened her notes. "Kupferstichkabinett Museum—did I spell that right?"

The man read it and nodded. "Since you're here, Professor Barbero is also a great Dante expert. Today's lecture is actually about his book on the Supreme Poet." He smirked. "But there's no way you'll get to see him—he's a rock star in this field. Still, you could attend the lecture. You might get a chance to ask him a question."

Not exactly a topic to bring up in a public forum—secrets about missing infernal drawings that could threaten humanity, with murders and tailing in the mix. Lorenzo shook his head. "Thanks for the suggestion. Good afternoon."

They retraced their steps. Disappointment smothered any trace of excitement, leaving only a heavy emptiness. "And now?"

Adrienne tapped the museum's name—Kupferstichkabinett—and copied it. "If I remember right, I was already planning to go to Germany. Let's see if it's the same museum." She opened her AI app, pasted the name, and typed something.

Lorenzo didn't have time to see the question before the loading icon rippled. The answer came back: "Yes, the Kupferstichkabinett Museum houses some of Botticelli's works on the Inferno, along with works on Purgatory and Paradise. Eighty-five drawings in total."

Adrienne tapped the message. "What a coincidence—the expert nicknamed after a watch turns up among Botticelli's drawings right after the murder of the art dealer who claimed to have found the missing ones. Will you come with me?"

Follow her all the way to Germany? Madness.

The only sensible thing to do at that point was to drop it. Especially given how much he was losing control around her. "I'm sorry, but I think this time I'll leave the investigation to you." A sharp pang stabbed him in the side. Not pain—turmoil. Still, it was the right call.

She bit her lip. "I understand."

Her stern expression couldn't quite hide her surprise; she must have expected another answer.

They walked in silence for a few steps, passing two young people kissing. A flicker of envy and desire stung him. How long had he been alone? Two years since Elisabetta's death, and Adrienne was the first woman to unsettle him enough to imagine something more. But she wore a ring.

He needed to kill these fantasies, and if he couldn't do it himself, he had to block the path entirely. "I'm sure your partner will be happy to join you in Berlin." He flicked a glance at the ring.

"This?" Adrienne twisted it around her finger. "No, it's just a way to ward off unwanted advances — but it's actually backfired on me."

"How so?"

"It scares off the good guys but attracts lovers looking for a fling. You, on the other hand, are in a relationship, right?"

Well, he'd asked for it. Like a coward, he'd sought confirmation she was taken so he could use it as a shield — only to find himself on a highway where she was the one asking for a ride. "Yes, I'm in a relationship."

"I thought so. Someone as capable as you… What's the lucky woman's name?"

"Eli…" His voice caught, as if a vice were tightening around his throat. He hadn't spoken that name aloud in years. To say it now, pretending she was alive, in front of her twin, was torture. He swallowed. "Elisabetta."

"Elisabetta," she repeated, her French accent giving the name a seductive elegance. "Beautiful name, very aristocratic. With such a selfless partner, she must be a very happy woman. And grateful."

"Selflessness is the foundation of any relationship." Especially with Elisabetta, who had always been so needy. As for happiness — Lorenzo forced himself not to go there. "That's what love means: giving. I never did it out of gratitude, but unconditionally."

She snorted, a sarcastic laugh. "The idea of loving without expecting anything in return sounds charming in fairy tales. But in real life, mature love needs a delicate balance between giving and receiving—because anything that isn't mutual is toxic."

His heart froze. Anything that isn't mutual is toxic.

Had his relationship been toxic?

Years spent chasing Elisabetta as a teenager, then obsessed with saving her as an adult—until he'd erased himself trying to give her a happiness she had never found.

His head spun. Lorenzo leaned against the wall.

"You all right?"

No—he couldn't breathe. Just dots and faces, faces everywhere: Elisabetta's. The rapist's. The bald head of the fake gallery assistant.

But the bald man had his back to them. He was scanning the room, turning his head side to side, searching for someone.

Looking for them—he wasn't just in Lorenzo's mind.

Lorenzo grabbed Adrienne's hand and shoved open the nearest door, knocking the "Do Not Enter" sign to the floor again. He pushed her inside, followed, and shut the door behind them.

Adrienne looked at him, puzzled.

A man's voice came from inside. "Sorry, is it time already?" The cadence was Piedmontese.

Alessandro Barbero smiled from behind a desk. He glanced at the clock. "I was sure the lecture wasn't for another half hour."

They were alone with the historian. A rock star, and an expert on Dante.

1.7

Barbero pushed his glasses up the bridge of his nose with his index finger. "Is it time for the lecture already?" He smiled — confident yet warm — glancing between Lorenzo and Adrienne.

It was an opportunity they couldn't waste. A scholar of his standing had precisely the kind of expertise that would be highly useful to their investigation.

Lorenzo caught Adrienne's gaze, her eyes now lit with a spark of hope. She smiled back and stepped closer to the professor. "Please forgive us — we're not here for your lecture on Dante. We came in by mistake; we hope we haven't disturbed you."

He smiled, shrugged, and waved a hand lightly. "Not at all. I was just reading."

He held a book with a well-executed cover — clearly not AI-generated — depicting armored medieval men facing off, while a ghostly figure whispered over the shoulder of a young man with a sword.

Spirits. Here too?

Lorenzo swallowed and pointed at the novel. "A history book?"

"More or less." Barbero lifted it for them to see. "Historical fantasy."

"Fantasy?"

"Of course. I love the genre. My favorite is still *The Master and Margarita* by Bulgakov. This one's about Guido Cavalcanti and Dante Alighieri. Having written my own novel about the Supreme Poet, I feel it's only fair to read what other Italian authors have done with him."

Adrienne seized the opening. "On that subject — if we're not interrupting — have you ever heard of Botticelli's drawings for the *Divine Comedy*?"

He nodded. "I know them. Botticelli was a Medici court artist and inevitably tied to the events of the Pazzi Conspiracy — not to mention Savonarola's Bonfire of the Vanities."

At that name, Lorenzo flinched, remembering Martina — she had followed that religious order.

Barbero studied him, puzzled. "You look troubled." He shrugged, then smiled. "Forgive me, I tend to slip into long monologues. These topics are just so fascinating."

What a modest man. The energy in his voice was infectious, and his reputation clearly well earned. "No, it's nothing. I was just thinking of something else." Still, he had to focus. Their questions suddenly felt clumsy, almost out of place. "Some of Botticelli's *Inferno* drawings are missing. We're trying to find out what happened to them."

Barbero tilted his head, his glasses sliding slightly down his nose. "Botticelli worked for a very, very powerful family. Think of the Vasari Corridor — a symbol of prestige and political might. It let the Medici move between Palazzo Vecchio and Palazzo Pitti without mingling with the crowds, preserving that royal distance."

Adrienne reached into her bag, rummaging. "We're less interested in the politics than in the religious side."

The professor nodded. "Well, the Medici even built their own churches. Art was a display of power — that's why the Vatican holds so many masterpieces."

"And Botticelli's *Inferno* in particular?" Adrienne pulled out a folded sheet from her bag — Manfredi's notes — but kept it closed in her hand.

"Well, back then Hell was considered very real. But Botticelli's work is more than that — it's where painting and literature meet. Something similar exists in the *Dante Urbinate*, but in Botticelli's version, Dante moves through the map — that's a huge difference. The *Cantos* are transcribed on the reverse of each parchment, with the image appearing first as a frontispiece."

Lorenzo pressed on. "Could there be archives that tell us what was in the missing works?"

The professor shook his head. "I couldn't say. If I recall, the famous map in the Vatican was used as a cover — or perhaps as a project proposal, a conceptual draft. Studying the drawings might allow someone to reconstruct the missing ones."

Barbero's brows arched with a flash of cunning. "But if you're hunting for something specific — say, hidden messages — an artist would hide them in the smallest details. I doubt a cover summarizing the *Cantos* would help much."

He had picked up the supernatural undertone of their questions, without any prompting. Lorenzo felt heat rise to his cheeks. "We…"

"Don't worry," Barbero laughed. "It's not the first time I've been asked strange questions about the mysteries of the past. It's in human nature to seek answers beyond the veil —

and who's to say that isn't the right path?" He turned the book toward them again, his face glowing with satisfaction.

A soft knock interrupted them. A polite but urgent voice came through the closed door: "Excuse me, professor — five minutes until we start."

Time was running out. It was clear there was no point in circling the subject any further. Lorenzo gathered his nerve. "Does the phrase 'the door is Mars, the solution is the light within the eyes' mean anything to you?"

Barbero shook his head. "I'm sorry."

"One last thing." Adrienne unfolded the page from Manfredi's journal, revealing the coat of arms. "Do you recognize this symbol?"

Barbero examined it, lips pursed. "Blue field, red band, rampant lion holding a silver sword." He sighed, pushing his glasses back up. "If I'm not mistaken, that's the Da Vinci family's coat of arms."

"Which Da Vinci? You mean *that* Da Vinci?"

"Who else could it possibly be?" Another knock. Barbero picked up his bag and smiled apologetically. "I'm afraid I have to go now."

The door swung open, and the doorway filled with flashes, shouts, and applause. People whistled and chanted as Barbero waved, all shy sincerity. A remarkable man.

Adrienne gripped Lorenzo's arm. "Do you realize?"

"Yeah — he's a real rock star."

"I mean the coat of arms. Leonardo da Vinci. How does that fit in?"

Lorenzo looked down at the drawing. Everything felt more tangled than before. In the chaos, he had even forgotten to tell her why he'd pulled her into the room. "Outside, I saw that bald guy—the fake gallery assistant. I'm sure they're following us."

She shivered, biting her lip. "You're certain it was him?"

"Yes." Unless it was another hallucination.

She trembled again and let out a long breath. "That's also why I need to understand why they killed my boss. I worked with him—I don't feel safe."

A knot tightened in Lorenzo's stomach; how could he leave her alone? "What will you do now?"

"Now?" Her eyes glistened as she blinked. "One thing at a time. For now, I want to visit the Vatican Museums. I know it's asking a lot, but... would you like to see Botticelli's originals in person?"

Going all the way to Germany would have been a stretch, but Rome... He couldn't let her go alone. He sighed. "Let's go."

Da Vinci Coat of Arms. A family originating from the castle of the same name. The great-grandfather of the famous Leonardo obtained Florentine citizenship in 1381. From Antonio, his son, was born Piero, who practiced as a notary and served as chancellor of the Signoria in 1484. From him was born Leonardo — an acclaimed painter, sculptor, architect, mathematician, physicist, hydraulic engineer, mechanic, musician, and poet — who died in France in the arms of King Francis I.

1.8

Rome

Lorenzo turned over in bed and sighed again. The canopy dominated the room: four small columns, carved from dark wood, supported the upper frame, from which hung drapes of fine red fabric. The headboard was carved with floral motifs and clusters of grapes—craftsmanship that left him speechless. Thirteen grapes in each cluster—counting them in an effort to fall asleep had been to no avail.

The clock on the opposite wall ticked steadily. Was Adrienne's room beyond that wall? Or on the other side? The wail of an ambulance tore away what little drowsiness remained; there was no point in lying there, staring at the ceiling.

He got up, crossed to the window, and drew back the curtain. St. Peter's Square seemed so close he felt he could touch it just by stretching out his arm. From the magazine rack, he pulled a leaflet bearing an image of the Basilica and unfolded it.

It read: "*The square, a masterpiece of the Baroque, designed by Gian Lorenzo Bernini in the 17th century. 320 meters long and 240 wide, it is encircled by two semicircular colonnades that embrace the space like open arms welcoming the faithful. At its center stands an obelisk over 25 meters high, supported by bronze lions and crowned by a coat of arms..."*

All very interesting, but as with paintings, the description could never stir the same feeling as seeing it in person. He lifted his gaze again—the view was extraordinary. His breath fogged the glass despite the spring temperatures.

Two chimes marked the hour; little rest remained before his appointment at the Vatican Museums. Above all, what did he hope to discover about Adrienne in Botticelli's original drawings? To see them in person was, in any case, a privilege reserved for the few.

Inferno.

Elisabetta would have been in the Wood of the Suicides, the place of punishment as described by Dante.

Lorenzo's eyes stung; he rubbed them. The anxiety refused to loosen its grip. Ever since he had been caught up in this whole affair, it had been a constant rollercoaster of emotions.

He knew little of Dante's work—perhaps there was a leaflet about the Vatican Museums and Botticelli's drawings. He bent over the magazine rack and rifled through the brochures: Castel Sant'Angelo, Trevi Fountain, Piazza Navona, Pantheon, Piazza di Spagna… They must have felled a forest to print the flood of informational flyers for tourists, yet there was nothing on the museums' treasures.

The phone's vibration broke the silence. Lorenzo sat on the edge of the canopy bed and took the smartphone from the nightstand. A glowing notification lit the screen: *You've won 10,000 points! Redeem them now.*

That stupid little game he'd played on the train.

Beside the redeem button, amid sponsored ads, was an advertisement for an artificial intelligence app.

He sighed and shook his head. In the end, he tapped the icon.

He completed the purchase in the online store. The progress circle filled in, then confirmed the start of the installation. He had actually done it.

"Welcome, Lorenzo. How can I help you?" appeared in friendly lettering. It was already calling him by name — it must have synced with his store account.

He leaned toward the microphone. "Give me a summary of the circle of suicides in Dante's *Inferno*."

In the middle of the screen, the usual pulsing dot formed. A female voice began to read the text appearing there.

"The circle of the suicides is found in the seventh circle of the Inferno. There, those who commit violence against themselves are punished. The sinners are transformed into trees and shrubs, unable to speak except when their branches are broken. Around them fly the Harpies, who tear at their leaves and branches, causing pain to the souls within and allowing them to speak through the blood that flows."

It hurt just to imagine it. Even if it was fiction, the Church's dictates weren't so far removed. And according to the priests, Elisabetta was there — damned forever in Hell. The tightness in his chest was too much. Lorenzo brought the microphone closer again. "Why?"

The application processed the request. *"If you are asking me what it represents symbolically, this contrapasso — the punishment mirroring the sin — depicts the negation of one's human form, as a penalty for rejecting the gift of life."*

"No." Lorenzo stifled a sob, stopped the text, and pressed the microphone. "Why would God allow this? Hell. Isn't God love?"

"And you? What are you?"

Lorenzo pulled the phone away from his face and stared at it.

What kind of question was that? It didn't sound like AI-generated text. The phone was hot—growing hotter by the second.

The text began to form again, but now the reading voice was male. *"You couldn't save her? Why didn't you?"*

His muscles tensed; he couldn't move.

Panic surged. The tub. The blood. Images forcing their way into his mind. "I—I tried to save her." The words came without him even pressing the microphone icon.

Yet the AI replied. *"Sure, you tried. Go tell that to Elisabetta. But first, remember to drain her lungs, filled with her own blood. Murderer."*

"I'm not a murderer, I..." He tried to throw the phone away, but it seemed glued to his hand. "I wanted to save her. I tried to make her happy, I—"

"Liar. Do you know which circle you belong in? The circle of traitors. You betrayed her trust. She died because of you!"

"That's not true, I wanted—" Then a cramp seized him, and he froze. Lorenzo could no longer move.

"Why?" The voice on the phone had changed—it was Elisabetta's, gurgling. *"Why didn't you notice?"*

The handset seared his palm, the battery icon fading bar by bar. A blotch on the screen took the shape of a bleeding tree—the suicide tree. Elisabetta screamed. "I'm dying. You've been killing me little by little. Why didn't you save me? Why did you make me do it?"

The sound of water in the tub. He had failed. Guilt over his beloved weighed on him. Lorenzo swallowed, heart pounding, short, hyperventilating breaths. "Please, I—"

"Sshh!"

"No, let me talk!"

"*Sshh!*" She was silencing him. And she was crying.

The battery dropped to one bar. The screen flickered.

His eardrums rang—then another scream. High and sharp.

Lorenzo dropped the phone and clamped his hands over his ears, but the screaming didn't stop. Then came laughter, deep in his own throat, laughter that never paused for breath. Just as Elisabetta wasn't breathing.

And then he was drowning; water sealed every orifice, burning down his throat. Blackness closed in, his face scalding as if he were in hell. He thrashed, struck something. He screamed in his mind, but no air came out. None went in.

A spasm—he'd be dead in moments. He forced himself, scraped with his tonsils, dragged in a ragged breath.

He was in the bathroom. Clutching the sink, water overflowing, his face dripping. He'd been drowning himself.

The faucet poured boiling water, hissing sshh, steaming up the mirror. The scream had become the wail of an ambulance siren. The phone lay at the bottom of the sink, still on. Waterproof.

On the screen, a friendly message: "*Welcome, Lorenzo. How can I help you?*"

Three or four streets separated the hotel from the Vatican Museums; he walked them in stony silence. Adrienne glanced at him now and then but asked no questions. His face must already have told her everything.

He was losing his mind—or possessed.

Or both.

The square was filling, an unstoppable river of tourists flowing in from every corner of the world. Among them, a few priests and bishops in black or purple cassocks skimmed over the cobblestones, woven leather sandals flashing beneath the hems as they walked. Oversized rings on the prelates' little fingers caught the sunlight—symbols of power that made Lorenzo's stomach turn that morning.

Adrienne caught his sleeve. "Stop for a moment. I can go alone if you're not feeling well. It's obvious something's wrong."

Go back to the hotel? Only to end up talking again to those damned voices on the phone—or worse, contemplating suicide in the tub under God knows what delusion? He kept going toward the museum. "Let's go. You said yourself it's not easy to get permission to view the original Botticellis. I'll feel better." He forced a smile that didn't even convince himself.

But Adrienne didn't move. She studied him with anxious eyes, ready to object. If she'd asked one more thing, he might have burst into tears right there in front of everyone.

He stepped back, took her hand, and guided her toward the entrance. "Come on." Time to change the subject. "Tell me how you managed to get permission in just one day."

Adrienne's soft, yielding fingers tightened at last. "The permits? Let's just say that working at the highest levels of the art world, as Mr. Manfredi's secretary, I have the right contacts."

The crowd thickened at the entrance to the Vatican Museums, set into the towering walls, where the line snaked for dozens of meters.

It would mean hours of waiting under the sun. The weight of a sleepless night — and of what lay ahead — pressed on Lorenzo's shoulders. "We'll spend the whole day in line."

"Wait." Adrienne stepped over to a security guard and said something. The attendant spoke into his radio, nodded as he pressed his earpiece, unclipped the red cord, and tilted his head toward the interior.

"Come on, they're expecting us." Adrienne led the way down a corridor lined with doors. Then she slowed and lowered her voice. "It was important you be in good shape — once we're inside, you have to do something."

"What do you mean?"

"Well, you see… I didn't tell you quite everything." Her short, quick steps were forced by the tight skirt. The sly look on her face was anything but reassuring.

Lorenzo cleared his throat and whispered, "Can you please be more specific?"

"Well, as I was saying" — their footsteps echoed under the high ceiling — "you can't just call the Vatican Museums, ask to see a Botticelli in person, and get an appointment. You need the right credentials."

"Which you have — you're the secretary of a famous art dealer."

"Exactly. And you're the art dealer."

He wasn't sure he'd heard right; he stopped. "Are you telling me that — "

A man in a black jacket with graying hair stepped out of an office and planted himself in front of them. He extended a hand to Lorenzo with a slight bow. "Mr. Manfredi, your reputation precedes you. It's a pleasure to meet you in person."

1.9

The curator of the Vatican Museums paused in the doorway. He smiled, the wrinkles in his face creasing, and with a sweep of his hand he beckoned them inside. His pale skin was mottled with ruby-red birthmarks.

How would an art dealer behave? Lorenzo inclined his head in thanks. He had to stay in character — play the part of Manfredi. Stepping through the doorway, he found himself in a room that was a riot of opulence. At its center stood a long table, surrounded by walls painted a pale yellow. On one side, a row of windows, draped in blue and trimmed with ivory, bathed the space in a warm, golden light.

The other walls were a shrine to art and history: marble plaques embedded in the masonry, their surfaces engraved with elegant Latin inscriptions; portraits of popes and patrons hanging at precise one-meter intervals around the perimeter.

"Don't ask me to open the windows." The curator traced the shape of an arch in the air with his hands. "We keep the climate controlled to protect the works. Everything in the Vatican Secret Archi— ahem." He brought a fist to his mouth and cleared his throat. "Everything in the Vatican Apostolic Archive is planned down to the smallest detail."

Incredible—he'd already given himself away. With that slip, he'd all but admitted the secret archives existed. Perhaps the missing *Inferno* drawings were kept there. Manfredi had been right: something was hidden.

Lorenzo seized the moment. "Curator, we'd actually be more interested in the secret archive than the Apostolic one." He shot Adrienne a look of satisfaction, but she pressed a hand to her forehead in embarrassed dismay.

The curator scratched his temple and shifted his mouth from side to side. "I'm surprised at you, Signor Manfredi. An art dealer of your caliber doesn't know they're the same thing? The Vatican Archive was originally called the Vatican Secret Archive. But in October 2019, Pope Francis changed the centuries-old title of *Archivum Secretum Vaticanum* to the Vatican Apostolic Archive."

Heat rushed to Lorenzo's face. "Of course, of course," Lorenzo steeled his features. My God, what situations this girl was dragging him into. "It's just habit—I know perfectly well that…" He glanced at Adrienne, who stepped in smoothly.

"It was a wise choice on the Pontiff's part. Not everyone knows that *secretum,* in the common medieval Latin sense, doesn't mean hidden, but private or personal. It referred to the Pope's personal collection, distinct from the other archives of the Holy See."

The curator nodded, folding his hands. "Yes, everyone's ready to accuse us of imaginary secrets. So many unfounded speculations about the Holy See. Now, back to the matter at hand—you wished to see one of our Botticellis depicting the *Inferno,* correct?"

He crooked a finger toward the open door. An attendant entered, pushing an aluminum cart that screeched over the polished parquet. Upon it lay two glass panels encasing an ancient page, yellowed with age yet meticulously preserved.

The curator stepped up to the cart. "Lately, the Dante–Botticelli Codex has been in quite high demand."

Adrienne straightened. "You mean someone else has requested to see it?"

"Miss," the old man raised his chin, his smile taut and self-satisfied. "We receive dozens of requests each week for our treasures."

With deliberate care, he slipped on a pair of white cotton gloves and lifted the glass panel. His movements held a reverence bordering on the sacred. Gently, he laid the ancient document on the table. "Here is Botticelli's panel depicting the first canto of Dante's *Inferno* — the Three Beasts."

Lorenzo's artist's eyes drank in the drawing, and his breath caught. Though it lacked color and was only a preliminary sketch, the image ignited something in him. He didn't just see the lines on the paper — he saw what they would become. Every stroke spoke of a mastery that had outlived centuries.

The *lonza* — a feline that could be either leopard or lynx — was rendered in graceful, fluid motions. The thick fur along its neck looked soft enough to touch. The lion commanded respect, even reverence, its mane a forest of inked lines. The she-wolf, though sketched in rough outline, radiated the gnawing hunger that defined her.

"I had my doubts about you." The old man's voice.

Lorenzo started. "What?"

The curator held out a pair of gloves. "I said, I doubted you when you stumbled over the Secret Archive. But now, seeing how you study the piece… you can only be a great art dealer. You can see it in the way your eyes linger on the old panel."

Pity his gaze was an artist's; though it couldn't have been far from the passion a dealer felt for art. "It's in our nature to admire beauty. Today, when something moves us, we take a photo; back then, they drew. A painting was a way to preserve a story—a window onto the world."

The curator nodded. "That's why those who ask to see one of Botticelli's *Inferno* drawings usually choose the famous Abyss—the only complete one, and by far the most captivating. Curious that you requested Canto I. It's the second time this week someone's asked for it."

"May I?" Adrienne slipped on her gloves and stepped closer to the drawing. Her gaze swept over its surface from top to bottom. "Have you checked for watermarks or other markings visible when held up to the light?"

"Of course. Nothing to report."

"Any details or specifics about the piece?"

"Well…" Once again, the curator lifted his chin. "Botticelli had a profound knowledge of Dante. In his innovative approach, he chose a panoramic format, with the binding along the top edge of the book. You would flip the pages from bottom to top, and on each upper-facing page you could admire the illustration accompanying the text printed on the following page."

Adrienne went back to examining the details. "And does the work follow the exact order of the *Divine Comedy*?"

"Certainly. The order is respected, except for the missing cantos, of which we know nothing. From the lesser sins to the most heinous, ending with the traitors in the last circle of Inferno."

Lorenzo's head spun.

The most heinous: the traitors. Exactly what he'd been accused of during that sleepless night—whether by a possessed artificial intelligence or by his own fevered mind, haunted by Elisabetta's voice. "I don't remember the cantos by heart—do you have Botticelli's drawing of the Wood of the Suicides, or is that among the missing ones?"

"Missing, unfortunately."

Perhaps that was for the best. In his state that night, he would have seen the drawing come alive, Elisabetta's features replacing the trees. "And has the Vatican ever searched for the missing works?"

For the first time, the curator's expression darkened. "In truth, the search for the Codex is recent. It was an Austrian art historian, Joseph Stricosky, who first discovered the connections between the Vatican's works and those in Berlin. Understandably so: in the 1700s Botticelli wasn't as famous as other artists. Imagine—they even spelled it *Bottirelli* on the binding of the Berlin collection. It seems incredible."

Adrienne lifted her head from the drawing, disheartened. "Why was the original collection divided in two?"

"We don't know. By 1632 the manuscript had already been split. Here we have seven drawings, including the map. Eighty-five are in Berlin, and eight have vanished."

They were closing in on the heart of the matter: who had made those works disappear? Lorenzo stepped forward—it was time to go on the offensive. "So, the drawings you have here in the Vatican are only from the *Inferno*?"

"Yes."

"And the missing works—are they only from the *Inferno* as well?"

"Considering that Botticelli never began the last two for the *Paradiso*…" The curator's tone was firm, but a flicker of awareness crossed his eyes. Step by step, the questions were boxing him in. "Yes. The only pieces missing from the collection are from the *Inferno*."

Lorenzo crossed his arms, savoring the final blow. "So, considering you have the works both before and after the missing ones, what can we conclude?"

The curator hesitated, then replied. "That the missing works were from our collection." The wrinkles around his eyes deepened.

Exactly. The lost drawings of the *Inferno*: either the Vatican had lost them, or it had made them disappear. The question was—why?

The curator pulled a pocket watch from his waistcoat and cast a deliberate glance at its face. He furrowed his brow in pointed emphasis. "I must admit I did not appreciate the veiled insinuations you've aimed at the Vatican. That said, I think it's time you left."

That was it? That was how he was dismissing them?

He picked up the work from the table—hands once so delicate now brusque and hurried. He set the glass back onto the cart. Lorenzo sensed they would get no more information from him, nor any further special permissions. He glanced at Adrienne, who was biting her lip hard.

Then she drew a deep breath and stepped forward. "May I ask you just one last thing? You said you showed the First Canto to someone else this week. Could you point us to a name?"

He laughed. "Obviously not. Who do you take us for? We take the privacy of our institution very seriously."

Hostile, unwilling to cooperate. Adrienne's gaze lingered on the glass plates covering Botticelli's drawing, a shadow of disappointment and dismay settling over her face.

It couldn't all fall apart now. Lorenzo was used to handling people caught in the whirlwind of emotion — he just had to find the right approach with this man too.

He steadied his voice. "Curator, we never meant to imply anything against you. Forgive us if we gave that impression. We're simply caught up in the excitement of searching for the missing works. If you help us in our investigation, the Vatican will be the first to be updated on any discoveries. You have my word as an art dealer."

The old man gripped the cart's handle, ready to push it away, but his gaze lingered on the drawing. The eyes of a man in love.

That was the power of art. Somewhere in him glowed the distant desire to recover the missing pieces. If the Vatican had caused their disappearance, he didn't seem to be complicit. The eyes of faith are like filters that refuse to see certain truths.

"All right," he said at last. "Look for Professor Guido Amilto: a Jesuit brother, a scholar, not a priest. He's specialized — obsessed, really — with Botticelli's *Inferno*. His office is here in Rome. I'll let him know that Mr. Manfredi has asked for him."

So, once again, Lorenzo would have to pretend to be someone he wasn't. Hope returned to Adrienne's face, softening and brightening it. Lorenzo had only once seen Elisabetta radiate such energy: the day they moved in together, far from her bigoted family.

That joy had lasted only a single day.

Perhaps Lorenzo wasn't truly searching for the missing works of the *Inferno*. He was searching for Elisabetta — his own

Inferno. And Adrienne, who resembled her so much, was his Virgil.

Now they had two names to pursue: the name in Berlin, noted in Manfredi's diary, and an Italian expert on Botticelli's *Inferno*. There was still hope — one of these two paths might yet lead to a breakthrough in the mystery of the lost drawings.

Drawing / draft by Sandro Botticelli depicting Canto I of the *Divine Comedy*, with the three beasts, kept in the Vatican Apostolic Archive.

The series of drawings for the *Divine Comedy*, created by Sandro Botticelli between 1480 and 1495 on commission from Lorenzo di Pierfrancesco de' Medici, includes the famous drawing *The Infernal Abyss*, which is housed in the Vatican Apostolic Library, the only complete one of the codex. Botticelli used a silver stylus with lead for the basic lines and then retraced the contours with pen and ochre, gold, or black ink. The series includes 92 known drawings on parchment, 85 of which are in Berlin and 7 in the Vatican (I, IX, X, XII, XIII, XV, XVI). Ten drawings are missing: 8 *Inferno* drawings considered lost (II-III-IV-V-VI-VII, XI, XIV) and the drawings for two *Paradiso* cantos believed to have never been started (XXXI and XXXIII).

1.10

Adrienne tore her gaze from the map on her phone and pointed toward a building. "That should be it."

The place they were looking for was built of sandstone, in a neighborhood so exclusive the Colosseum served as its backdrop. The façade exploded with flower boxes spilling petunias and geraniums; at the entrance, a dozen gleaming plaques listed the businesses within.

Out front, a cluster of ten or so workers in hard hats and oil-stained overalls clogged the lane. They swarmed around a gaping hole in the asphalt; traffic had been diverted with orange cones and metal barriers. The constant blare of horns mirrored the drivers' frayed tempers.

What chaos.

Lorenzo skirted the construction site. They were hauling rusted pipes from the ground, the metallic clank of tools an irritating, unending soundtrack. He stepped closer to Adrienne and raised his voice. "What exactly does this Guido Amilto do?"

"I'm not sure. The curator said he's a Jesuit brother and a Botticelli expert. I don't know him." She ran her finger down the intercom panel and tapped a name. "Here: Studio Amilto."

"Wait!" Lorenzo moved her hand aside. "Wouldn't it be better if—" A jackhammer shattered the concrete in an earsplitting volley.

"What?" She cupped a hand to her ear.

Talking over the racket was useless. Beyond the tree-lined avenue, he spotted a small café. "Let's get a coffee and decide what to say, so I don't make a fool of myself again pretending to be an art dealer."

She laughed and nodded. Within a few steps, the noise was bearable. The café had about ten outdoor tables, the warm breeze tugging at the corners of plaid paper napkins. It looked inviting.

Adrienne craned her neck toward the display case, her lips rounding in surprise. "Look—they even have ciriola, the typical Roman bread." Her Roman accent was flawless, her speech shifting easily between French and excellent Italian.

"You speak well. Where'd you learn?"

"I have Italian roots—my mother." Her phone rang. She pulled it from her bag, glanced at the screen, and froze. The spark in her eyes vanished. "Hello, Inspector..."

The police? Maybe there was news.

Adrienne's eyes flicked left and right, avoiding his. Her face had gone pale. "I'm out of town right now. I'll be back in Florence in a couple of days."

Lorenzo started to speak, but she pressed a finger to her lips. Whatever it was, it wasn't good.

"All right, I'll let you know." She ended the call.

"Well?"

"Nothing. He called me in—unofficially." She headed toward the café.

"But have they found something?"

She twisted her mouth, weaving between tables until she reached the door. "He wouldn't say. And in any case, I don't trust the police. Remember how they treated me?"

Of course he remembered. But who else were they supposed to trust if not the authorities? Lorenzo paused in the doorway. Maybe it was time to restore her faith, at least a little. "I work with the police all the time. You're letting strange ideas get into your—"

The television above the counter was showing an interview with Martina, the girl raped by a demon.

The scrolling caption read: *Satanist rapist commits suicide in demonic ritual.* The footage cut between a spoon filed to a sharp edge, the cell floor marked with geometric designs traced in blood, and a photo of the rapist beside an AI-generated sketch.

He couldn't breathe. Muffled voices and laughter merged with the distant clatter of construction.

Another episode—right in front of Adrienne, who was watching him, worry etched on her face.

He swallowed, struggling for air. "Just a moment," he murmured. "I need some air." He headed down the tree-lined avenue toward a roundabout where a wide patch of sky opened above. Voices began to echo in his head—laughter, then screams. Martina's screams. He had to stay calm, get away, find air. He quickened his pace and stumbled.

A root jutted from a crack in the sidewalk. The branches overhead swayed and creaked, reaching for him. Seeking revenge. Elisabetta, in her suicidal form, claiming him for Hell. A shiver of terror ran down his spine.

Two yellow eyes flared among the leaves. "'Ffhh'!" hissed a branch. It snapped and fell on him; claws raked his cheek. The sting was nothing compared to the shock.

"Get away, you mangy cat!" Adrienne shouted.

The black cat hissed and sprang aside, perching on a block of concrete, curling its tail around its paws.

"You're bleeding." Adrienne held out her hand to help him up. "Oh, Madoné. Are you all right?"

No. He took a deep breath, fighting the dizziness, and accepted her hand. He needed an excuse. "I'm fine. Just afraid of cats." He brushed dust and twigs from his coat. His sick mind was trying to push him over the edge.

"Listen, should we postpone?" She opened her bag and handed him a tissue. "You looked like you couldn't breathe."

"Nothing serious." He dabbed beneath his eye, looking at the tissue now streaked red. Some café customers were staring and whispering. The TV had switched to a report on solar panels. On the ground lay broken branches; across the way, the cat sat motionless on the concrete block—yellow eyes, and between its ears, a small white patch shaped like a flame. Martina had claimed her attacker spoke to a cat.

Lorenzo didn't know what to think, what to believe.

Dear God, what was happening to him?

Adrienne handed him another clean tissue. "So, what do you want to do—postpone?"

If he didn't bring this to a close soon, it would drive him mad. "Let's go now. Just give me some water and a coffee, then we'll ring Guido Amilto's bell. See what he has to say."

———————— ❧ ————————

Lorenzo crossed the threshold of Mr. Amilto's office, Adrienne at his side. The antechamber's walls were swathed in salmon-colored wallpaper, adorned with gilt-framed paintings of saints and lit by crystal-trimmed lamps.

Once again, the opulence of power. The scholar, he thought, must be the usual type—an academic with an imposing presence.

A young woman with blonde hair swept into a chignon greeted them, extending her hand toward the other door. "Please, go right in—the professor is expecting you." Her long black dress brushed her ankles, buttoned primly to the very top. The Jesuit must keep strict rules in his domain.

"Thank you." Adrienne stepped through first.

The room beyond was lined with bookshelves on all four walls. Not a single painting—only books.

Behind the desk stood Mr. Amilto, waiting for them—a gaunt, wiry figure, the exact opposite of what Lorenzo had pictured.

The professor rubbed his hands together. "Welcome. Please, sit. The curator of the Vatican Museums told me you'd be coming." His voice was soft, yet carried an unexpected weight of authority.

Adrienne took the lead, moving toward the desk; two candelabra stood upon it, along with a laptop, a pad of paper, and an elegant old-fashioned telephone—upright, dignified, steeped in nostalgia. "Pleased to meet you. I'm Adrienne Dupont, and this is—"

"No." Amilto took her hand, shaking his head. "He is not Manfredi." He turned to Lorenzo, fixing his gaze on the bruised cheekbone, but said nothing.

A stab of fear pierced Lorenzo. "I…" And now what was he supposed to say?

The Jesuit held Adrienne's hand far longer than courtesy required. "I knew Mr. Manfredi well before you became his secretary."

He let her go and extended his hand to Lorenzo. "Don't trouble yourself over the lie. I understand how an obsessive search for answers can push one to the edge of morality."

Lorenzo's first impulse was to bolt, but he took the offered hand and shook it. The grip, for all its seeming fragility, was firm and steady. "Pleased to meet you. Lorenzo Berti. I'm a..." Yes—what was he? And what was he doing here? "...a forensic sketch artist."

An artist he most certainly was not.

Amilto gestured to the chairs and took his seat. "So Manfredi discovered who made those drawings vanish — and they killed him."

Lorenzo and Adrienne exchanged a glance.

They sat. Adrienne, a tremor running through her, folded her arms across her stomach and murmured, "How do you know that?"

"After hearing that Manfredi would be visiting, I did my own research to get up to speed." He swept an arm to encompass the shelves. "Knowledge is power—especially in negotiations. Word of his murder is already circulating in that world."

The death of the art dealer was public knowledge, but the Jesuit shouldn't have known about his interest in works that portended the Apocalypse. Adrienne fell silent, momentarily thrown. Lorenzo needed to step in. "But you know details that haven't been made public—about the Botticelli works, for example."

"Of which I am the foremost expert. As I told you, Manfredi came to me some time ago, and we shared a passion for that enthralling mystery: those drawings are missing for a reason."

"What reason?" Adrienne asked.

He laughed. "I don't know. I had theories, which I shared with Manfredi. You need only read his notes—in the leather-bound notebook."

Too bad it was in the hands of the police.

Amilto looked from one to the other and smirked. "They're not letting you read it, are they? I'd wager the police have it and haven't permitted you to study it."

Indeed, knowledge was power.

Adrienne sighed. "What did you reveal to Manfredi?"

"Are you believers?"

She nodded, while Lorenzo held back his answer, lifting his palms in bafflement. "What does that have to do with anything?"

"I am a Jesuit brother, which means I believe in the principle of double truth. Do you know it?"

"I do," Adrienne answered quickly. "The simultaneous validity of one conclusion reached through philosophical inquiry and another, contradictory, accepted through faith."

"Exactly. Double truth: the rational truth comes from observation, while the truth of faith belongs to the religious sphere." Amilto fixed his gaze on Lorenzo, leaning forward over the desk. "You will never uncover the truth about the Inferno drawings if you are a skeptic. So... are you, or are you not, a believer?"

Was he?

Until a few weeks ago, she would have said no. But now... "Let's just say I believe there's something beyond."

The Jesuit smiled. "Fine by me. Then we'll work together. I'll tell you what I know, and you'll tell me what you discover.

Tell me: how did the examination of the drawings at the Vatican go?"

"Nothing new," Adrienne said. "The curator didn't share anything we didn't already know."

Amilto smirked. "The Holy See can be jealously protective. Interesting, isn't it? They're the only ones who hold the Hell drawings—the most complete set. The *Abyss*, above all, but also the few colored Cantos—10 and 15—safely locked away in their archives."

"All the colored drawings are in the Vatican?"

"No, they're missing one. One colored piece is in Berlin, and it has a peculiar detail: only one figure left uncolored—just one. Geryon, described as the most colorful being in Hell. And yet, in that panel, he's the only one left blank. Why?"

"You tell us."

But he laughed. "I have no idea. I can only tell you that Geryon was inspired by figures from the final, agonizing torments of the Apocalypse. To find answers, you'll have to look beyond the tangible. You must investigate Botticelli."

He rose, crossed to the bookshelf, and pulled down a brown-covered volume with gold lettering. Opening it on the table, he flipped through the pages until he stopped at a portrait of a woman. "What do you notice about this Botticelli painting?"

It was a half-length portrait, the woman turned slightly to the side, her gaze fixed on the viewer. It must have been painted in tempera on panel, the pigments diluted in water. Aside from the imperfect perspective, Lorenzo saw nothing unusual. "I wouldn't know what to say."

"It's the *Portrait of Smeralda Bandinelli*—the first documented depiction of a woman looking directly at the viewer. Before her, women were always painted in profile. Do you know why? Because in profile, the viewer looks at the woman—she becomes an object. Women were expected to keep their eyes lowered."

He turned a few more pages and stopped at *Primavera*. "And this—isn't it a masterpiece? *Primavera*, a painting teeming with pagan deities, created in the heart of the Christian world. And then there's what we might call Botticelli's greatest gamble."

A spark lit his eyes as he turned to *The Birth of Venus*. He pointed to the Goddess's feet. "It's thought to be the first depiction of a fully frontal nude. For the first time, the female nude was painted to celebrate beauty, not to condemn it. Do you see the enormous difference?"

The words "female nude" etched themselves into Lorenzo's mind, conjuring the image of Adrienne, and desire surged through him. Not Elisabetta—Adrienne.

It was the first time he had fantasized about another woman.

He shook his head, trying to focus. "What are you trying to tell us?"

"That Botticelli often used his art to break the era's codes of modesty. A twofold truth. The Medici commissioned him to produce several works with pagan themes, including his depiction of *Inferno*." He leaned back in the leather chair, which tilted slightly. "I have a suspicion about what Botticelli wanted to hide in his works. And I told Manfredi."

He paused—whether for dramatic effect or to remind them that knowledge was power, it was hard to tell. He was seeking prestige from them. Lorenzo, resigned, asked the question the Jesuit was waiting for. "Then tell us: what did Botticelli hide in the missing Inferno works?"

A satisfied grin spread across his face. He leaned forward, almost sprawled across the desk, and spoke in a voice barely above a whisper, the way one utters secrets: "A map."

The depiction of Geryon in Botticelli's drawing of Canto XVII of the *Inferno* is located in the upper left corner. He is described as a multicolored being, yet in that panel — one of the few the artist colored — he is the only one left in white.

The Portrait of Smeralda Bandinelli, created by Sandro Botticelli around 1475, is housed at the Victoria and Albert Museum in London. Botticelli employs the tempera-on-drawing technique, using pigments diluted in water to create a velvety and luminous effect. The contour line is precise and fluid, but the perspective remains somewhat immature, with a slight tilting of the support plane where the hand rests. This is the first documented portrait of a woman looking directly at the viewer (it competes for primacy with *The Portrait of Ginevra de' Benci* by Leonardo da Vinci). Women were expected to look downward.

1.11

"As I was saying, this isn't a talk for skeptics." Amilto rose from his desk and strode to one of the countless bookcases lining the walls. Had he really said map? A map for what?

The Jesuit's hand brushed along a row of volumes until it paused on the worn spine of an atlas. He drew it from the shelf, returned to the desk, and laid it on the oak surface with almost reverent care. Flipping through the pages, he stopped at an old map of Italy. "Do you know how to pinpoint an exact spot on a map?"

The lines formed a grid; horizontal parallels marked latitude, vertical meridians longitude. Easy. Lorenzo traced the frayed lower edge with his finger, then slid it up the side. "You need two coordinates to meet—one horizontal, one vertical."

The Jesuit shook his head. "In the sixteenth century? Moreover, thinking in terms of a map, that only gives you an area—a quadrant—not a precise point. And you'd still have to know which map those values refer to. I want to identify a place—one point in the world—as a man of the Renaissance would. How do you do that?"

Lorenzo and Adrienne exchanged a glance, excitement quickening; it felt like joining a treasure hunt. The question pulled them back to a time when such knowledge was within everyone's reach; now, people relied on satellites and Google Maps. But in 1500?

Amilto chuckled. "I see you're stuck. I'll tell you: triangulation!"

Of course. Now that he'd said it, it seemed obvious. Lorenzo nodded. "Three points on the ground used as the triangle's vertices; draw the angle bisectors to locate the point inside."

"Exactly." Amilto's fingers glided across the map, brushing cities and rivers. "Geologists use it to find earthquake epicenters. The military, to locate the enemy. Archaeologists, to locate a site. Botticelli used it in his map, drawing on Dante's *Inferno* — the three beasts."

A wave of dizziness hit Lorenzo; he gripped the desk, heart pounding. Could that reasoning really hold?

The air seemed electric. Amilto moved toward another bookcase. He took short, quick steps, his enthusiasm palpable. Lorenzo, too, found it hard to stay still; his hands trembled. He looked at Adrienne, who followed the Jesuit's movements with astonishment in her eyes.

Amilto pulled down a leather-bound volume stamped in gold. "Reproductions of Botticelli's surviving drawings. The illustrations for Cantos Two through Seven are missing, but we still have the first — the one with the three beasts." Burning with anticipation, he set the heavy tome down on the desk, creasing a corner of the map beneath it.

He opened to the plate for the First Canto and pointed to the lion. "Tell me: this is the first beast — pride." He set the book aside and returned to the map of Italy. "Which city does this animal represent?"

"The lion?" Adrienne said. "If I have to match it to a city, it can only be the Lion of Saint Mark — Venice!"

"Exactly!" In one swift motion, Amilto yanked open a desk drawer, grabbed a marker, pulled off the cap with his teeth, and drew a thick black circle around Venice. He looked at them. "Now, the she-wolf of greed. Which city?"

Lorenzo's mind went straight to the Eternal City, with Romulus and Remus suckled by the she-wolf. "Rome — where we are now."

"Perfect!" Amilto circled the capital with another black ring, then flung the marker to the floor in a burst of anger. "That leaves the beast of lust to complete the triangulation: the 'lonza.' I've never found it." The Jesuit hunched over the map, puzzled, two points out of three marked.

Lorenzo thought it over — the 'lonza'… He had no idea what animal it even was, and he was ashamed to show his ignorance. Adrienne ran her palm over the incomplete map and repeated, "In medieval Italian the 'lonza' is a wild feline: it could be a leopard or a lynx. A leopard or a lynx…"

"But it doesn't stand for any city." The Jesuit brought the reproduction of Botticelli's drawing closer again. "Look how it's drawn; do you see the spots on its coat? Notice the hint of a mane at the neck?"

Lorenzo leaned toward the drawing: true, the animal had both the spots and the faint mane. "What does it mean for it to have both?"

"Exactly what I've just said. Not all lynxes are spotted, and leopards don't have that mane. Look at the drawing: Botticelli has drawn both animals — it's both a leopard and a lynx. Other artists illustrating the First Canto always chose one or the other. This animal is ambiguous!"

His head throbbed; what connection could there be? Three beasts: triangulation. It was fascinating. But it was also a risky interpretation.

The map's worn edges curled upward; Lorenzo smoothed them with his palm. "How can you be sure Botticelli's Codex hides a map?"

"Think of the cover—the infernal abyss. Isn't that a map of Hell? Tell me, did Manfredi give you any other clues?"

The art dealer's dying words whispered through Lorenzo's mind: *the door is Mars. The answer is the light within the eyes.* He was about to speak, but Adrienne pressed her foot on his under the desk and gave a small shake of her head. She didn't want him to reveal it.

Amilto sank into his chair with a huff. "Botticelli served Florence's aristocracy, who used him for pagan works. Then he got tangled in the Pazzi Conspiracy—political murder. Finally, he was swept up in the Bonfire of the Vanities and with Savonarola, burned at the stake as a heretic—a prophet of his own death."

The Jesuit's gaze locked first on Adrienne, then on Lorenzo. Determination burned in his eyes; his lips curled into something more snarl than smile. "Botticelli moved in the circles of the hidden forces that steer the world. I believe he uncovered something supernatural—something beyond—and hid it in his art. Then the Vatican made them disappear. One thing's certain: those drawings were in that collection."

"But why a map?" Adrienne asked. "And why leave the First Canto while the rest disappeared? Wouldn't they have erased it all?"

Amilto shook his head. "If you had to hide a route from point A to point B, you'd need a clear starting point and a trail of clues to the destination — clues only your intended readers could follow. The three beasts triangulate the start; the missing Cantos chart the route."

"The route... to what?" Adrienne asked.

The Jesuit's voice was a resigned whisper. "I don't know. But Botticelli illustrated only one Canto twice. And only one infernal character twice."

"Who?"

"The devil."

Canto 34, with the depiction of the devil, is the only one that Botticelli represented twice.

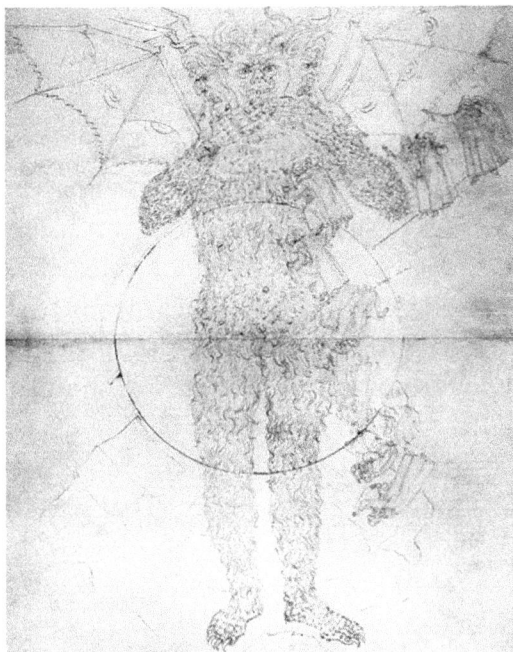

1.12

Leaving Amilto's office, they headed down the stairs. Lorenzo kept one hand on the railing; his head was spinning. Too many thoughts jostled for space: the map, the devil, the triangulation with the three beasts—the leopard, the lonza… Adrienne, walking beside him, was equally lost in thought, her brow deeply furrowed.

Outside, the din of the construction site engulfed him once more. Hoists were lowering new conduits into the hole in the asphalt, replacing the rusted ones piled at the roadside.

Adrienne pointed toward the café where they'd had breakfast not long ago. "Let's sit for a while."

A good idea—it was about lunchtime anyway.

They wove past the barricades and the deafening jackhammers, following the scent of coffee like a beacon. Adrienne's phone rang. She pulled it from her bag with a quick, almost anxious motion, glancing at the screen while angling it away from him. Her lip curled; she silenced the call and slipped the phone back into her bag.

Suspicion pricked at Lorenzo, and now he felt comfortable enough to give it voice. "That was the inspector, wasn't it?"

She straightened, hesitating as she often did when cornered by awkward questions. Then she nodded. "I don't trust him. Or them." She covered her mouth, a sob slipping through her fingers. "I don't trust anyone."

Poor thing—she must have felt she was in danger. The sight of a corpse isn't something you forget, especially when it's someone you're attached to. Right, Elisabetta?

The root he'd tripped over earlier was still there, close to the café tables. The black cat still sat on its concrete perch, watching him with golden eyes. Between its upright ears was a small patch of white fur, shaped like a flame. It almost seemed to be waiting for him.

Calm down, Lorenzo—it's just a cat.

They took a small outdoor table.

A deafening crash erupted from the construction site, and a cloud of dust filled the street. Customers hurried to shield salads, toasted sandwiches, and drinks. A little boy hid his focaccia under his T-shirt, earning a sharp scolding from his mother. They hadn't ordered yet.

The waiter approached. "What can I get you?"

Lorenzo glanced at the paper placemat menu. "A toasted sandwich and a Coke."

Adrienne raised two fingers to the young man, then pulled out her phone again. "Let's do a quick search—see what artificial intelligence has to say about this 'lonza'." She began typing.

Her app wasn't meant to be possessed. Lorenzo had uninstalled everything as soon as he'd fished his phone out of the sink, where he had tried to drown himself, in the grip of visions.

The cat meowed.

It almost sounded like it was commenting on his thought.

"Here we go." Adrienne read from the screen. "The word 'lonza' can mean two things: a boneless cut of pork from the back, lean and elongated, which can be roasted whole or sliced and pan-fried. Or, in medieval Italian, a wild feline—specifically the leopard or the lynx. In Italian, literally 'leopardo e la lince.'"

Nothing they didn't already know.

Another crash from the worksite. "Careful!" a worker shouted. "A leak—too much pressure!"

The tree Lorenzo had tripped over creaked; the crack in the asphalt where its roots pushed through widened by several centimeters. The base of the trunk splintered with sharp snaps.

The cat watched intently, the tip of its tail twitching. It meowed again. The workers rushed to the tree, pried up chunks of asphalt, and forced the gaps wider with crowbars.

"You all right?" Adrienne's voice pulled him back.

Calm down, Lorenzo. "Yeah. Sorry—I just haven't been sleeping well lately. It's just… everything feels strange. I mean the atmosphere. Don't you think so?"

She paled, nodded, and folded her arms across her stomach. "I haven't been sleeping well either. For a while now."

Her, too? Lorenzo opened his mouth, but the waiter arrived and set their order down on the small table. He was about to tell her what he'd been seeing, but the moment suddenly felt wrong. The cat meowed. Again.

My God— could he really be influenced by a cat? Adrienne was watching him, puzzled. He had to tell her something. He steadied himself. "I've been having strange dreams too. I found myself sleepwalking—it's never happened to me before. And then all this: Inferno. The *lonza…*"

"Right. A leopardo, or la lince."

The words buzzed in his head. Lorenzo began repeating them to himself: *Leopard, the lynx.*

Leopardo, la lince.

It stirred something in his memory, a connection just out of reach. The thought kept needling him: *Leopard, the lynx.*

Leopardo, la lince.

Leonardo da Vinci.

The cat meowed, the sound reverberating inside his skull. "Adrienne, whose coat of arms was in Manfredi's notes — the one linked to the first canto?"

She dug into her bag. "The Da Vinci family — Professor Barbero told us that." She pulled out the page and showed him the drawing.

"Exactly." He leaned across the table. "'Leopard, the lynx.' Doesn't that make you think of Leonardo da Vinci?"

A loud crash came from the tree, and the workers jumped back. At the base of the trunk, blood began to gush; the branches trembled under the pressure. A red pool, streaked with mud, spread at their feet.

A child pointed. "Mommy, the tree is bleeding."

A worker called toward the construction site, "It's water and rust — shut off the old line!"

No. It was blood. The infernal tree of the suicides was bleeding, though they couldn't know that. It was Elisabetta trying to speak to him — just as in the *Divine Comedy*, where the suicides became gnarled, twisted trees, and from their broken branches came a voice mingled with blood.

The metallic tang of rust mingled with the aroma of coffee and warm sandwiches — except blood smells like rust too.

And the cat seemed to be smiling. It padded to the pool of blood and drank; the white patch between its ears was stained crimson.

"Look." Adrienne's voice snapped him back. She was showing him her phone. "I asked it to explain the Da Vinci coat of arms."

The cat meowed.

It kept staring at him—unnervingly. Lorenzo forced himself to ignore it. "What did the AI say?"

"Da Vinci coat of arms: a blue field crossed by a red fess supporting a golden lion, head turned, holding in its mouth a silver sword adorned with gold. When the lion is shown walking with its head turned toward the viewer (*passant guardant*), it is termed 'leopardised'—that is, a heraldic 'leopard.'"

She looked at him, eyes wide. "You might be right—'leopardised,' you see? The Da Vinci coat of arms has a lion shown as a heraldic 'leopard.' The leopard. The *lonza!*" She tapped at her phone again. "And look—while you were staring at the tree, I used Street View to find Leonardo da Vinci's house. Look at this!"

She turned the screen toward him: a bas-relief carved into a brick wall, with a rampant lion and a shield awaiting a coat of arms. Lorenzo could hardly believe it. "We need more confirmation. But think—what if Leonardo da Vinci's house was the third point in the triangulation, together with the lion of Venice and the she-wolf of Rome?"

She nodded. "The three beasts. And the beginning of Botticelli's hidden map."

A map for what—for the devil?

A metallic screech came from the construction site, and the tree stopped bleeding. The cat had vanished. "What does Leonardo da Vinci have to do with Botticelli?"

Adrienne shrugged. "I don't know. But here, between Castel Sant'Angelo and Vatican City, there's a huge museum about Leonardo. Shall we go ask?"

On the wall of Leonardo da Vinci's birthplace, his coat of arms is displayed. The house consists of three spacious rooms, including an entrance hall with a 15th-century fireplace adorned with a coat of arms carved on the pediment. On the façade, there is a rampant lion holding a shield where the heraldry should be. In the Da Vinci family's coat of arms, when the lion is passant and with its head turned toward the viewer, it is referred to as 'leopardito.'

1.13

Domenico

Seated behind the wheel of the parked car, Domenico pulled on the glove — a barrier between his skin and the gaudy luxury of the vehicle's interior. Even the feel of such opulence sent a faint shiver of disgust through him.

From behind his sunglasses, he glanced toward the café. Adrienne and the illustrator were deep in conversation, their untouched order still sitting on the small table. Those gluttons wasted even their food.

A sudden hiss, followed by a gush of water, filled the street. A leak had transformed the area into a small urban swamp, muddy runoff coating the asphalt. Workers rushed in to contain the problem. At least all the commotion would make him less noticeable.

The phone on the dashboard vibrated: the Grand Girolamo.

The thought of hearing his spiritual guide made his heart tremble. His saintly mentor wanted a report. "Hello?" His voice shook. "Master, they've been all mor —"

"I know where they've been," thundered the deep, commanding voice on the other end. "The Lord reveals their every move to me! And you — where are you?"

"Close to them, parked. I can see them sitt —"

"How close? You don't need to watch them every moment. Your task is to follow them discreetly and be ready to act if necessary. They've already seen you more than once, Domenico. Be diligent."

"Yes, yes, of course. I was only looking at them for—"

"There is no 'only for.' Every action must be deliberate, every step considered."

The rebuke struck like an arrow to his chest. The Grand Girolamo was right—how petty of him to risk sending everything to hell. "Master, I'll do penance at once."

"No. Simply exercise greater caution; let Savonarola's assiduity be a beacon and an example to guide you in this undertaking."

Despite the encouragement, the thought of having disappointed the Master sent a shiver of fear down his spine. "I will meditate on Savonarola's zeal—his passion will give me strength."

"Good." The Grand Girolamo blew into the microphone. Domenico longed to breathe in the saintly breath. "The Lord has revealed that they've been researching Da Vinci; Dupont even looked up his house on Street View."

The Almighty had blessed the Grand Girolamo with mastery over technology—what a miracle! "That Da Vinci?"

"Could there be another? Call me as soon as they move, and I'll send you their location so you can follow without being seen. Understood?"

"It will be done!" Domenico bowed his head, pressing his forehead to the glossy leather steering wheel. Too bad it wasn't a video call—how he wished the Master could see his contrition.

The call ended, and he set the phone down.

He needed to regain focus. Penance was forbidden; instead, he could only meditate on the Saints' passion and bear the weight of his failings. He closed his eyes.

During the first and third phases of his trial, Savonarola was tortured repeatedly. The friar and the other prisoners were subjected to the Strappata as many as ten times in a single day: the victim was tied by the arms, raised ten meters, then dropped until he hung mere centimeters from the ground — tearing at bones and muscles with searing pain.

The Saint had also endured rope torture: bound by the wrists behind his back, hoisted into the air until his shoulders dislocated and muscles tore. Sometimes the rope was slackened and stopped abruptly; sometimes weights were tied to the feet or the soles burned. The ordeal left permanent deformities — a true martyrdom.

A cat's meow broke his reverie. Domenico opened his eyes. The animal was perched on the windshield. It had interrupted his memories.

He opened the door to shoo it away, glanced toward the café — and saw the illustrator's and Dupont's chairs empty. Where had they gone?

The cat meowed again; its head was wet, with a tuft of pale fur between the ears shaped like a flame, and tinged red.

Domenico touched it: water and rust. No — blood. A sign for the Keepers of the Flame! The cat jumped down, slipped along the side of the car, and sat by the exhaust. In that direction, Dupont hailed a taxi and got in with the illustrator.

They were on the move. Domenico slid into the driver's seat, grabbed the phone, and dialed. "Master, they're leaving."

"Good. Get behind the wheel, I'll send you their position. Follow them from three streets away." The line went dead.

The cat meowed again, almost smiling. A sign from the Saint himself. But Saint Francis spoke to animals — and he too preached a certain sobriety within the Church. Not like Savonarola; his purification was fiercer, more virtuous. The Grand Girolamo, though, spoke with Angels.

Domenico slipped the glove back on and clipped the phone into its mount. This devil-spawned machine offered air conditioning and every comfort. A stab of nausea clenched his stomach. He'd rather walk on nails than wallow in such luxury.

The phone beeped — the GPS showed the heretics' real-time position. Swallowing back bile, Domenico started the sedan, this time keeping the distance that would preserve his anonymity.

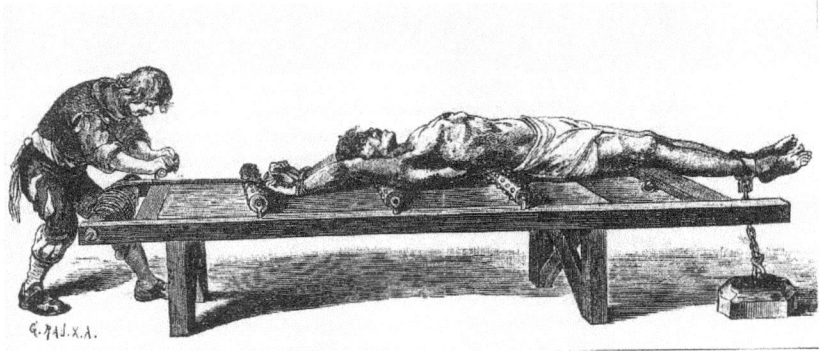

The rack was a medieval torture device used to extract confessions and information during interrogations, as well as a form of punishment for committed crimes. It consisted of applying a rope around the victim's chest or wrists; a violent pull caused pain and internal injuries.

The practice of Strappado.

1.14

Leonardo da Vinci Museum – Rome

Lorenzo slipped on the headphones, and the world went muffled. The museum's audio guide would lead him through the multimedia tour—a technology that had probably put someone out of a job. A forerunner of AI.

Adrienne let down her high ponytail and used the headphones like a headband. Her black hair, with its bluish sheen, fell sleek and glossy over her shoulders—exactly like Elisabetta's. Not to mention the heavy makeup and the tight black dress: she looked like a sexy witch.

How he longed to draw her nude…

She rubbed her chin. "Did I spill coffee on myself?"

"No."

"Then why were you staring? Do I have something on my face?"

Damn it. "No, it's just…" He reached for an excuse. "I feel silly wearing earbuds. I preferred when real, flesh-and-blood people acted as guides."

She wobbled her hand in a so-so gesture. "There are upsides, too. This way we're not stuck in a big group—we can still get detailed information, just the two of us."

"And who do you ask your questions to—a recorded voice?"

The cashier handed them brochures. "Soon you'll be able to ask questions as well. The audio guide with integrated artificial intelligence is currently being tested."

He'd suspected as much.

The woman activated the turnstile, and they stepped through.

The hall stretched on endlessly. A few steps in, a jaunty little jingle played through the headphones, followed by a male voice: "Welcome! You will have access to over 500 square meters divided into five themed areas. On display are codices, manuscripts, and fifty never-before-seen, fully functioning machines built from the Master's designs. You will also find reproductions of twenty-three paintings, including the *Mona Lisa* and *The Last Supper*, works certified and faithfully recreated at life size using the traditional methods of Renaissance workshops and the same materials employed by the artist."

A red carpet ran over beige marble, marking the route; in the background stood machines that would have looked futuristic in their era. Finally, a series of dark walls displayed reproductions of paintings.

Adrienne hurried to the first machine—a weapon: a cannon with dozens of barrels. Curiosity lit her face, then shifted to astonishment. He wondered what the voice in her headset was telling her.

Lorenzo stepped closer, and his own headphones chimed a jingle. "In front of you is Leonardo da Vinci's multi-barreled cannon—a battery of thirty-three small muzzle-loading barrels arranged on a rotating frame in three rows of eleven.

This bronze multiple cannon was designed to support infantry actions. Its mechanism…"

Interesting, certainly, but not why they were here. How could a museum visit reveal the links between Leonardo, Botticelli, and Dante's *Inferno*? They needed an expert.

And with the headphones on, how were they supposed to talk?

Lorenzo pulled his off, stepped up to Adrienne, and tapped her back. She uncovered one ear. "Let's take a quick lap and see if anything might be useful. No headphones, so we can talk about it."

"Fine." She tugged hers off too, her hair falling in messy, static strands across her face — like waking up in the morning. Imperfect, and all the more beautiful for it. That hint of disarray felt like home.

At their first meeting, she'd said: *So it's true – imperfections create beauty.*

And they did.

God, Lorenzo, get a grip.

He quickened his pace and passed the pavilion of Leonardo's inventions. Marvels of engineering — in their time they must have provoked the same disquiet modern AI does. But they were investigating paintings and drawings, and those were in the next section.

The paintings hung on plain black walls. Lorenzo slipped along the route to get a general look, passing the reproduction of *The Last Supper, Lady with an Ermine,* and the two versions of *The Virgin of the Rocks.* Then *The Annunciation, The Musician,* and other works whose names he couldn't recall.

In front of the *Mona Lisa,* Lorenzo stopped short. The museum's soft lighting wrapped the painting in a mystical aura. Mona Lisa's smile was everything and nothing at once — joy and melancholy fused into an indecipherable expression.

Joy and melancholy: the same feelings evoked by the memory of Elisabetta. He stepped closer, his draughtsman's eye taking in every detail — the softness of the contours, the masterful shading, the perspective that...

His eyes went out of focus; he struggled to take in the work. Something hypnotic kept him from roaming across the portrait. Maybe it was the eyes.

Those eyes — many eyes. Not human: divine. Spiritual.

The same eyes that haunted him. That watched him and pierced him. Dead, like Elisabetta's, staring from beneath the amber surface of the water; yet alive, like Adrienne's. Not honest eyes — they accused, and they ached.

They wanted him dead, but only after they'd used him.

"Careful!"

Lorenzo jolted, bumping into a display case. He'd been backing away without realizing it. He was running away. On that wall hung a fragment of parchment depicting a hanged man. The paper was identical to that used for Botticelli's *Inferno* drawings; the technique seemed the same as well.

Beside him, Adrienne stared at the drawing, her face frozen in shock. "It's... it's identical."

He wasn't the only one who thought so.

The audio guide was already explaining, so they put their headphones back on: "...depicts the hanging of Bernardo Bandini Baroncelli, involved in the Pazzi Conspiracy. This sketch is part of the *Portraits of the Infamous*. After taking part in the plot against the Medici, Bandini fled Florence but was captured and executed on December 29, 1479. His hanged body was drawn by Leonardo da Vinci, who was present at the execution. The work reflects not only his skill as an artist but also his interest in historical and tragic events such as the Pazzi Conspiracy."

Portraits of the Infamous.

A shiver slid down Lorenzo's spine. What they had found represented a significant connection between Botticelli and Leonardo, revealing a deep artistic and historical link.

Adrienne tore off her headphones, her hands trembling. "Botticelli was commissioned for the *Inferno* drawings the very next year. It's incredible, but—the *lonza*, the leopard, the lynx; the paper and the technique that seemed identical; the Pazzi Conspiracy and the *Portraits*... Botticelli really could have chosen him as the starting point for triangulating the map."

Lorenzo's head swam yet again, skepticism giving way to doubt. If their assumptions had any truth to them, then Manfredi's fear might be justified: the Apocalypse.

This was too big for them. "Let's go back to Professor Amilto. We'll triangulate the location of Canto I and see where it takes us."

He didn't say the rest out loud, but he thought it: *Let's pray.*

Leonardo da Vinci, drawing of the hanged corpse of Bernardo di Bandino Baroncelli (1479)

He was the assassin of Giuliano de' Medici, the younger brother of Lorenzo the Magnificent, who was killed on April 26, 1478. Bandini was one of the masterminds behind the famous Pazzi Conspiracy. Shortly before the attack, the conspirators realized that Giuliano was absent, as he had stayed home due to illness. Bernardo Bandini Baroncelli, together with Francesco de' Pazzi, then went to the Medici palace to fetch Giuliano. While walking towards Santa Maria del Fiore, he embraced him, pretending to be a close friend, only to check whether he was carrying a dagger or wearing armor, which, in his haste to get ready, he had not brought with him. Bandini struck the first stab at Lorenzo's younger brother and, along with Francesco Pazzi, completed his task by bringing the young man to his death.

1.15

Professor Amilto's distraught gaze shifted from one to the other. "Leonardo da Vinci," he murmured, struggling to speak, his mouth hanging open in astonishment. "Leopardo, la lince, to you, these would be symbols evoking Leonardo da Vinci?"

Granted, it was a flimsy clue, but all the other elements pointed toward the same conclusion. Adrienne stood off to the side, clutching her stomach. Poor thing—for her, this wasn't just historical research: she was convinced her life was in danger. And given that the fake gallery assistant had been following them, she had every reason to worry.

On the desk lay an open volume containing reproductions of Botticelli's drawings of the Inferno. Lorenzo pointed to the lonza in the illustration for the first Canto. "You pointed out how this figure embodies both animals, and the similarity in their names is undeniable. What's more, the da Vinci coat of arms bears a lion with its head turned—a so-called 'leopardised' lion."

"True, I'm familiar with heraldry," Amilto replied.

Adrienne shook her head and stepped away. She brushed her fingers along a row of books, then leaned back against the solid walnut side of the bookcase. "Not to mention the *Portraits of the Infamous*. Leonardo also portrayed one of those responsible for the Pazzi Conspiracy. He and Botticelli worked together; both served the Medici."

"Who didn't, in those days?" Amilto scratched his clean-shaven chin, his expression a mix of puzzlement and thought. "Now that I think about it..." He rose, went to one of the bookcases lining the walls, and began scanning the spines.

He selected a hefty volume and hurried back to the table. Pages rustled as he flipped through it, stopping at Botticelli's *Adoration of the Magi*, famous for the self-portrait of the artist looking directly at the viewer.

Amilto pointed to that very figure. "Here Sandro painted himself among the powerful. Every figure in this work is someone of great importance. The Magi are Cosimo, Piero, and Giovanni de' Medici, followed by Lorenzo the Magnificent and Angelo Poliziano, tutor to Lorenzo's children. Also depicted are Pico della Mirandola, Gaspare Lama, and many others."

Tracing a circle with his finger around the central figure of Jesus, the professor continued, "In this work, Botticelli introduces stylistic innovations later adopted by Leonardo da Vinci and Filippino Lippi in their own *Adorations*, now displayed at the Uffizi."

And they were magnificent—Lorenzo had seen them many times. But Leonardo drawing inspiration from Botticelli didn't bring them any closer to an answer. "But what does that have to do with the *Inferno*?"

"Well, the setting is classic fifteenth-century. The ruins symbolize the end of paganism after the birth of Christianity. And notice—Botticelli isn't looking at Christ; it's as if he isn't interested. He's looking at the viewer. Do you see anyone else turning away from Christianity?"

Adrienne hurried to the painting and stood beside Lorenzo. There was another young man turned slightly aside—his eyes not quite meeting the viewer's gaze, his face turned away from Christ. She pointed. "Him."

"Exactly." Amilto laughed and held his head in his hands. "Many scholars have suggested it, but I always thought it was nonsense. Look."

Once more, he dashed to the bookcase and pulled out two volumes. He opened the first to a bronze statue—a curly-haired David armed with a sword. "Modeled by Andrea del Verrocchio; according to tradition, Leonardo da Vinci posed for his master. The face of this David is said to be Leonardo's at about eighteen years old. Guess who commissioned it?"

Adrienne sighed. "The Medici."

"Exactly. Now look at this one." He opened the other book to a portrait of a young man who closely resembled him, holding a sheet of paper. *"Portrait of a Musician.* We don't know who Leonardo painted here. When it was cleaned in 1904, restorers found that he holds a musical score in his hands, concealed beneath a later overpaint. This led some to believe it was Franchino Gaffurio, but the identification is uncertain. Leonardo was a musician and built several instruments. It's likely this was his first self-portrait."

He set side by side the bronze statue, the portrait of the musician, and the section of Botticelli's painting showing the figure turning his back on Christ. They all had the same face.

Identical.

"C'est incroyable!" Adrienne breathed, astonished.

In his work, Botticelli had depicted only two figures turning their heads toward Christ: himself and Leonardo da Vinci—in an allegory where the crumbling ruins stood for paganism.

A few years later came the enigma of the vanished Inferno drawings, which had disappeared without a trace.

No, Lorenzo couldn't believe it. "That's a bit of a stretch to support the triangulation theory with the three beasts, don't you think?" He looked at the others: they, too, seemed unable to find the words to voice their doubts.

The professor stroked his chin again and sighed. "We have one last test to run — to see whether the three beasts mark the starting point of a map hidden in Botticelli's drawings."

"What?"

"Let's triangulate the location and verify it."

Would this be a beginning... or an end?

Lorenzo's legs trembled; curiosity burned through him as fiercely as excitement. Amilto began closing the books scattered across the desk, stacking them carefully, one atop the other. He bent, slid the bottom volume free, and heaved the pile up with a grunt.

Beneath lay an atlas, open to an ancient map of Italy — one mark near Venice, another on Rome. The corner of the page was creased; they'd crumpled it themselves in the heat of their investigation. And now, they were about to close the circle.

The professor turned toward a chair, set the books down, opened a desk drawer, and retrieved a marker and a ruler. "The three beasts. Triangulation," he said, his voice pitched a little higher than usual.

He smoothed the map with the flat of his palm, bit the cap off the marker, and spat it out. The tip touched Venice. "The lion."

He drew down to Rome. "The she-wolf." His voice shook.

He moved toward Tuscany, gauging the distance with his fingers, and circled a point. "Leonardo da Vinci's house — the 'lonza'."

With the ruler, he joined the three cities, forming a triangle. Then, with a protractor, he drew the bisectors of each vertex, calculating where they converged: a spot in Tuscany, near Arezzo.

The professor studied the area, eyes scanning the names of the towns. He scratched his chin repeatedly. "Impossible... then it's... It's true," he murmured—and began to laugh.

Lorenzo's heart hammered so hard it felt as if it might crack his ribs. "What? Don't keep us in suspense!"

The man only laughed, clutching his head.

Inside, Lorenzo felt the same laughter bubbling up, as if in sync. Uncontrollable. No—this wasn't the moment. He pressed a hand to his chest, struggling for breath. Should he ride out the attack or call for help?

No one noticed. Adrienne held her palms out toward the professor. "Will you tell us what you've discovered?" But he just laughed, half-mad.

Sounds dulled; Lorenzo shut his eyes and swallowed. Calm—he had to calm down. The voices returned, as if he were rising from underwater. Or from a bathtub.

Amilto stood by a bookcase, a volume in his hands—when had he taken it? "...you understand? D'Annunzio wrote verses in a priceless copy of Dante because he believed the book would never be lost. Do you realize how deeply the Divine Comedy has shaped the world?"

Adrienne huffed. "Yes, but get to the point."

The professor laid the book on the atlas. "By triangulating, we pinpoint an area that includes Poppi. In 1307, Dante was in exile there, a guest of the Guidi family in Poppi. That same year, he began the Inferno."

The triangulation led to the very place where the Supreme Poet began writing the Inferno. "What... what does that mean?"

"That it really is a map. A map of Dante's journey through Hell! Botticelli had uncovered—or preserved—the clues to reconstruct it, hiding them in his works so the path could be followed. And I've figured out where it leads. I know why the riddle was hidden in the missing opening Cantos." His laughter rose again, bordering on hysteria.

Lorenzo and Adrienne exchanged a glance. She had gone pale, trembling. Barely above a whisper, she asked, "Where does the map lead?"

"Leaving aside the other missing drawings, in Cantos two through eight, Dante travels through Hell and reaches a city. Dis—the infernal city." He slammed his palm down so hard the books on the chair toppled to the floor; then he spun and dropped into his armchair, the wheels rolling him back several meters.

He looked at them, eyes alight with the gleam of a man who had just given purpose to his life. "Don't you see? It can't be a coincidence that triangulating the clues leads exactly to the place where the Inferno begins—where it was begun. The work itself is a path. In the missing drawings lies the road to the infernal city of Dis. Hell exists."

Lorenzo repeated the words to himself, dizzy: a map to the infernal city of Dis. On Earth.

In order: the second character depicted with his gaze turned toward the viewer in *The Adoration of the Magi*, the *Portrait of a Musician*, and the bronze *David* by Verrocchio, in which, according to tradition, Leonardo da Vinci posed for his master.

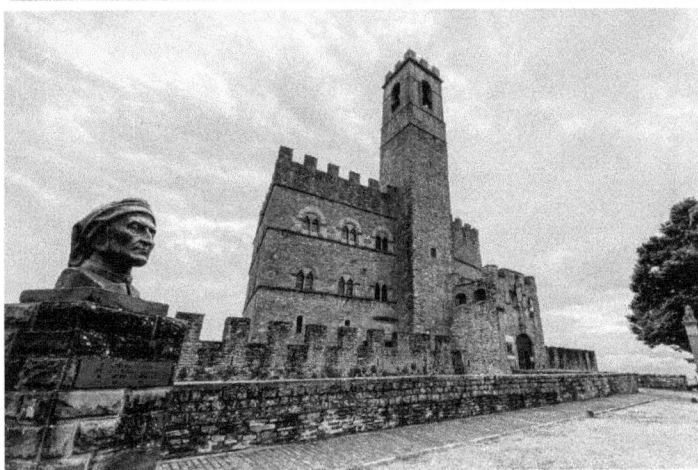

Bronze bust of Dante Alighieri placed in the square in front of the Castle of Poppi, where he was hosted in 1310 by Count Guido Simone.

Part
II
Purgatory

2.1

The secretary brought in a tray with a pitcher of water and three glasses. The hem of her long black dress brushed the floor with a faint rustle. She set the tray in a corner of the table. "Do you need anything else?"

"No, thank you," Amilto replied softly, almost singing the words. He paced the room with an ancient map of Italy in his hands, stopping now and then to study it intently before resuming his walk.

The discovery had clearly shaken him to the core, and Adrienne was just as unsettled — her pale, stricken face had yet to regain any color after the latest revelations.

The triangulation seemed to point to a tangible clue. Dis: *the infernal city*. Could it be real? Lorenzo poured himself some water, sipping slowly. Its cool freshness jarred against the dense air of tension. He had to get to the bottom of this.

Who had found the path, only to hide it in a map? Dante himself, Botticelli — or perhaps both? The three beasts were Dante's idea. But the *lonza*, drawn so it might resemble either a leopard or a lynx and used to triangulate the starting point with Leonardo's house as a marker — that was Botticelli's work.

"*Très bien,*" Adrienne's voice broke the silence. "What's the next step?"

"To do what?" the Jesuit countered. "My research is purely academic. What are *your* intentions?"

A good question. If they found the map, it could lead them straight to Hell; but the very act of searching for it might set off the bogus attendant, ready to send them to the other world.

Amilto pressed his point. "As far as I'm concerned, I've found what I was looking for. I'd advise against going any further—some truths are better left hidden."

Sage advice. But Adrienne let out a long sigh, her voice breaking. "All I know is I can't leave this story unfinished. I haven't slept since I got caught up in this madness."

Neither had Lorenzo. And yet he hadn't felt this alive in years—not since that day by the tub.

The memory burned: the drenched sleeves of his sweater heavy with Elisabetta's blood. He had thrown it away—he could never wear it again. From that day on, he never painted a happy picture again.

In fact, since then he hadn't managed to paint at all, except for work. Adrienne had brought his inspiration back.

He couldn't give up a miracle like that—but to make it real, they first had to resolve this. And the Jesuit was the only one who could help them. "Professor, you were the one who spoke about the principle of double truth, correct?"

"And so?"

"Our aim is to answer both truths—the rational one and the spiritual one. And who's to say they aren't the same?"

The Jesuit furrowed his brow, bit his lip, and rubbed his smooth chin. Then he chuckled. "The next step? Forget the drawings—they're gone, and there's nothing we can do. But we know the *Divine Comedy*. After the three beasts, what comes next?"

Adrienne's eyes rekindled with fervor; even her lips regained their color. "The gate," she said. "After the three beasts, Dante and Virgil pass through the gate of Hell."

My God. The dying voice of Manfredi echoed in Lorenzo's head, and he repeated his last words. "The door is Mars."

She straightened, her eyes widening as she made the connection. She turned quickly toward the professor. "Are there any Botticelli paintings that involve Mars?"

"Yes — *Venus and Mars*. It's in London. Why?"

"The door is Mars — that was in my boss's notes."

Professor Amilto's face became a canvas of astonishment. His lips curved into a smile, and he rushed to the bookcase. "London is a long way off, but I'm sure I have a copy of that drawing in my archives." His fingers danced along the spines of the books as if playing a piano, stopping on a hefty volume, which he pulled down.

He set it on the table and opened it to *Venus and Mars*. The reclining goddess radiated calm and awareness, her gaze fixed on Mars, who lay sleeping, spent.

They looked like lovers who had just made love.

The effect came from the posture of their bodies and the expressions on their faces — Botticelli's artistry at its finest.

Around them, mischievous fauns were having a field day with Mars's weapons. There seemed to be a mistake — Venus's leg. It was lost in the folds of her silky gown until it disappeared.

The door is Mars; and yet nothing in the painting seemed to connect to that phrase.

Nor to the other one Manfredi had murmured: *the solution is the light within the eyes.* Mars's eyes were closed—there was no light.

Adrienne studied the panel too, shaking her head. Her phone buzzed; she dashed to her bag, glanced at the screen, silenced it, and went back to him, dejected. "Do you notice anything?"

Only that the gods had made love—and that he wanted Adrienne as his Venus. "No. You, Professor—what can you tell us about this painting?"

He shook his head. "I'll do some research, it will take—" He broke off abruptly, a hand flying to his forehead.

"Now that I think of it, there's another work by Botticelli that references geography, maps, and positions."

"You mean it reproduces a map?"

"No—some instruments. And it also contains a reference to Mars. It's a mural: *Saint Augustine in His Study*, in the Church of Ognissanti in Florence. Dated around 1480, the same period when the *Divine Comedy* illustrations were commissioned."

That meant they could view the original. And the thought of returning back home—to Florence—with Adrienne warmed his chest. He could put her up there. He pointed to the print of *Venus and Mars* and met his Venus's eyes. "What if we went to see it, while the professor carries out his research?"

"Back to Florence?" Adrienne's lips pressed into a thin line.

The inspector had summoned her to Florence. Her phone's buzz earlier—it could have been him. "If we want to continue researching Botticelli and Dante, sooner or later we'll have to go back to Florence."

She remained impassive for several breaths.

Her fingers played with the ring—a symbol of a commitment only in appearance, devoid of any real fidelity. Then she nodded.

"Let's be clear," Amilto thundered. "I'm helping *you*. But you'll keep me informed of everything. Deal?" He held out his hand.

Adrienne shook it, and so did Lorenzo. On the desk, the image of *Venus and Mars* still lay open. The fauns, drawn to the gods' passion, had stolen the god of war's weapons. The theft of his lance was a fitting symbol of his disarmament before love. And so was he before that woman.

In his mind, it was easy to replace the goddess's face with Adrienne's. It was harder to replace Mars's with his own. He was no warrior, let alone a god. He was a failure who had let the woman he loved die—and he had been drawn into this story for fear of losing the only woman who had made him rediscover love.

Venus and Mars (1482)
The meaning of the painting is obscure, but it almost certainly should be interpreted according to the philosophical themes of the Neoplatonic Academy. After the adulterous affair between the two gods, Mars lies exhausted in the 'little death,' the state that follows the sexual act, from which not even a trumpet blast in his ears can awaken him. The fact that the little fauns have taken away his spear also symbolizes his disarmament in the face of love.

2.2

Florence

They had arrived. The train hissed, releasing pressure through the braking system. Lorenzo and Adrienne grabbed their rolling suitcases, stepped down from the carriage, and slipped into the stream of passengers. Three chimes rang over the loudspeakers, followed by the metallic voice of an announcement: "The train 'Frecciarossa' from Rome Termini, now arrived at Florence Santa Maria Novella, will continue to Milan Centrale in five minutes."

The murmur of travelers echoed beneath the canopy. Lorenzo caught Adrienne's eye and pointed toward the exit. "This way!"

She nodded, wheeling her trolley after him. In her other hand, her smartphone screen kept lighting up insistently. She glanced at the name and grimaced. Ignoring the call, she slid it into her purse—it was surely still the inspector.

They left the tracks and, through an underpass, emerged outside Santa Maria Novella station. A line of taxis waited at the curb. Adrienne tilted her head toward the snaking line of white taxis. "Do you have a hotel in mind for tonight? There's no time to see the Church of Ognissanti now."

The station clock read four in the afternoon. At that hour, there was no point in visiting the other Botticelli painting the expert believed to hold references to Mars. It was the perfect excuse to invite her to spend the night at his place. He would behave—he only wanted to talk to her, to have her close. But was it the right thing to do?

Lorenzo's phone vibrated in his pocket. He pulled it out: the screen showed a number displayed plainly, not in his contacts.

"Wait!" Adrienne glanced at the screen and made the same grimace as before. "Don't answer."

My God—she recognized the number. The inspector was calling him too. "Adrienne, if it's the police, we can't just play dead."

"Better to play dead than end up really dead." She blinked twice, her doe-like black eyes kindling a quiet laugh inside him.

But Lorenzo couldn't ignore a call from the authorities—he worked with them. For now, at least. "Your fear is unfounded."

"It isn't. There are things you don't know."

"Then tell me."

She stayed silent, shaking her head while the phone kept vibrating in his hand. She needed a push. He showed her the screen, then pressed the button to reject the call. "I won't answer—for now. I want to trust you. Now you trust me and tell me."

Her tense features almost broke into a smile; she appreciated the gesture, but didn't want to show it. Then her expression hardened. "The inspector—they've got to him. He serves two masters."

"And who would that be?"

"Others. Very powerful ones."

"And how do you know that?"

"I know because…" She stopped and bit her lip. "I just know. Let that be enough for now." She pulled her coat sleeves over her hands, her hunched shoulders betraying her discomfort.

He wasn't going to leave her alone.

He hadn't been able to help Elisabetta, but it would be different with Adrienne. "No hotel. You'll stay with me." The words landed halfway between a statement and a question.

Again, she stiffened her expression to hide a smile. "And your girlfriend?"

My God—he'd forgotten he'd told her that lie. Now he stood at a crossroads: keep lying, or tell the truth and risk breaking the fragile trust between them.

He chose something in between. "We're on a break." The shame pricked twice—betraying both Elisabetta's memory and Adrienne's trust.

"I thought so," she murmured. "I noticed you never called her while we were in Rome." She lowered her head; color rose to her cheeks.

She had noticed. Maybe even hoped. "And you never called anyone either. Your parents, for example."

Her gaze stayed fixed on her shoes, transforming her into someone else—not the sensual woman, but a child. At last, she looked up and sighed. "I don't have them anymore. And that's part of why I don't trust the police. Do you remember the Bataclan attack in Paris in 2015?"

"Of course. I remember the news."

"My father had multiple sclerosis, and by then the disease had confined him to a wheelchair. He was a journalist." A tear slid down her cheek. "In a world where a father is expected to be physically strong, mine was strong in spirit." The words caught in her throat.

She pulled a tissue from her pocket and dabbed her nose. "His disability let him buy reduced-price tickets, with a companion. I was the one who wanted to go to that concert. When the group of religious fanatics attacked the Bataclan, my parents were among the ninety victims."

Lorenzo felt the weight of Adrienne's guilt pressing on him. He understood. That was why he felt such a kinship with her. She went on, "One of the terrorists was arrested four months later. He was known as a dangerous jihadist, yet at the time the authorities weren't monitoring him. Negligence, they said. In reality, they were either corrupt or fanatics like him."

"I'm very sorry." He tried to put a sincere, reassuring note in his voice. "But think about it—I don't believe all police officers are corrupt."

"Not all—only where it counts. Think of Nassiriya, the 2003 attack on your Italian base. The investigation revealed that some members of the Iraqi National Guard were actually in league with the attackers. The failure to search the tanker carrying the explosives was once again chalked up to negligence or collusion—what a coincidence. The truth is, fanaticism and money are two gods with many followers."

She glanced around uneasily, perhaps looking for the bald man who'd been following them. After a past like hers — coming face-to-face with yet another corpse and ending up investigating Hell itself—her wariness was understandable.

Lorenzo moved closer, took her arm, and stole the carry-on from her hand. "My place is quiet and safe. It's time we got some rest."

Lorenzo slid the key into the lock; the Batman keychain clinked against the brass. He opened the door and switched on the ceiling light. "Sorry for the mess."

Adrienne looked around, her gaze moving over every detail as if appraising a painting. "And this is what you call a mess?!" She stepped farther inside and spun on her heel; the sight of her lean silhouette turning in a slow circle caught Lorenzo's words in his throat.

Excitement was building. He turned his back to her and closed the door. He had to keep it together, stay calm. The familiar walls and the intimacy of the space teased his imagination, but now was not the time to do something he might regret. All in good time—if something was meant to happen, it would happen naturally.

He lined the luggage up by the entrance, took a breath, and turned toward her. "You take the bedroom, I'll sleep on the so—" But Adrienne was staring toward the bathroom's half-open door, where the dim light revealed the bathtub. Just like that afternoon.

She sighed. "*Mon Dieu*—can I take a bath?"

Lorenzo's shirt sleeves suddenly felt heavy, clinging to his arms again, soaked in warm water—just like when he'd pulled Elisabetta out of the tub. He tried to steady his breathing. "No, um, the tub's drain is clogged. But there's a shower."

"Ah, what a shame." Adrienne stepped out of her heels and picked them up from the floor. "I was really looking forward to relaxing a little." She slipped a hand under her dress strap, reached to her neck, and removed a necklace: a rosary. Strange that she would wear such a symbol of faith after the stories she'd told about religion.

His thoughts leapt to Martina and the rosary she'd been working through during the failed composite sketch. A shiver ran through him. Her hallucinations of being raped by a demon had planted the seeds in his mind — surely the reason for the strange things he'd later seen himself. "As I was saying, take the bedroom. I'll sleep on the sofa."

She nodded, her eyes tracing the room's perimeter until they settled on the easel leaning against the wall.

Lorenzo could have listed every scratch and stain on those wooden legs from memory. Piled beneath them was a jumble of pencils, charcoal, and graphite; sable-hair brushes; the palette; oil paints, tempera, and the rest...

Adrienne ran her forefinger along the easel and held it up, gray with dust. "Looks like you haven't used these in a long time."

"Yeah." After that day, his art had grown dark and repetitive, haunted by the memory of those moments — until he'd stopped drawing altogether, except for work. He'd give her some excuse. "These days I mostly use a graphic tablet — it saves time. And money."

She shook her head. "But the smells? The feel? I couldn't imagine creating a sculpture with a 3D printer, no matter how much time or effort it saved."

"Maybe it's just nostalgia — or a generational shift."

"Meaning?"

"My art teacher used to look at my eReader and say he could never give up the smell of books. I get that it's nice to hold them, to smell the pages — but that doesn't mean you can't use them alongside more practical tools."

She nodded. "So it's the same with artificial intelligence."

"No." Irritation tingled on his tongue; anger rose in his chest. "It's something else."

Adrienne shrugged, then smiled. "I have a proposal. Let's take a little trip into nostalgia." She gestured to the art supplies. "Would you draw my portrait?"

My God. He'd wanted that for days—thought of little else. He hadn't painted another woman since that day, except for work.

She was watching him, waiting. "Well? Will you draw my portrait?" The light within the eyes.

Lorenzo felt a throb in his head and murmured, "The answer is the light within the eyes."

"What?"

"Nothing." He shook his head; even now he couldn't stop those phrases from slipping out. Tomorrow they'd be examining the painting on Mars itself. "I was just thinking the paints will be dry by now."

"Use charcoal. Something quick." And she smiled.

He couldn't wait to capture that smile—so much like Elisabetta's, and yet so different.

With Adrienne, he had found a little happiness. A little. With Elisabetta, too, he had never felt more than a little happy—never completely. Back then, he'd told himself he'd get there, fully, when things worked out between them.

Now, a little happiness was all he wanted.

He moved to the easel in the corner and lifted it, the dust on its latch rising in a faint swirl. He set it in the middle of the room. His chest felt light, as if filled with warm honey; how he had missed that ritual.

He opened the box of charcoal sticks and set out a clean rag. He would draw her clothed but shade deeply enough to let the hidden curves of her bare body emerge. The firm shapes, the soft lines. It would be like making love.

He turned to Adrienne, who had brought over a chair and settled across from him. From where he sat, just behind her, the bathtub came into view. The room lay in an unnatural half-light, thick and palpable. A head with long hair leaned over the rim of the tub—a translucent figure, its eyes like burning coals.

The light within the eyes.

The demon had no features, only the oval of a face and lidless eyes. But the mole on its cheekbone left no doubt—it was Elisabetta's. It raised a hand clutching a kitchen knife—the same one she had used to slit her wrists, later found when the tub was drained. It set the blade horizontally where a mouth should have been, and cut itself a lopsided smile from which blood and water spilled into the tub.

Lorenzo swallowed, every muscle locked, frozen in place. A terror so intense it pulled him out of himself, as if he were watching himself from the outside.

"Not happy with the light?" Adrienne asked, seated before him. Puzzled, she glanced toward the bathroom, saw nothing, and faced forward again. He shut his eyes, then opened them again. The room was empty. Hallucinations— nothing real. Perhaps. Yet the unease weighed on him. "Would you mind if we switched places? I'd get better light that way."

Adrienne nodded, and they changed seats.

Now the bathroom was behind him. He set the blank canvas on the easel and took up the charcoal. The air at his back turned icy, but he refused to look. A cold breath brushed his ear, leaving an unsettling prickle. No one was there.

Adrienne laughed, a little awkwardly. "What's wrong? Am I that hard to draw? How should I pose?"

"Turn three-quarters; I'll draw you from the bust up." He touched the charcoal to the canvas, mapping out the space. The demon's breath still grazed his ear. His hand trembled, vision blurring. Under the mounting pressure, the charcoal snapped cleanly in two, and Lorenzo crumpled to the floor, swallowed by sudden darkness.

2.3

The Church of San Salvatore in Ognissanti stood just beyond the square. Lorenzo stepped out of the café, the bitter aftertaste of espresso still clinging to his tongue. Adrienne gently stroked his shoulder. "Are you sure you're feeling better? I don't want you fainting on me again like last night." What a fool he'd made of himself. "I'm fine." When he'd woken, the canvas he'd meant to use for Adrienne's portrait still bore the smear of charcoal from where he'd collapsed onto the floor. "Come on—let's just go in."

They set off, the golden morning light caressing the church's façade. The alterations over the years had left their mark: the coat of arms of Florence now took pride of place on the façade, replacing the historic Medici emblem. Dominating the façade was Rapolano travertine, a material alien to Florentine tradition. Yet it presented itself with an aristocratic elegance. The façade was articulated in two tiers, each tripartite with decorative pilasters, niches, and window surrounds.

Crossing the churchyard, they stepped inside—a single nave. Cool air pricked at the nape of the neck. At the far end, a transept cradled several chapels. Natural light filtered through rectangular windows, evoking a mystical aura.

A clean-shaven young man with a bright, open face approached. "Welcome. Are you here for the services or sightseeing?" Adrienne extended her hand. "I'm Miss Dupont, and this is Lorenzo. We spoke on the phone yesterday about—" "Ah, yes, the art dealers. Pleased to meet you. I'm Mattia, an intern here. Come, I'll tell you a bit about the place." He shook both their hands, then led them further in. "Are you sure you only want to see the Botticelli? This little church isn't well known, but it holds some remarkable works—Giotto, Ghirlandaio..." He gestured upward.

Lorenzo's legs trembled faintly; the thought of being surrounded by such masters was both humbling and intoxicating. A full day wouldn't have been enough to take in the details of a single work. "We just need to see the Botticelli."

Mattia nodded. "The fresco or the tomb?"

"What do you mean?"

"You didn't know Sandro Botticelli is buried here?"

Lorenzo froze. Adrienne's mouth fell open in shock. Buried here—just steps away? The very artist who had hidden such an astonishing enigma in his infernal drawings. "Please—show me his tomb."

"Of course." With a sweeping gesture, Mattia led them through the church's right transept.

He pointed to an oil painting near the altar. "This is *The Altarpiece of Saint Didacus of Alcalá Healing the Sick* by Jacopo Ligozzi, 1595. Next is the Chapel of Saint Peter of Alcántara, with the vault and springings frescoed by Matteo Bonechi, and the side walls by Vincenzo Meucci."

Lorenzo forced himself to move on, though every part of him wanted to linger over each brushstroke. Then, with a certain solemnity, Mattia pointed to a corner of the floor. "Here lies Sandro Botticelli."

A marble disc inlaid with the Filipepi family crest marked the spot. Lorenzo held his breath, a shiver running down his spine. To think that one of the Renaissance's greatest masters lay just a step away knotted his gut. Nearby hung a painting uncannily similar to the self-portrait Botticelli had hidden in his *Adoration of the Magi*, its features unmistakably his.

Adrienne bent to examine the crest more closely, brushing the stone with a reverent hand. "I don't even have a flower to leave on the tomb."

Lorenzo bit his lip; he, too, wished for something to leave behind. In their investigations, they'd uncovered the man behind the art—his works piecing together a life and emotions that Sandro had scattered like secret clues.

He wondered if Botticelli had died content.

Adrienne straightened. "Let's remember this detail and move on. The fresco with Mars, then?"

Right—the door is Mars.

Mattia tilted his head, puzzled. "Mars?" Then his eyebrows lifted, as if a thought had just fallen into place. "You must mean *Saint Augustine in His Study*. This way."

They made their way back along the nave. Mattia pointed to the left, at a confessional above which hung a vast fresco. "There's Ghirlandaio's *Saint Jerome*, and opposite, Botticelli's fresco. They were once near the altar, but during the seventeenth-century renovations they were detached and moved here, facing each other."

He made his way toward the Botticelli, though he kept pointing at the other fresco. "The two works reflect the distinct temperaments of their creators in approaching the sacred theme. Ghirlandaio's *Saint Jerome* radiates a calm, contemplative air, with painstaking detail influenced by Flemish models; Botticelli's *Saint Augustine*, on the other hand, shows jewel-like precision and a profound introspection in capturing the saint's mystical rapture."

They stopped before the latter. The colors blazed with intensity, filling the space with masterful harmony. Whether they could unravel its riddles was another matter.

The saint's presence was magnetic; from the first moment, you felt a connection with him. His posture, the way light brushed his pensive face, gave weight to his thoughts. The deep red of the episcopal robe stood out against the pure white of the tunic, lending an aura of sanctity. His study formed a miniature world of humanist learning: shelves lined with ancient books, an astrolabe, and an armillary sphere resting on the table.

Lorenzo pointed them out, speaking quickly to Adrienne. "Look—Professor Amilto mentioned instruments linked to astronomy and geometry."

She nodded, her eyes scanning the scene for clues. Aside from the astrological instruments, there was nothing that seemed connected to Mars. Lorenzo turned to Mattia. "Where's the reference to Mars?"

"Mars? There's no reference to Mars."

What? "But earlier you smiled knowingly when I asked about the work that mentioned Mars."

Mattia looked puzzled. "So you don't know?"

"Know what?" Lorenzo shook his head, then looked back at the fresco. The colors were majestic, the details plentiful, yet he had no idea what he was searching for. He turned to Mattia with a shrug.

Mattia laughed. "Not *Marte*—Mars. There's *Martino*."

"Martino?"

"Yes. The name *Martino* comes from the Latin *Martinus*— meaning 'dedicated to Mars.' This fresco hides one of the

Renaissance's most curious and amusing details, which is why I assumed you knew it. See the open book above the saint's head?"

Lorenzo focused on the book. Adrienne stepped closer. Inside, the pages were filled with notes and geometric sketches. "They're not actual words—more like scribbles."

Mattia nodded. "Exactly. They're purely decorative marks—except for one line, marked on the left margin by a tiny cross."

Lorenzo narrowed his eyes until he spotted it—a small cross next to a single line of text. "And that line? That's real writing?"

"The only one." Mattia gestured toward the fresco. "It reads: *Where is Brother Martino? He has fled. And where has he gone? Outside the Porta al Prato.*"

The guide chuckled, palms raised. "Likely a playful nod to a friar's amorous escapades—episodes Botticelli may have witnessed while working in the church—consummated near one of the city gates: Porta al Prato. It's a rare glimpse of the artist's humor, since he's so often remembered as melancholic and sharp-witted. But you wouldn't believe how much speculation those words have stirred."

Lorenzo and Adrienne exchanged a look—they could believe it. However lighthearted the reading, the phrase carried both the reference to Mars and to the gate. A detail painted just when Botticelli began his infernal work. And Botticelli's remains were kept there. And what if Porta al Prato really was the Gate of Hell on the map leading to Dis?

Time for a site visit.

Saint Augustine, Bishop of Hippo, is depicted as the typical humanist of his time, caught in a moment of divine illumination within his study, which is filled with precious books and other scholarly objects, such as a solar calendar and an armillary sphere.

A distinctive detail is the open book above the saint's head, featuring geometric illustrations. The written words are actually elaborate decorations, except for one line, marked on the left edge by a cross, where it reads: *Where is Brother Martin? He has escaped. And where has he gone? He is outside the Porta al Prato.'*

2.4

Lorenzo opened the taxi door and offered his hand to Adrienne, who accepted with a timid smile. Once again, she had been the one to pay. It was humiliating, but the truth was he didn't have a cent to his name. Ahead of them loomed the majestic Porta al Prato tower, its medieval stone rising over the street.

Tram tracks cut across the road in front of the monument, with an asphalt street stretching behind it. Not exactly the most flattering setting for something of that age. In another country, they might have gone to greater lengths to showcase such a treasure. But in Italy, history was everywhere—turn your head and you'd find another fragment from the past. One tower more or less hardly seemed to matter.

Adrienne glanced at her phone. "Martino: from the Roman supernomen *Martinus*, later used as a given name. It is a theophoric construction based on the name of the Roman god of war, Mars—meaning 'consecrated to Mars,' 'dedicated to Mars,' or 'belonging to Mars.'"

The phrase hidden in Botticelli's painting was far too vague to connect Porta al Prato to the Gates of Hell, the beginning of the path to the city of Dis. Lorenzo exhaled sharply. "But there aren't any other clues?"

"The drawing of the Gates of Hell is one of those that disappeared. The clues that brought us here are exactly what Manfredi told you: the door is Mars."

The opening where the gate had once stood was crowned by a large arch. The upper level bore windows, while the roof looked different—newer. "Have they done work on it?"

"I'll check." Adrienne typed into the AI app, then read from the screen: "The tower was lowered in 1529 and altered to make it less vulnerable to cannon fire. Originally, it would have resembled Porta San Niccolò."

Lorenzo let out another huff. "So we don't even have the tower in its original form!"

A sudden burst of car horns cut him off. Down the street came a lively procession, led by a gleaming sedan decorated with white ribbons twined along its handles and mirrors, fluttering in the wind.

Through the open window, a bride waved at the crowd, her face radiant with joy. Passersby waved back, blew kisses, shouted good wishes. An elderly woman crossed herself and began to pray.

Adrienne watched the scene, her eyes bright as they followed the bride leading the procession as it drew farther away. "Beautiful, isn't it?" she whispered, her voice tinged with quiet longing. "My father won't walk me down the aisle."

A sharp pang struck Lorenzo's chest; his thoughts flew to his own father, killed at the concert.

Why was it so hard to find the right words? He wanted to take her hand, to let her feel his warmth, his support—but holding hands in front of a bride seemed far too symbolic. Instead, he placed a hand lightly on her shoulder, but he couldn't find the right words.

She shook her head. "They'll have used that new formula — *I welcome you.* I can't stand it."

"In the vows, you mean?"

"Yes. They replaced *I take you as my wife/husband* to avoid misunderstandings. As if anyone thought 'take' meant owning someone. And this new *I welcome you* — doesn't it have the same problem? Worse, actually."

"Worse?"

"Of course." She folded her arms tight against her chest. "*Welcome* makes it passive, like someone showing up at your door and you just let them in. Where's the desire in that? If something has to be taken for granted, let it be good intentions — not desire. But it's wrong to make the union with someone you love sound passive. *I take you* isn't about possession — it's about passion."

She shook her head and inhaled sharply through her nose. "Sorry. Forget it." With small steps, she started toward the tower rising above the road.

It was the second time she'd let her guard down. Her father's memory was her soft spot. Just the thought that he wouldn't walk her down the aisle set off a whirl of thoughts.

Lorenzo followed her beneath the monument, wondering what it had looked like in its original state. She caught her breath and pointed to a plaque set into the wall, engraved with Latin inscriptions. "There's a string of Roman numerals. Doesn't it remind you of the inscription on the Gates of Hell?"

School lessons stirred in Lorenzo's mind, his teacher's voice reciting: *Through me the way into the city of woe, through me the way to eternal pain, through me the way among the lost people...* Such marvels, the entire work of Dante — its beauty and rhetorical mastery so perfect it made you wonder if it was divinely inspired. "But what does it say?"

"Let's see." Adrienne snapped a photo with her phone, still using the AI app. Had they really reached the point of translating and examining everything through a screen?

The loading symbol vanished. "This plaque is affixed to Porta al Prato in Florence, listing the measurements of the walls, the tower, and the defensive moat, according to the decree of 1311."

Interesting—similar enough to spark connections with their investigation, but not enough to be sure. And now that they were here, what could they do? Lorenzo nodded toward her phone. "Want to ask it what the next step is?"

"*Mon Dieu,* I doubt it could go that far. We're chasing drawings we can't even examine. But if we wanted, there's another lead we could follow…" She let the sentence trail off, hinting at Germany.

Lorenzo stepped in front of her. "You've known for days that Walter Obermann—the guy from the notes—is at the museum in Berlin and has the other pages of the Botticelli Codex. Why keep chasing leads that go nowhere?"

Her expression darkened. "I haven't gone to Berlin because you said you wouldn't come. On my own, I wouldn't know how to manage it."

She held his gaze, eyes pleading. Then her back straightened and she turned—just as a police car rolled past. She must have felt like a fugitive.

The vehicle rounded the corner and she exhaled, but her face remained clouded. "If I have to go alone, tell me now."

Anxiety tightened his chest; his heart was torn. "I can't afford a trip like that."

"It's all paid for—by me. Well, by the company I work for. I still have the credit card from Manfredi Arte, and it was his wish to shed light on this mystery."

So that was her source of funding. Maybe that was also why she feared the police—she was spending a dead man's money, whether or not he would have agreed. And there was no way to ask him.

It was time to take a stand. Berlin wasn't just another stop—it was the next chapter in their search. With luck, they might finally uncover something concrete from the elusive Walter Oyster Obermann—like the clock. "All right," he said. "I'll go to Germany with you."

The marble plaque of Porta Al Prato, from 1311, where the measurements of the walls, the tower, and the defensive moat are recorded.

Porta al Prato and next to it Porta San Niccolò (as it must have been before the lowering works).

2.5

The departure announcements alternated with the low murmur of travelers. At the check-in counter, Lorenzo checked the boarding passes. He lifted the suitcase and set it on the conveyor belt, which swallowed it.

In the end, he was going to Germany for her. Work wasn't an issue — ever since law enforcement had turned to AI for composite sketches, he'd been rendered obsolete.

He made his way back to the waiting area. Adrienne had settled into a small armchair. Sitting there in that unusually short sheath dress, she was showing more skin than usual. The skirt had ridden halfway up her thighs.

Her left leg, elegantly crossed over her right, swung with a nervous rhythm. A black sandal clasped her ankle with delicate grace. Her toenails were neat, painted white, the curve of her foot recalling a ballerina's stance — perfect, sinuous.

Lorenzo swallowed, resisting the urge to let his gaze sweep over her like an X-ray. My God, how he longed to capture her on canvas in that pose — so natural, yet so sensual. He sat beside her. "They should call us to board in about half an hour."

"Perfect." She smiled and buttoned her blouse, only for it to part again with her breathing. The neckline drew the eye, called to him. She'd saved the extra fabric for the long sleeves that reached her wrists, hiding the tattoo she was afraid to reveal.

Beyond the wide windows, a plane taxied toward the runway. The air behind its engines shimmered in the heat before it took off. With majestic slowness, it rose from the ground and carved a path across the sky. Watching a plane lift into the air was always captivating; his thoughts drifted to Leonardo da Vinci's flying machine they had seen at the museum.

The day humankind stops chasing its dreams, it will become nothing more than an automaton — no different from artificial intelligence. Adrienne was right — he shouldn't fear that technology. "You know," he said. "I think I'll reinstall the app you're always using."

"Artificial intelligence? It's useful — you just have to use it the right way. For example, last night before bed, I did some research." She smiled.

From the couch, he'd noticed the light seeping from under her bedroom door late into the night. How many times had he wanted to knock and go to her. "And what did you find?"

"The provenance of Botticelli's drawings kept in the Vatican. Remember how part of the collection is in Rome and the rest in Berlin? Well, regarding the Vatican drawings, there's documented evidence of the first person who owned them. Do you know who it was?"

"Who?"

"Queen Christina of Sweden, a Protestant who converted to Catholicism. After her death, the sheets passed to Cardinal Pompeo Azzolini, then to Bishop Pietro Vito Ottoboni. And guess what role he eventually took on?"

Her tone hinted at an extraordinary rise. "He became pope?"

"Exactly—Pope Alexander VIII. The drawings then became part of the Vatican Library's collection."

Adrienne spoke as if those drawings might have played a role in their owners' ascent to power, as if they held mystical qualities. "Interesting. And the Berlin collection?"

"I don't know. I didn't find much—the path of those drawings seems a bit more compli—" The crash of a suitcase hitting the floor echoed through the waiting room, and she jumped in her seat.

A man bent to pick it up—tall, thin, with the gleam of a shaved head. From behind, he could have passed for the fake usher.

Lorenzo glanced at Adrienne—her hand clutched the armrest so tightly her knuckles had gone white. Her breathing was ragged, her lips trembling.

The bald man straightened the suitcase and rose, turning to show his face. The likeness dissolved—his eyes held a different intensity, his nose was less pronounced. It wasn't him.

Adrienne exhaled, her body relaxing from taut bowstring to slack, though a faint tremor lingered in her hands. "Mon Dieu. Thank goodness."

Only then did Lorenzo notice the pounding in his own chest. He wasn't built for physical confrontation—never had been.

Adrienne stroked his arm. "Thank you for being here. Without you, I wouldn't feel safe."

Of course—nothing to fear with him around. Lorenzo stifled a snicker. "Don't worry—if the fake gallery assistant shows up again, I'll fight him off with hideous portraits. I'll do his face in Cubist style, his body in Realist style. He won't survive it."

She burst into laughter and leaned against his shoulder, the sharp scent of cinnamon rising from her hair blotting out every other aroma.

She sat up straight and wiped a tear from beneath her eye, tracing the line of her makeup. "I meant that seriously, you know."

"So did I. Do I look like someone who could take on a killer?"

Adrienne studied him, her lips tightening into a thin line. "Do you remember when I told you about my father's illness?"

Multiple sclerosis. Even the word felt unpleasant to say. "I remember."

"And in your opinion, didn't my father make me feel safe?"

Pins of pain pricked his throat—he hadn't meant to imply otherwise. But she went on before he could speak. "At the Bataclan, from his wheelchair, he threw himself over me and my mother to protect us. He made himself our shield. My parents are the reason I'm still alive."

Lorenzo's voice dropped. "That's terrible. I'm sorry—I didn't mean it like that."

She smiled. "Don't worry—I didn't misunderstand you. What I mean is... you don't feel protected by someone who offers you their physical strength, but by someone who offers you their strength of will."

The words were more than a sword to the heart: they were a blade that pierced the soul. And they cut away anything else he might have said. Lorenzo simply nodded, his eyes filling, while she shed a single tear.

A voice over the loudspeakers called for boarding.

Lorenzo swallowed and stood. He offered Adrienne his hand to help her up, and he didn't have to struggle to keep from looking at her legs; it was her eyes that drew his attention.

And still, he hadn't been able to paint them.

But perhaps that was for the best, because the more he got to know her, the more he would paint them together with her soul, which to him was beautiful beyond words.

2.6

Berlin

The suitcase thudded against the steep staircase, step after step. They had taken too long—far too long. There was no time to stop at the hotel now; the museum would close in fifteen minutes.

The last step opened onto a vast square, as wide as a football field, ringed by massive, sharp-edged buildings, all in the stark style of German architecture.

The Kupferstichkabinett Museum stood ahead—square, orderly, the very image of national rigor. Lorenzo pulled his phone from his pocket: the installation icon for the AI app was frozen halfway. No use—his plan didn't cover data abroad. "Does your phone work?"

Adrienne shook her head. "Battery's dead." Her words tangled with her labored breathing. "But my plan should work all across Europe."

Ten long strides later, they stepped into the reception area—a bright, spacious room with a light-wood counter at its center. A smiling young woman beckoned them over.

They were the only visitors left; the museum would close in ten minutes. "You talk," Lorenzo said, ceding the lead. "You're better at English."

She nodded and moved toward the receptionist.

To their right, past a velvet rope, the last visitors were filing out. The walls were dotted with posters. One, an abstract explosion of vivid color and cryptic shapes, promoted a contemporary art exhibition. Lorenzo didn't get the style; for all he knew, it could have been slapped together by artificial intelligence.

In fact, AI might have done it better.

Adrienne was still speaking with the receptionist. Lorenzo wasn't following the exchange, but the name *Manfredi* caught his ear. The receptionist pressed her lips together, picked up the internal phone, and spoke in German. The art dealer must have been well known—just his name was enough to open doors.

In a corner, an interactive touchscreen map invited visitors to explore the layout. Even here, machines had replaced human guides. What was the point of resisting change? You adapted, or you were left behind.

"Okay," the receptionist said, hanging up. "The professor can see you tomorrow morning at 10:00 a.m."

Adrienne's face lit up. "Thank you. Thank you so much!" She turned to him. "We have an appointment—tomorrow!" She was radiant.

It felt good to see her happy. Elisabetta had never smiled like that. Finally, they could look for a hotel. Lorenzo held the door for her with a small bow. "After you."

Adrienne mimicked the gesture and stepped out, passing a stand crammed with colorful flyers. She plucked one and began flipping through it as she crossed the threshold.

Lorenzo followed—until his trolley snagged in the door, jerking him to a halt. The receptionist laughed; sometimes he really was too clumsy.

He freed the suitcase and let the glass door swing shut. In its reflection, something caught his eye—a black car across the square, gleaming like a pool of oil in the sun. Lorenzo turned and squinted: a bald man sat in the driver's seat.

Even at that distance, partly hidden, it was him. He'd drawn that face; he knew every proportion, every detail. A black cat clambered onto the dashboard, a white patch between its ears—the same cat from the construction site, the one that had scratched him before drinking from the bleeding tree.

Lorenzo swallowed. Now the question was different: was this real, or just another hallucination?

The headlights flared, and the car shot forward. A cyclist, pedaling casually, swerved hard at the last moment, barely staying upright. "Verdammter Idiot!" he shouted.

Not a hallucination. The man had followed them to Berlin.

"Do you like this?" Adrienne's voice.

"What?"

She tapped a photo in the brochure. "It lists nearby hotels—there's one just around the corner. Shall we go there?" She was smiling, oblivious.

Her cheerful tone made it clear she was enjoying the day. This wasn't the moment to tell her. "Sure, if that works for you."

"Then this way."

Remorse and worry rose in his throat. Was it right to keep it from her, just to spare her the fear? What difference would it make if she knew? They'd been followed from the start—that much was certain now.

They turned the corner; the hotel sign was only steps away. She kept chatting, and he answered with short, distracted replies. Another squat, blocky building. They went inside.

A blonde woman with her hair tied high greeted them and took their documents. She glanced at Adrienne's. "Oh là là—Dupont?" And just like that, they switched to French. The receptionist said something with a questioning lilt, and Adrienne gave a start.

She froze.

"What did she ask you?"

Adrienne met his eyes and swallowed. "She wants to know if we're taking a double room or a single."

His knees weakened. There was a hesitation in Adrienne's voice, a weight that gave the question a different meaning. And the softness in her gaze made her meaning almost explicit.

Lorenzo flushed; suddenly, his coat felt like one layer too many. "What would you like?"

Adrienne bit her lip and raised a finger toward the receptionist. "*Une chambre, s'il vous plaît.*"

Lorenzo pressed the keycard to the door. It clicked open. He opened it and stepped aside, as he always did, to let Adrienne in. She smiled as she passed, her feet gliding over the carpet like the softest of breaths, her gait carrying a rare uncertainty.

She was nervous.

And so was he.

Adrienne flicked on the light. A warm yellow glow filled the room. On the desk, a sprig in a scent diffuser released a trace of lavender; beside it lay a few unlit incense sticks. She brushed her fingers over them, then nodded toward the bathroom. "Maybe... I should take a shower." Her voice trembled, as if the words had slipped out with embarrassment.

But she didn't move. She stood there, looking at him with wide, uncertain eyes — different this time. As though she were seeing him for the first time.

That look weighed on him like a stone. It crushed him. How long had it been since he'd been with a woman — two years? His heart pounded in his chest, and still, she was waiting.

A few days earlier, she had spoken about the desire between husband and wife: *I take you.* That was the gesture she had hoped for. He stepped toward her, drawing her into his arms, his eyes never leaving hers.

She smiled, her posture melting at his touch — then stepped back. "Wait," she said. "If we keep going now, everything will change. Think."

"Think, you say?" True — everything would change. But maybe the time had come. "Thinking too much doesn't make you happy." And he kissed her.

Cinnamon in her hair, the spicy bite of ginger on her lips. What could a single second mean in the face of eternity? And yet, in that second, their lips met.

She began pushing him toward the bed, pressing her body to his. She pulled away, stepped back, and unfastened the sheath dress, letting it slide down her hips, her sandals still on.

How beautiful she was. A goddess. A Venus.

And he would be her Botticelli.

He couldn't wait—he had to draw her.

"Undress," he said.

He rushed to the bed, yanked the blanket free, and tossed it aside. The sheets were white—exactly what he needed. Stripping them from the mattress, he opened the wardrobe and wedged the sheet into the hinge space. Closing the doors stretched it taut, a perfect vertical canvas.

Adrienne followed his movements, mouth slightly open, eyes bright with surprise and mischief. She pulled off her top, leaving her in her bra and panties. "What exactly are you planning?" she asked, starting to slip off her heels.

"No! Stop." Lorenzo picked up one of the diffuser sticks—cedar. Perfect. Next to the incense was a box of matches; he struck one and charred the tip of the stick.

The heat made him sweat. He stripped off his shirt and pants. "Naked. On the bed." His voice was clipped, urgent, possessive.

The stick was now a small, smoldering charcoal that would crumble more than once, but it would do. Desire swept over him—yet inspiration, even more so. "Get on the mattress, close your eyes, and think of yourself, Adrienne. Think of who you are, what you want. What you dream of. Then, when you feel like yourself, choose a pose and hold it."

She hesitated. But she closed her eyes.

Her hands moved behind her back, unclasping the black bra. She slipped it off, revealing small, firm breasts. Her panties slid down next, and she climbed onto the bed on all fours, then knelt.

She breathed deeply, chest swelling, then exhaled, her sensual collarbones catching the light.

She was searching within herself, just as he'd asked.

Searching for Adrienne.

Then she opened her eyes and fixed them on him. She lay down on her side, ankles crossed; her thighs neither parted in vulgarity nor closed in modesty. Her sex was shaved — save for a small black tuft, clearly visible.

Leaning against the headboard, she lifted her right arm to rest across her forehead, putting on display the tattoo she had once hidden. She had called it a youthful mistake — an adolescent impulse — now worn with pride.

Lorenzo rolled the charcoal between his fingers, the ash darkening his fingertips. He calculated the spaces on the canvas: four eighths of the canvas for the legs, three for the torso, one for the head.

He began with the outline of her face, the curve of her jaw, then down her neck. Each stroke was an exploration, savoring the imagined touch of his lips along her throat, near her collarbone.

Then the curve of her lips — even from here, he could taste the ginger of the kiss they had shared. The swell of her breasts — soon he would touch them, explore them; drawing them stretched the moment, made it last.

The charcoal slid down the sheet, tracing the curve of her waist, her hips, the suggestion of a bent leg, poised to open for him.

The tension rose; the waiting tortured him.

And his arousal grew. At last, he reached her expression — he had to pour into it the same desire with which she was looking at him. She was waiting. Finally, the tattoo on her wrist, the very last line before the charcoal snapped.

Adrienne gazed at the work in silence, her eyes shining. "It's… beautiful."

Because she was so beautiful.

Adrienne shook her head, incredulous. "It does look a lot like me, but I don't have that mole. And the tattoo ink seems to be melting—what an imagination you have."

A mole?

Lorenzo glanced back at the sheet: he had drawn Elisabetta. The tattoo with the dripping ink was her slashed wrist, bleeding.

A laugh he couldn't hold back curled in his chest.

"Come on, come here now." Adrienne crawled to the edge of the mattress, took his hand, and pulled him onto the bed. She pressed herself against him, body to body, kissing him again and again. And all the while, someone was laughing. Laughing without a single breath.

No. Not now!

She glistened with sweat, gripped him by the nape, and guided his lips to her neck. "Kiss me. Please."

Lorenzo let her guide him, bit her—and his mouth grew wet. But it wasn't the sharp tang of sweat. It was blood. He looked at her and shuddered; it was Elisabetta's lifeless face staring back at him, eyes rolled so far back the whites gleamed. Her hair fanned across the pillow as if she were underwater. "What's wrong? Don't you want me?"

"Of course I want you."

"Why are you laughing?"

He hadn't laughed. Not him, anyway. But someone was laughing in his throat, and it never drew breath. Just like when they'd raped Martina. "I'm laughing because I'm happy."

Elisabetta kissed him, vomiting black blood. "I'm happy too," she said, her voice guttural and cavernous. Sliding her hand down, she gripped him, guided him inside. Wrapping her legs around his hips, she tightened them, drawing him in.

Lorenzo held back nausea and hysterical tears.

Meanwhile Elisabetta laughed and moved her hips in a steady rhythm. And laughed. Without once drawing breath.

After two years without a woman, this wasn't making love, but letting himself be abused. By the demon of the woman he had let die.

Domenico

Domenico flicked on the turn signal and pulled over near the German hideout of the Guardians of the Flame, just a few hundred meters from the museum. Their temporary base of operations was nothing impressive — only a garage in a small underground depot.

All the way to Germany, he had been forced to shadow those two sinners. It had gone well enough; he had barely avoided running over that damned cyclist. That would have drawn far too much attention.

The cat meowed and leapt back onto the dashboard. Twice now, the animal had made itself the unlikely guardian of his cover. During the stakeout at the museum, that meow had alerted him to the draughtsman's glance from across the street, an inquisitive look trying to place his face. Apparently, the man hadn't succeeded — he was too far away. And since he hadn't alerted Dupont, he clearly hadn't recognized him.

He'd had no choice but to follow them in person; they'd switched off their devices as soon as they reached

Germany. Tailing them this way was risky, but Grand Girolamo had promised to resolve the issue — though he still hadn't called. Domenico checked his phone: three bars. Nothing to do but wait and hope he wouldn't lose them.

Beyond the windshield, an advertisement sprawled arrogantly across the façade of a building: a man and woman locked in a lascivious embrace, the entire image contrived to flaunt the gold Rolexes on their wrists. A shiver of disgust ran down his spine. He would have gladly smashed those watches over their heads.

"Vanity, the mother of all sins," he muttered. Signs of spiritual weakness, crafted to seduce and deceive. A crude mask to hide an inner void behind a glittering façade.

The city's skyline was nothing like what he was used to. In Germany, buildings rose hard and unyielding, a hymn to pragmatism — less offensive to him than Italy's obsession with beauty.

Yet it grated on him, almost beyond endurance, that these streets belonged to the homeland of the Lutherans. They, too, had rebelled against the Church, but had chosen the heretical path, following false doctrines that tore at the fabric of the true faith.

"Lutherans," he hissed, the word itself venom on his tongue. "Heretics disguised as reformers."

The cat meowed, as if in agreement.

The phone's screen lit up. Praise be to the Saint — at last, his Master. "I'm here, Grand Girolamo."

"Domenico, stop tailing those two wretches in person. Have they seen you?"

"No, Master. All according to the Lord's will."

A long sigh came through the line. "Good. Our venerated Savonarola has come to our aid. The two checked into a hotel near the museum an hour ago. Where are you?"

"At the address you gave me — our base."

"Good. Go to the refuge; that garage is like a sanctuary to us. The heretics have just connected to the hotel Wi-Fi. They're updating their mobile plans for use abroad."

"It will be done, Master."

"Be steadfast, Domenico. Soon we will need your zeal. Sharpen your spirit — not through the mortification of the body, but through study. Keep your body strong; shed no blood for the Saint."

That command to refrain from penance meant action was close. "I will, Grand Girolamo."

"Good. The Apocalypse is at hand; the fifth seal is about to break. Through the work of the Guardians of the Flame, we will reveal the abyss to the world and open Dis."

"*Amen*, my Master."

The line went dead. Domenico crossed himself, reached for his backpack, and rummaged until he found the key with the beer-mug keychain. He pressed the remote: the garage gate rolled open. He started the engine and drove down the ramp.

Cell number forty-five — the days of Savonarola's imprisonment and torture. A double garage, with a cot and a cupboard at the far wall. He parked, switched on the light, and lowered the shutter. The air was dense with mold. Cramped and cold — fitting enough.

The cat meowed.

"Yes, I know you need to eat."

He opened the trunk and took out the bag for the cat, poured water into a bowl, and opened a can of tuna. The sharp, salty scent of fish filled the air.

The cat sniffed the food, lifted its head, and stared at him.

What a strange creature — turning its nose up at fish with almost aristocratic disdain. The only thing it had eaten eagerly was lamb, always rare. "I don't have any now. I'll get some tomorrow."

The cat meowed and padded over to the shutter. It sat and waited.

"You want to go hunting?"

It meowed.

Domenico chuckled — it truly was wild. "Go on, then. But be back soon; we're leaving tomorrow morning." He opened the door a hand's width, and the animal slipped out.

Alone again. He couldn't perform penance, but in the Guardians of the Flame's safehouses there was never a shortage of Savonarola's writings.

He walked to the back, gripped the wardrobe handle, and pulled. The doors opened with a long, sinister creak — hinges untouched by oil for far too long. Inside was an arsenal that would have made a Templar jealous: throwing knives with razor edges, long and short swords with mysterious engravings, daggers of exotic make…

No firearms — unworthy of the Saint. Some of the more discreet blades might prove useful tomorrow.

Beside them sat a chest. He opened it. Inside lay the tools for bigger jobs: detonators, timers, insulated wire — all arranged with obsessive precision.

Perhaps the books were in the low cabinet, tucked discreetly into the cupboard's shadow. Yes — volumes and manuscripts, pages steeped in faith, prophecy, and fervor.

He scanned the spines, looking for the right text. Given what awaited him, the *Sermon on the Art of Dying Well*, November 2, 1496, was perfect. He lay down on the sagging cot; the springs groaned under him. He opened the book, the scent of old paper rising from its pages. The copy was identical to the original, woodcuts and all.

Savonarola had recognized the power of movable type to reach the masses, sending an impressive number of sermons and homilies to press. The images were rough sketches, not meant to glorify vanity in art but to carry the message.

A stark contrast to the endless wandering among Botticelli's works; that traitor to Savonarola's followers had, after the Holy Martyr's death, returned to painting art and beauty. Not like his brother Simone Filipepi, faithful to the end.

Sadly, it had been Botticelli himself who studied Alighieri's *Comedy* and uncovered the path to the true gate of the infernal city of Dis. Once the Guardians of the Flame found that entrance, the Apocalypse would be certain.

Fifth seal, Revelation 6:9–11: the souls of the martyrs beneath the altar crying out for justice. Then the sixth and seventh seals — earthquakes, eclipses, falling stars, cosmic upheavals. And silence in heaven for half an hour, awaiting God's judgment.

Domenico had to prepare. Once the seal was broken, Grand Girolamo would administer what remained on earth. He prayed to the Saint and began to read: *"In omnibvs operibus tuis memorare novissima tua, et in aeternum non peccabis…"*

Woodcut from one of the four Florentine editions of Savonarola's sermon on the art of dying well, given on November 2, 1496.

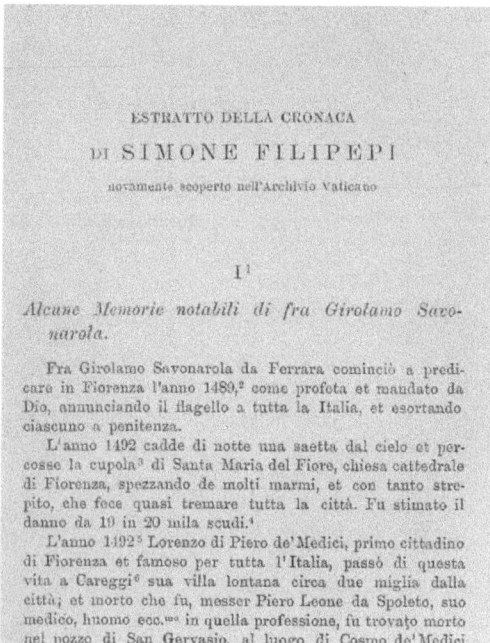

Testimony of Simone Filipepi (Botticelli's brother) taken from a collection on Savonarola in a volume published in Florence by G. C. Sansoni, Publisher 1898

2.8

Lorenzo leaned forward in the padded chair of the waiting room, shielding his eyes from a shaft of morning sunlight streaming through the window. The art museum's atrium was beginning to fill with the low hum of visitors as they waited for their meeting with Walter Obermann. Beside him, Adrienne watched the flow of people and kept shooting him discreet glances.

After one more glance, she sighed. "You're sure you're not hungry?"

"Sure, thanks." The memory of the night they'd spent together — Adrienne's face merging with Elisabetta's — turned his stomach. Was it really possible he still couldn't let it go? After two years?

Adrienne leaned forward, caught his gaze, and offered a sympathetic smile. "Do you feel guilty about Elisabetta?"

"What?" Lorenzo jerked in his seat. How could she know about his guilt over his partner's suicide? "Who told you? How do you know?"

She lifted her hands in surrender. "Calm down. You told me you were technically engaged but on a break. I meant — do you feel guilty about what we did yesterday?"

Lorenzo let out a long sigh. True—he'd lied to her. It wasn't the best way to start a relationship, but he had done it anyway. "It's more complicated than that."

"How so?"

He might as well tell her. Maybe if he laid that burden down, he'd stop seeing Elisabetta's face in hers. "The truth is... she died two years ago. She took her own life." The words burned on his tongue. "I feel guilty. But not about yesterday—it's... more complicated."

He stopped there. One truth at a time. It wasn't yet the moment to confess that he hadn't been able to save her.

Adrienne leaned back, silent for a moment. "Why didn't you tell me right away?"

"Because once I say it out loud, I can't pretend everything's fine anymore. I wanted to show you my best side—not weigh you down with my problems."

"What are you talking about? And me? Haven't I told you about my past?" Her expression tightened, hurt that he hadn't offered the same trust. Then it softened. "Think about what I told you before: anything that isn't mutual is toxic. Remember?"

Of course he remembered. That sentence still haunted him—and now she was using it to ask him to share the weight. His eyes burned, but he kept the tears at bay. "Thank you. Everything will be fine."

"Of course it will." Adrienne rubbed his back. "And you should start drawing again—it would do you good. Why did you throw away yesterday's sketch?"

Because it had been a nightmare. "It didn't do you justice."

"Then we'll redo it." She gave him a conspiratorial wink. "I'll help you get back into it. I saw the canvases and the dusty

art supplies at your place. You shouldn't have stopped —
maybe it would have helped you."

"Drawing did help me — but only when she was alive."

She frowned slightly. "What do you mean?"

It wasn't an easy answer. Lorenzo turned away. Visitors
kept streaming in: families with restless children, couples
holding hands, clusters of students with backpacks. Just
shadows, their laughter a grating noise in his ears.

She deserved the truth. "I loved Elisabetta, but I wasn't
happy with her. When she was alive, I used drawing as a
refuge — something to keep me going."

"And why did you do it?"

"Drawing gave form to my fantasies. A writer does it with
words, a musician with music. Anyone who lives in an
imaginary world does it because they can't bear the real one.
And when she killed herself, I realized she couldn't bear hers
either. Which meant I hadn't given her what she wanted. I
hadn't seen it, and I couldn't stop her."

Every step, every laugh, every photo snapped by the
people around them seemed amplified, grating in his
perception. This time, a tear tickled his cheek.

Adrienne took his hand. "It wasn't your job to stop her. It
wasn't your fault."

Lorenzo nodded, offering her a half-smile that wasn't real.

Some wounds can't be healed with reasoning; emotions
can't be subdued with logic. Scars never vanish completely. As
in a painting: erase a brushstroke and it still leaves a trace —
you have to accept it, weave it into the composition. That
would take time and work.

The receptionist beckoned them over with a wave.

Adrienne stood and offered her hand to help him up.

He took it, but instead of rising, he pulled her close and kissed her. It was time to pull himself together, to focus. Who knew — maybe Walter Obermann would shed some light on things.

———— ❧ ————

Accompanied by a security guard, Lorenzo and Adrienne climbed another flight of stairs and turned into yet another corridor — the place was vast. The corridor's cool air mingled with the softer warmth drifting out from the inner offices.

They stopped before a dark wooden door. The guard knocked, then opened it without waiting for a reply. He said something in German; a woman's voice answered with a formal cadence. Stepping aside, the guard gestured for them to enter.

Lorenzo went in first. Behind a desk, a secretary looked up from the planner she was filling out. Her smile wavered into uncertainty. Rising, she gestured toward the chairs in front of her. "Please, have a seat. Professor Obermann will see you shortly." She spoke in Italian — music to their ears.

"Thank you." Lorenzo pulled out a chair for himself, then the one beside it for Adrienne. He sat, the chill of the metal seeping through his clothes into his skin.

Grey filing cabinets crammed with folders, a computer, and a photocopier filled the space. In one corner, a small plastic plant made a half-hearted attempt to liven the room. A promotional calendar on the wall displayed images of artistic masterpieces — the only faint nod to the world of art.

From the door behind the secretary came a torrent of angry German. She acted as though she hadn't heard a thing. Her eyes, an indistinct grey, moved from Adrienne to Lorenzo, then back to Adrienne. She raised her eyebrows in an inquisitive arc, lips pressed into a thin line. "I've never seen you working with Mr. Manfredi," she said to Adrienne, her tone carrying a thread of professional curiosity.

"He hired me about six months ago."

The woman nodded. "Professor Obermann is very busy today, but when he heard that Mr. Manfredi's associate had requested a meeting, he rescheduled an appointment for you. Is there any news regarding the investigation?"

Lorenzo gripped the armrests; word was spreading in the field. The thought of travelling across Europe under his name made him feel guilty. Adrienne shook her head. "No news so far. That's exactly why we're here—we believe Professor Obermann might be able to help us."

"And what does Botticelli's *Inferno* have to do with this—the files you requested from us?"

"It was the last project my boss worked on," Adrienne replied without missing a beat.

The secretary pursed her lips and turned to Lorenzo. "Are you with the police?"

A pang in his chest. My God, what had Adrienne told them to get this meeting? He shot her a glance; the last thing they needed was to pretend he was a police officer after already passing him off as Manfredi.

"He's a forensic consultant who works with law enforcement. Why all these questions?"

Again, a burst of agitated German came from the inner office. The secretary stood. "Because, as I said, the professor is extremely busy. I need to be sure you're not here to waste his time."

She moved to the metal filing cabinets, opening one drawer, then another. The rails slid with a rough scrape, making it plain how heavy and overstuffed they were. She pulled out a thick dossier.

Returning to her desk, she set it down, opened it carefully, and began leafing through the pages with deliberate precision. "Here's the complete history of the Botticelli Codex — at least the part belonging to the Berlin collection. I'll just check if anything is missing."

Lorenzo couldn't help leaning forward, curiosity tugging at him. "Could you give us a preview?"

"About what, exactly?"

Adrienne craned her neck to look. "How the works arrived at your museum, if possible. That way we'll take up less of Professor Obermann's time."

The woman's face brightened — just the mention of saving her boss's time had done the trick. "Between 1780 and 1790, the drawings were in France. In 1803, the bookseller James Hedward, returning to Paris, reported that they were owned by Claudio Molini, a bookseller of Italian origin."

"Molini? An Italian bookseller in France?" Lorenzo repeated, glancing at Adrienne. "So Botticelli's drawings passed through your homeland too?"

The secretary pressed on, leaving no room for interruption. "It's likely the works had previously been gifted to the King of France. Then, in 1819, Molini sold the drawings to the 10th Duke of Hamilton, who added them to his art collection."

Adrienne leaned toward the document. "So the drawings went to England?"

"Scotland. But only briefly—they fell out of fashion, and the entire collection was put up for sale. In 1882, Friedrich Lippmann bought the lot for £80,000, including the Botticelli drawings, whose existence and significance were unknown at the time. The collection was shipped from Scotland to Berlin in eighteen zinc crates, loaded onto four ships."

"Could the missing *Inferno* works have been lost during that move?"

"Who can say?" The secretary smiled faintly. "But here's where it gets interesting. The Hamilton collection contained only eighty-three illustrations for the cantos of the *Divine Comedy*. Only later was the connection made to the drawings in the Vatican, once part of the Queen of Sweden's collection. At first, the few drawings in Rome were thought to be sketches, not part of such an extensive work. Later, when the collections were compared, it was discovered that six cantos before Dis were missing, along with four other drawings."

The door burst open and a sweaty man stormed out, shouting in German: "*Ich werde dich verklagen!*" He swept past without a glance and hurried down the corridor.

From the other room, a deep male voice continued to thunder in German, ending with an unmistakable: "*...du Idiot!*"

The secretary closed the file, stood, gathered the documents, and headed toward the inner office. "Professor Walter Obermann will see you now."

Hamilton Palace was a grand country residence located northeast of Hamilton, Scotland. Built in 1695 and demolished in 1927, its decline began in 1882 when William Douglas-Hamilton, 12th Duke of Hamilton, after losing significant capital in gambling, sold most of the collections accumulated by his grandfather and kept in the palace. Among these were the 85 drawings by Sandro Botticelli for the *Divine Comedy*, whose existence and importance were unknown in Berlin at the time.

2.9

Lorenzo and Adrienne crossed the office threshold, their footsteps muffled by a Persian rug woven with intricate geometric patterns. The room radiated a minimalist elegance; an Apple computer dominated the clean and orderly desk. Little else furnished the space: two brass floor lamps and a rustic-style bookcase.

Obermann sat behind the desk, setting down the file the secretary had left. His face was still drawn with the anger of an argument with his previous visitor. His gaze, hot with irritation, landed on them. He cleared his throat, softening his stern expression. "Please, have a seat." He spoke in Italian. He gestured toward the chairs in front of the desk; the gold watch on his wrist was massive and gleaming.

It was no accident that Manfredi had used that Rolex model to give him the nickname recorded in his notes: *Oyster*. Adrienne extended her hand. "Thank you for seeing us."

"Manfredi and I were friends and colleagues. I only learned yesterday what happened. And—since you're here on behalf of his agency—I don't recall ever seeing you with him."

"He hired me about six months ago." Adrienne tilted her head toward Lorenzo. "On the day of the murder, we were both there. Essentially, he passed the baton on his research to us."

The truth was more complicated, but that explanation sufficed to justify their presence. Lorenzo inclined his head slightly. "Thank you for taking the time to see us."

Obermann leaned toward the file. "From what I gather, you're here about Botticelli's drawings of the *Inferno*."

"Exactly." Adrienne nodded eagerly. "Your name appeared in Mr. Manfredi's diary. Could you tell us anything about that?"

The man stood and stepped aside; the cut of his suit was accented with buttons stamped with the Versace emblem, and the leather of his shoes bore the word Prada. He was the embodiment of designer elegance. "As it happens, not long ago I received a registered letter from Manfredi. Which is odd, considering that nowadays everything is handled by email."

Adrienne leaned forward, perching on the edge of her seat. "What did he say?"

Obermann snorted. "Why should I tell you? Isn't that something for the police, given the circumstances?"

"He's with the police." Adrienne pointed toward Lorenzo.

Oh God, not this again. Lorenzo straightened in his chair, forcing his voice to remain steady. "Yes, I'm a consultant who works with the police."

The professor pressed his lips together, unconvinced. "The letter contained a key and the address of a safe deposit box. I've never been there; I had no reason to. My time is limited."

"Could you give it to us?"

"No." The man laughed. "But I can check what's inside. It'll take a few days, though—the letter went to my villa in the mountains."

Lorenzo bit his lip. Any delay gave that fake gallery assistant more time to manipulate events. But there wasn't much they could do. The important thing was keeping him away from Adrienne. "Can we see the Botticelli drawings kept in your museum?"

Obermann shook his head. "No luck—they're at the labs for restoration. Where are you staying?"

"At the hotel near the museum."

"I know the place. I have an apartment nearby—my refuge for long nights of work. Did you come by car?"

"No."

"In that case, you could take the train to the labs... they're two or three hours from here. You could go in the next few days, while I retrieve Manfredi's correspondence. I'll give you a pass."

Better than nothing. Time was ticking for them too. One piece of information was still missing. Lorenzo inclined his head respectfully. "Thank you for your help. Any idea what Manfredi might have hidden in that safe deposit box?"

Obermann exhaled sharply and rubbed the back of his neck.

There was a knock at the door; the secretary's voice said something in German. Obermann picked up a sheet of paper. "Einen Moment, bitte." He drew a gold pen from his breast pocket and began to write. "The fact is, the last time I spoke with Manfredi, he shared some rather bizarre theories with me."

"Theories?" Adrienne rose from her chair. "Please, tell us. We're going crazy trying to piece together my former boss's research."

"Well…" He twisted his mouth into a half-grimace. "The subject of the *Inferno* lends itself to a certain aura of mystery, don't you think?" He stopped writing and folded the note. "For example, I've never understood one thing about the Christian religion: if the devil punishes the wicked, why is he the bad guy? Doesn't that seem contradictory to you?"

Maybe this professor harbored some spiritual doubts of his own—but to be sure, Lorenzo would have to prod him. Lorenzo swallowed a lump in his throat. "Are you a believer?"

"If you're asking whether I think there's something mystical in life, yes. But I don't follow any religion."

Adrienne stepped forward. "You mean you have faith, but you're not practicing?"

He laughed. "What is faith? Certainly, in Dante's and Botticelli's time, faith was experienced very differently—more tangibly."

Adrienne's face darkened. "I can assure you that even today, some people live their faith all too tangibly." Her eyes said *Bataclan*.

Obermann handed the folded note to Adrienne and returned to the desk. "Of course. But who can say who's right and who's wrong? Many Satanists have more faith than those who call themselves believers. There's a passage in the Bible that says: the demons believe, but do not obey. So what are we really talking about?"

Indeed—what were they talking about?

Another knock at the door; their time was up. Lorenzo pointed at the note. "Is this our pass?"

"Along with the address of the labs. We'll touch base in three or four days. I'll have someone call you at the hotel. If you are people of faith, I'd be careful. But even if you're not — the devil is on earth, the Bible says so clearly. Not only that — if he was able to offer the kingdoms of the earth to Christ to tempt him, it means they belong to him." Another knock. Obermann got up and opened the door.

Lorenzo and Adrienne stepped out, passing a suited man with a briefcase. In the hallway, the security guard was waiting. He escorted them outside. Lorenzo glanced at the address on the slip of paper — two lines in German accompanied it. "And now?"

"Tomorrow we'll go see the drawings. For now, let's head back to the hotel." Adrienne looked across the street toward a row of shops. "Actually, you go up to the room — I'll join you in a bit. I need to take care of something."

Lorenzo pulled back the curtain of the hotel room; Adrienne was still nowhere in sight. From the window drifted the faint hum of traffic and the muddled voices of the street below. The square, orderly buildings lent the scene a certain tidiness, but little to stir the senses.

He sat on the edge of the unmade bed; they'd hung the Do Not Disturb sign to keep housekeeping away. First, they had to deal with the painted sheet, crumpled in the corner to hide the portrait of Elisabetta. It was a pity Adrienne was meant to be the one gracing that makeshift canvas.

He glanced at the wall clock—nearly an hour had passed since they'd parted. Anxiety pressed on him. He should have told her he'd spotted the fake waiter sitting in that parked car...

Stupid, stupid, stupid! Whatever she'd gone to do, how could he have let her go alone!?

Heels clicked in the hallway and stopped at the door. The electronic key beeped, the lock clicked open, and Adrienne stepped inside, radiant, two bags in hand. My God—thank goodness!

Lorenzo rose to meet her, masking his worry behind a hardened expression. "What did you get?" He reached for the bags.

Her eyes swept the room, pausing on the balled-up sheets, a shy smile on her lips. "We had a problem to solve."

She handed him one of the bags. Lorenzo peeked inside—a new sheet. He chuckled and set the package on the table. "Well, now we can take down the sign and let them clean the room."

"Not now—tomorrow." Behind him came the rasp of a zipper, a sound that sent a jolt of ice through his veins. "Don't turn around. Today that sign stays right where it is."

Her tone left no room for argument. Lorenzo froze, eyes fixed on the bag. Behind him, the rustle of clothing sent heat climbing through him.

"Stay still," she repeated. Her heels clicked toward the bathroom, each step echoing in his head. She must be naked now, wearing only those shoes—just as he liked.

The rush of running water made him shiver.

No. Not the tub. Don't fill it...

Thankfully, the tap shut off, but the problem wasn't solved. What if the visions came back? What if, when he turned, he saw Elisabetta again, dripping blood? He swallowed hard. What if all of this was already just in his mind?

The world seemed to slow. Behind him, a gust of air snapped into the sound of fabric flaring—he pictured the sheets flung wide, settling over the bed. Light taps against the mattress.

Excitement tangled with fear. Then Adrienne cleared her throat. "Now, you can turn around."

His heart stopped.

Lorenzo closed his eyes and turned. There was no laughter in the darkness behind his lids, so he opened them. Adrienne was an epiphany—bare skin, loose hair, black sandals drawing the eye down her legs. Her nakedness was both power and vulnerability. She showed him her palms, smeared with dark paint.

The old sheets, now unrecognizable, concealed every trace of the bed. Elisabetta's portrait had been smeared with dark handprints—the little taps he'd felt earlier on the mattress.

Adrienne shrugged. "I saw how you looked at that picture—with fear and disgust. I thought we should redo it—my way." She pointed to the nightstand.

On the bedside table she had arranged a palette of water-based tempera paints, a glass of water, and some brushes. She crawled to the center of the bed, lay back, and ran her paint-smeared fingers from her neck between her breasts, leaving a black streak. "No sheet today. I'll be your canvas."

Lorenzo stood still, emotions churning. Adrienne's act—so intimate, so bold—struck him deep. A gesture of trust and complicity, defying every expectation.

She watched him, waiting.

She was a Venus imbued with art. To paint, at its purest, was more than laying images on canvas—it was seeing beyond the surface, turning pain into beauty, shouting a message to those who would not hear.

The naked muse offering her body was the embodiment of a woman taking control of her life, deciding for herself what to do with it.

He closed his eyes; her presence alone filled the room with beauty and sensuality.

Lorenzo moved along the side of the bed, picked up a brush, and tested its make—it was badger hair. He leaned over, teasing her sternum with the bristles, drawing a shiver from her. She trembled.

His canvas: a mortal body ready to host an abstract idea on its skin. The distillation of human spirituality, of faith, and of hope.

And Hell.

His own private Hell, too: Adrienne's gesture had silenced the laughter in his throat and the nightmares in his head.

Hell could wait—for now, he would savor the sin.

Once she was painted, they would wrap around each other, becoming one, transferring the design from skin to skin—until sweat erased every trace, except from memory.

2.10

Lorenzo opened his eyes again; the other side of the bed was empty. On the nightstand lay a sheet of paper, folded in half. He unfolded it: *Hi, I went out to run an errand.* Punctuated with a lipstick kiss. They'd stayed up late the night before.

He sat on the mattress. In the corner, the old sheets lay crumpled again, now just a single multicolored blot. The day before, they'd spent the afternoon making love, tidied up a bit, and gone out for dinner. Back in the room, they'd stayed in bed talking—hours spent holding her without doing anything. Not a moment wasted.

The thought of her being out alone unsettled him. He picked up his phone to call her—he had service now, even abroad. The screen read three o'clock in the afternoon.

Three? My God, they'd missed the train to visit the labs! He hit the call button. A vibration came from the side table: Adrienne's phone was there.

She'd never be careless enough to go out without it. Anxiety gripped him. He jumped out of bed and pulled on his pants—he'd run out and—

The door opened. Adrienne walked in, her forehead shiny with sweat. "Ah, finally awake. Good morning."

"Where were you? You're out of breath."

"I took the stairs—the elevator was busy. I went to withdraw some cash and... But why are you so worked up?"

Calm down, Lorenzo. Get a grip. He was unloading his paranoia on her, and it wasn't fair. "Nothing. It's just—it's three o'clock. We had a train this morning for the labs."

She nodded. "I woke up and saw we'd already missed it, so I took it easy. I booked another one for six p.m."

"But we'll get there so late. Today's Saturday, and tomorrow they're closed."

Adrienne stepped closer and pressed a kiss to his lips. "*Chéri,* then we'll just sleep there and go to the labs Monday morning. We don't have an appointment, just Obermann's pass. I'll book a hotel for tonight."

She was calm, at ease—unlike him.

Lorenzo drew a deep breath. Adrienne's composure softened his anxiety. Nothing was actually wrong. "You're right. Let's straighten the room and head out."

She glanced around, then winked. "In a bit—we've still got half an hour…"

* ❧ *

Monday, at the laboratories

It was cold, the kind of cold that felt like it could cut through your skin. Luckily, Sunday had been gentler, letting them spend Sunday strolling through the city like two sweethearts. Lorenzo checked his phone: nine o'clock sharp, well rested—just as Adrienne had predicted.

The security guard looked them over, his face stern under a stiff cap, then opened the door to the labs. Beyond it: cameras, security grilles, a secretary behind bulletproof glass.

Adrienne stepped forward and handed over Obermann's note. The secretary read it, stood, and picked up the phone. Behind her, an analog wall clock showed eight o'clock.

Eight?

Lorenzo pulled out his phone—nine. There was a one-hour gap. Odd. He leaned toward Adrienne. "Different time zone here?" He gestured toward the clock.

She frowned, tilted her head, then raised her brows. "No—last night was the switch to daylight saving time. They must not have changed the wall clock yet."

So that was it—the time change. His phone had updated automatically. A faint irritation rose in his throat; technology had become so woven into daily life he barely noticed how much it did for him. It would be the same with AI, he thought—you just had to adapt.

The heavy door clicked open; the woman behind the glass motioned them inside and spoke to the guard. He escorted them down a long corridor into a climate-controlled, sterile room, the air vents like those in the Vatican Museums. At the center stood a table with a flexible arm ending in a magnifying lens.

A woman in her fifties, dressed in a white lab coat, waited for them with composed dignity. On a metal cart beside her lay two parchments under glass: the Botticellis from the Berlin collection. "Italian?" she asked, her German accent hard-edged as an anvil.

Lorenzo nodded; Adrienne did too, less convincingly.

The woman smiled. "Forgive me if I don't speak well, but I can try. We often work with the Holy See, so many of

Professor Obermann's colleagues speak Italian. He told us of your visit. Botticelli, correct?"

"Yes," Adrienne replied. "Could you tell us something about your collection?"

"The works we hold include *Purgatorio* and *Paradiso*, unlike those in the Vatican Archives, which are only of the *Inferno*. The closer you get to Paradise, the more detailed the drawings become. You can see some intriguing details of Botticelli's work."

She spread a white cloth across the table, the fabric soft and pristine. Slipping on cotton gloves, she lifted the drawing with a delicacy bordering on reverence. "In one *Paradiso* drawing, you can see Botticelli changed his design: at first, Beatrice was looking toward the sky, but later he turned her gaze to Dante—so the two lovers would meet each other's eyes."

She laid the drawing on the table, and Lorenzo stepped closer to study it. He leaned toward the protective glass: the artist's confident hand, soft yet precise, had captured the two of them gazing into each other's eyes. But there was also a faint, faded line—where Beatrice had once been looking up at the sky.

Botticelli had wanted the lovers to meet not only in space, but through their gaze—a bridge between the two souls the poet had described with such passion.

"May I?" Adrienne shifted her arm, running the magnifying glass over the drawing. "Are there other erasures?"

The restorer shook her head. "Botticelli began by marking the outlines with an awl on the parchment, then sketched the preliminary lines with a metal stylus, and finally inked in the details. Each step was meant to minimize mistakes—parchment was expensive in those days."

It was true—and one of the reasons ancient works carried such value, shaped by a craftsmanship alien to modern haste.

Adrienne exhaled sharply. "That's all very interesting, but we're looking for the missing pages from this work. The ones from the *Inferno*."

"I understand. We have no information about the missing Infernal Cantos. But I can tell you something about the last two drawings of the *Paradiso*, which are also missing. We believe Botticelli may never have sketched them at all."

"Never sketched them?" Adrienne set the magnifying glass on the corner of the table. "You mean he died before drawing them?"

"No. It's more likely he abandoned the work because of the rise of woodcut printing, a technology revolutionizing art at the time."

Lorenzo stepped closer, perhaps unsure he'd heard right. "Forgive me—are you suggesting Botticelli set aside his work because a new technology threatened to smother his art?"

"Yes. In fifteenth-century Italy, printed illustrations were gaining ground. Book miniatures were no longer painted by hand, but carved into wood and mass-produced. In 1578, an edition of the *Divine Comedy*—nicknamed *Del nasone*—was published with ninety-six woodcut engravings." Her mouth turned down, regret etched in her expression. "Botticelli's illustrations paired with the text of the Cantos belonged to the past. It's likely he never completed the work out of sheer discouragement."

And now, centuries later, they were staring at unfinished drafts—abandoned because the artist had lost faith in himself, daunted by the dawn of printing.

For Lorenzo, it was the progress of AI.

How he longed to see Botticelli's completed drawings. The master was celebrated for his colors. What a loss for the art world. Lorenzo bit the inside of his cheek, branding the thought with a stab of pain. He had to shake it off—he couldn't give in. Change wasn't to be stopped, but embraced.

"And that one?" Adrienne pointed to the cart, where another panel lay. "Is it from the *Inferno*?"

The restorer shook her head. "*Paradiso* again, but a very unusual one. The angel carries a banner with Botticelli's name on it, as if pleading with the Almighty for forgiveness. Had it been colored, the inscription would have been hidden—known only to him."

Lorenzo's mind flashed to Adrienne's bare skin, when the sweat of their passion had erased the design he'd painted there. Those lines, too, had been theirs alone.

The *Paradiso* drawings were exquisite, and there was one detail which, if true, would make the work immortal. "For Beatrice's portraits, did Botticelli draw inspiration from the woman he was said to love—the same one he painted as Venus?"

"Of course—Simonetta Vespucci. They shared a special bond; just think where she's buried."

"And where is that?"

The woman knit her brows in dismay. "In the Church of Ognissanti—where Botticelli rests as well. They lie side by side."

It hit him like a blow to the heart: they had been there only days before and missed it. Lorenzo fought back his emotion. Was that the artist's calling—to give voice to suffering?

Paradiso and *Inferno* in the union of two souls: Dante and Beatrice, Botticelli and Simonetta. Lorenzo and who?

He searched for Adrienne's gaze, but she was too absorbed in the drawings and the investigation.

When she finally looked up, it wasn't at him. "This is all very beautiful, but we're searching for the missing works of the *Inferno*. These details don't help us."

The woman lifted the drawing from the table and set it back on the cart. "There's no definitive proof, but the missing drawings are more likely in the Vatican collection than in ours."

Adrienne sighed and looked at him, her eyes full of frustration. "Our only option is to see what's in Manfredi's safe-deposit box."

She hadn't been thinking about him.

About them.

Lorenzo swallowed a bitter taste, a laugh echoing in his throat.

In his ears, the rhythmic drip of a drop falling into a brimming basin.

Unlike Dante, he kept making the journey over and over—from *Inferno* to *Paradiso*, and from *Paradiso* back to *Inferno*.

The only question was where he would finally stop between the two. Perhaps that was the purpose of the map—to lead him to Dis.

In this drawing of the *Paradiso*, it is possible to see Botticelli's correction on Beatrice's head, where the artist wanted her to look at Dante rather than at the sky.

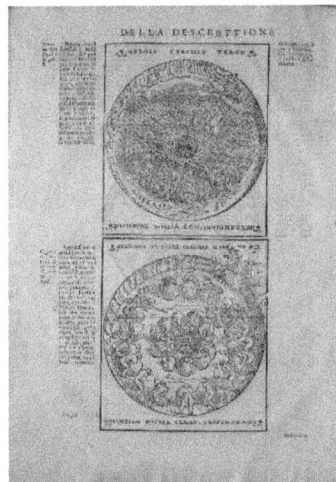

Divine Comedy – Nasone Edition. So called because of the image on the frontispiece – 1578 (with 96 woodcut engravings).

2.11

They stepped out of the station—Berlin once again before them—under a leaden sky heavy with the promise of rain. They would book the same room at the hotel near the museum and press for another meeting with Obermann. Three days had passed since their last conversation—the agreed time to verify the contents of the safe-deposit box.

Adrienne turned, the light catching on her pulled-back hair, tinged with a bluish sheen. "Shall we walk?" Her voice was a caress. "If I'm not mistaken, it takes just as long on foot as by car." Without waiting for an answer, she set off, her high ponytail swaying in time with her steps.

Lorenzo followed, drawn to that kind of decisiveness—perhaps because he lacked it himself. Falling in beside her, he said, "I wonder what Obermann found in the safe-deposit box."

"Hopefully something useful," she murmured, her dark eyes fixed on the pavement. "Some detail we overlooked." She was too consumed by the investigation.

As for him...

He was here for Adrienne—driven by a desire that burned in his veins, by her magnetism that pulled him in, and by her resemblance to Elisabetta, which pushed him past the bounds of reason. There was a risk she, too, might lose heart if they failed to find the answers they sought. "This isn't becoming a problem for you, is it?"

"What?"

"These investigations. You're obsessed—well beyond what's reasonable. Is it because of your boss's death?"

She hesitated, biting her lip. "Partly."

Had she told him everything? "Were you involved with him?"

She stopped and shot him a sharp look. "Mon Dieu, what's gotten into you?"

"Well, you know full well that continuing with these investigations is risky."

She shrugged and resumed walking. "I can't stand leaving things unfinished."

"Unfinished? What does that have to do with this?"

"You see—" Adrienne stopped again and met his gaze. "Manfredi was a good man. So were my parents. He was murdered by religious fanatics." Her voice broke; she was fighting back tears. "I need answers. Without them, I'll never be at peace."

Poor thing—she was carrying guilt that wasn't hers. Just as he did with his own past. Lorenzo brushed her cheek gently. "It wasn't your fault. Things just happen—it's fate." The words left a faint taste of bitter hypocrisy in his mouth.

She started walking again. "I know it wasn't my fault. But even if we can't choose our fate, we can give it meaning."

A reply that floored him.

There was nothing more to say.

As they neared the hotel, a burst of urgent voices reached them. They turned the corner into chaos: police cars blocking the street and sidewalks, blue lights slicing through the monotony of the heavy gray sky.

"What's going on?" Adrienne's voice betrayed a note of worry.

Lorenzo pulled her close. Adrenaline surged in his veins; his excitement and apprehension were mounting. "Let's find out."

He took her hand and they moved forward. Three German police cars stood at the hotel entrance, officers speaking with two men in Italian uniforms. One wore a jacket marked *Polizia* — not regulation issue, but still bearing the insignia of Italian law enforcement.

"What are the Italian police doing here?" Lorenzo whispered, more to himself than to her.

She squeezed his hand tighter, her steps faltering. The little trust she had in the police seemed to weigh on her shoulders like a sodden cloak.

The Italian officers looked up, their dark uniforms stark against the reflective vests of their German colleagues. Adrienne froze and tugged at Lorenzo's sleeve. "We'd better go," she murmured.

"Miss Dupont, Mr. Berti!" The voice of the Florence inspector rang out from the street perpendicular to theirs.

My God, what was happening?

"I've been looking for you repeatedly," the inspector said, signaling to his colleagues to join them. "If I'm not mistaken, you were ordered not to leave Italy. And yet, you look perfectly at ease." He gave a knowing glance at their joined hands.

The tension mounted. They let go, and Adrienne folded her arms across her chest. "Has he been following us?"

"I came here for you—to coordinate with the German police. Then something terrible came to light." The inspector regarded them, hands clasped behind his back, his stance both authoritative and thoughtful. "Mr. Obermann has been found dead." The calm with which he spoke made the words feel almost unreal.

Lorenzo's breath caught; the shock hit him like a blow to the gut. Beside him, Adrienne turned pale, her gaze fixed on nothing—staring into space.

"Stranger still." The inspector brought his hands forward, revealing a small notebook. He flipped it open and leafed through its pages—"Professor Obermann had your names in his diary."

The suspicion was understandable. A wave of indignation and unease swept over Lorenzo. "That doesn't mean it was us!" His voice came out sharper than he'd intended, betraying his nerves. "When did it happen? We only just got back."

The inspector looked up, locking eyes with him. "I know you were outside Berlin, but the murder took place before you left." His tone remained neutral, which somehow made the air grow colder. He knew his stuff; that much was undeniable.

He bent over his notes again, eyes tracking the lines of ink, then shifted his attention to Adrienne, as if trying to read her— something beyond words. "You said you were only recently hired by Manfredi. Correct?"

"Yes. But what does that have to do with anything?"

"That you never specified the circumstances of your hiring, Miss." His tone sharpened, edged with accusation. Adrienne lowered her gaze to the floor.

What was going on? Lorenzo searched her face for a clue, anything that might make sense of this. But she stayed motionless, swallowing hard, refusing to meet his eyes. She seemed somehow smaller, her face a mask.

The inspector continued. "The previous secretary suffered a mysterious accident that left her bedridden for months. Run over by persons unknown—just when Manfredi began his research on Botticelli's *Inferno*. Then you appeared. When her convalescence ended, the young woman recovered but was paid a generous sum not to return. And you received a very comfortable contract renewal. Doesn't that strike you as odd?" He seemed to relish it.

Lorenzo froze, a shiver crawling down his spine. Why was he starting to doubt? These were conjectures, not evidence. She wasn't deceiving him… was she?

He reached out, pulling her close by the shoulder—he would stand by her. "Your accusations are baseless. The killer is the bald man we ran into at the Uffizi."

"Because you say so, Berti."

"No. Witnesses in the queue saw him too."

"They saw him leaving, not attacking Manfredi. Three people went into that restroom, and only two came out. You had his blood on you."

"The weapon!" Adrienne burst out. "The murder weapon wasn't in the restroom—you said so yourself. Which means it couldn't have been Lorenzo." She defended him without a heartbeat's hesitation.

And yet, why did he still feel betrayed?

The inspector nodded. "I'll give you that. That's why Mr. Berti isn't in prison." He allowed himself a thin, mocking half-smile. "But for you, Miss, the situation has changed. You claimed to know nothing about Manfredi's research. If it was just a job, why push so hard to investigate? Was it of personal interest?"

Lorenzo didn't hesitate, repaying the loyalty she had just shown him. "She only wants to finish the job and find her former boss's killer—it's her fight against religious fanatics."

"Really? Against fanaticism?" The inspector laughed and winked, self-satisfied. "Then tell me—why were you hired by the art dealer thanks to the Vatican's persistent recommendations?"

"You?" Lorenzo stepped back from her. "You were hired because of the Vatican's recommendations?"

Adrienne lowered her head and stayed silent. The inspector delivered the final blow. "The same Vatican that houses some of the Botticelli Collection and is searching for the missing pieces recommended a young woman who claims to be at war with religious fanatics? Call them conjectures if you like—but don't you think there are a few too many coincidences?"

2.12

A fine, needling drizzle began to fall—too little to hide the tears. Not that Lorenzo had any. The realization that Adrienne had betrayed him had drained even the urge to cry. Maybe that would come later.

She kept her gaze on the cobblestones, now speckled with dark, wet spots, and said nothing. Then she lifted her head, avoided Lorenzo's eyes, and fixed her gaze on the inspector. "You still haven't told us whether we're suspects in Obermann's murder."

Lorenzo nodded. They'd been away for three days, and the professor had authorized them to open Manfredi's safe deposit box. The only question was whether he'd been killed before or after that. He turned to the inspector. "When exactly was Obermann killed, and how?"

The man shot him a sideways look. "If you don't mind, I'll be the one asking questions. Where were you last Saturday between three and four in the afternoon?"

Adrienne's mouth tightened. "We left that Saturday evening. Before that, we were at the hotel—in our room."

Heat surged into Lorenzo's cheeks at the memory of that afternoon tangled in the sheets. The time frame the inspector had mentioned was uncomfortably precise. "Why exactly three o'clock? Is that when Obermann died?"

The inspector's jaw clenched, his irritation plain. "As I said, I ask the questions." His words came out in a hiss that left no room for reply.

Every moment of that Saturday afternoon was etched in Lorenzo's mind as if it had happened yesterday. Adrienne had arrived late—stepping into the room at exactly three o'clock—a detail that now seemed crucial in deciding whether to trust her. He tried to sound firm. "I'm asking so I can give you a precise answer. Are you only concerned with the time between three and four on Saturday?"

"Yes."

Lorenzo let out a sigh and smiled. Legally, nothing had changed: during that hour, they'd been together, making love. Neither could serve as the other's alibi. But his trust in Adrienne had changed—an hour earlier she'd been out running errands. "At that time we were together, in our hotel room. The key card logs every entry—you can verify that."

The inspector shook his head. "The card only shows that someone entered the room. Could've been just one of you."

Lorenzo lowered his gaze; the fine rain traced patterns on the ground, merging into a single gray wash, while a dry halo remained directly beneath him. He needed more to clear their names. "Will you at least confirm that's the murder window? If you're accusing us, we need to defend ourselves!"

The inspector weighed the question for two breaths. "Yes, that's the time. The coroner gave us a three-hour window, but we narrowed it down. Professor Obermann wore a very distinctive watch."

"A Rolex Oyster. I get it: you gave us that window because they broke it in the struggle, and it stopped sometime after three on Saturday?"

"The hands had stopped, but not at that time. And it wasn't broken, only scratched."

"Scratched?"

"Yes." The inspector flipped up his coat collar. "Someone had marred the crystal—a gesture of hatred."

Then why were they so sure about that time frame? Lorenzo's confusion deepened. "How could the hands have stopped if the watch wasn't broken? And at a different time, you said."

"Because it's an automatic watch, powered by movement. When fully wound, it runs thirty-five hours without being worn. We subtracted those hours from the time on the stopped hands and arrived at the window between three and four on Saturday. In any case, not before three."

Lorenzo's gaze drifted into the rain. He pulled Adrienne to him by the shoulder, but she stayed stiff. And silent. She didn't defend herself. She didn't speak.

It was strange behavior.

And yet—even though she'd been late that Saturday—she had entered the room at three, so she couldn't have been the killer. True, she'd kept her Vatican business—whatever it was—from him.

Could he trust her?

A thought flashed through Lorenzo's mind—an idea that made Adrienne guilty. He ran the numbers again, and they still fit: she could have done it. Anger flared; he spun her to face him so he could look her in the eyes. "Were you there?"

She didn't answer.

My God—Adrienne's eyes were guilty.

Lorenzo dropped his hands from her shoulders and stepped back. She could have done it.

2.13

The drizzle had stopped, leaving a thin film of water on their shoulders and clothes. A few passersby slowed, curious about the police presence. They cast the occasional accusatory glance before moving on.

A German officer gestured to the inspector, who nodded and turned to the nearby Italian colleagues. "Keep an eye on them, but don't cuff them. Not yet." Without another word, he walked away.

Lorenzo tried again to catch Adrienne's elusive gaze, but she kept her eyes fixed on the ground. The fear that his suspicions were right sent his heart hammering toward the edge of tachycardia. But the doubt had to be settled — one way or the other. "Obermann had a place near our hotel. They got the timing wrong, didn't they?"

Adrienne didn't look up, but her brows lifted. "Just ask me."

The officer stood two or three meters away, fiddling with his phone. He wasn't paying attention, but it wasn't worth the risk. Lorenzo pulled Adrienne into an embrace; the contact sent a shiver down his spine. He whispered, "Was it you?"

At last she met his eyes, letting him see she wasn't lying. "No. It wasn't me."

"But you were there, weren't you? You were late that morning because you were there."

She turned away, but Lorenzo caught her chin and guided her face back toward his. He knew he was right, but he needed to hear her say it. " The clocks had changed halfway through. They should have subtracted 36 hours, not 35, because we had moved the clocks forward by an hour. The murder happened at two p.m., when you weren't in the room."

Adrienne stayed still, holding his gaze. The familiar cinnamon scent of her hair had become a nauseating stench. Her eyes fixed on some vague point on the ground, but it was clear she wasn't seeing anything around her. "It's... complicated. He was already dead when I got there."

The confirmation. "And all the other lies?"

"They weren't all lies."

"Oh no? And the Vatican?"

Adrienne huffed. "You think they hand a Botticelli to just anyone? Making you pretend to be Manfredi was a way to draw you in. I really did need you."

"To use me."

"No! You." She sighed. "Just you." Her eyes, bright with tears, radiated sincerity—but how could he trust her? Adrienne sniffled. "The Bataclan story was true, as was my struggle. Even Botticelli was a Savonarola once—a fanatic."

"Savonarola," he repeated, aghast. Rage flared, clouding his vision. "Who the fuck cares about Savonarola and Botticelli! I made love to you two years after my girlfriend killed herself—do you get that or not?!"

She lowered her head. A long, suspended silence followed. Then Adrienne pulled her smartphone from her coat, unlocked it, and opened her contacts.

"Hey!" the officer let out a sharp whistle. "Miss, you can't use your phone right now."

Adrienne hesitated, then straightened. "Are you trying to stop me from calling my lawyer?"

The officer faltered, then sighed and nodded.

Adrienne scrolled through her saved numbers, stopping at Sandro B., and placed the call.

Lorenzo's knees trembled. "Who are you calling?"

The line rang three times; someone picked up, then immediately hung up. Adrienne handed the phone to Lorenzo. "I'll explain everything. You have to trust me."

What was she talking about? How could he possibly trust her?

A laugh began to swell in Lorenzo's gut—Elisabetta's laugh. And then he was laughing too, loud enough to draw stares. But he didn't want to laugh, so why was he?

He was mad—completely gone.

In a burst of rage or madness, he smashed Adrienne's phone against his own head. Idiot! Nothing but an idiot! His rain-wet forehead ran with warm blood. Maybe he could crack his skull, join the forest of suicides too! A weakling, a sucker, an idiot of a dreamer!

"What are you doing?" the officer shouted, rushing over. He seized Lorenzo's wrist and forced his arm down, stopping him from hurting himself further.

Adrienne backed away, frightened. Two tears slid down the cheeks of that liar. Lorenzo bared his teeth and shouted, "Stop pretending!"

At the beginning of the street, a black car screeched to a halt, its door already open. Adrienne spun and bolted, leaping inside just as the vehicle roared away.

Sirens. Chaos. Confusion.

Several cars gave chase. The inspector barked an order to a colleague, who snapped the cuffs onto Lorenzo's wrists.

As if he cared.

He'd been wrong to chase those fucking drawings—he didn't need an investigation to find the infernal City of Dis. His life was already Hell. It was his past, his present, and it would be his future.

And in all three, it was his fault.

2.14

Domenico

A security guard buzzed the door open, muttered something in German, and motioned for Domenico to move along. He left the vault behind and returned to the bank's lobby. Everything he saw made his stomach churn; it felt more like a temple devoted to gold than to God.

Cold, sterile light bounced off surfaces polished to excess — marble floors as frigid as the hearts of the sinners who walked them, towering windows designed not to frame the sky but to tarnish it with their latticework. A place consecrated to the hoarding of fleeting riches.

Disgusting.

A banker signaled him over, and Domenico stepped back to the lacquered mahogany counter at the teller window. It reflected the light with gaudy pride, as though that shine could disguise the sinful nature of the transactions carried out there. He took back the forged document and forced a smile — may Savonarola forgive his falsehood.

Moments earlier, surrounded by safe deposit boxes, he had nearly vomited. Inside those steel coffers, the souls of the wealthy locked away their material sins, imagining they could keep them separate from their consciences. Fools.

But soon, the world would change.

Surely the Saint, after destroying the Great Harlot of False Religions, would move on to raze the banks — perhaps starting with this one. The image of that sanctuary of sin reduced to smoking rubble lifted his spirits.

And it wasn't the only memory to kindle his spirit: that greedy slave to Obermann's pleasures had got what he deserved. Everything was unfolding as planned; surely it was the Saint's will that he had found instructions for retrieving Manfredi's research on the person of that impious man with the ostentatious watch.

Clutching the papers from the safe deposit box, Domenico walked toward the double security door, nausea gnawing at him. The cylinder closed behind him with a muffled clang, and a recorded voice instructed him to place his finger on the scanner.

Again... Domenico pulled off his glove. The thought of touching that cursed device with bare skin sent another wave of gagging through him. It was like passing through Purgatory — a necessary but painful step on the way to liberation from this Hell of perdition. He pressed his index finger to the reader, and the second door slid open.

He was free — and he had the notes.

He spat into the alcove behind him, moistened his fingertip with saliva, and rubbed it clean with his sweater. Much better. He slipped his glove back on, picked up his phone, and returned to the car.

Grand Girolamo answered on the first ring — he must have been waiting. "Have you recovered Manfredi's notes?"

What joy to bring him such news. "Yes, Master."

"Have you examined them? Do they reveal the location of the city of Dis?"

Domenico closed his eyes, savoring the moment. It was a day for celebration. "Yes, Master. They indicate where the infernal city lies. I'll head there at once and break the seal."

"No! I must be there too. Do not proceed without me — swear it on the Holy Martyr!"

Domenico's stomach tightened — how could he ask him to swear? "Master, forgive me if I offend you, but the Divine Word commands us not to swear." The light turned green, and he stepped into the street. "Least of all by taking the Saint's name in vain."

From the receiver came only Grand Girolamo's breathing. "Almost right, Domenico. I wanted to test you: one does not swear by the Saint's name. But take care not to utter another blasphemy. What we are doing is no trivial whim."

Domenico stopped in the middle of the crosswalk and knelt. "Master, I have sinned." The walking-man signal turned from yellow to red. He closed his eyes. "Savonarola, if you wish to take my soul, do it now," he murmured, as car horns blared around him.

"What are you doing? We have a mission! Guard your body, Domenico — you hold the key to breaking the seals."

Strange that Grand Girolamo would doubt the Saint's work. But who was he to judge? Domenico rose and finished crossing, heading for the car. "I'll wait for you before breaking the seal, Master. Manfredi's notes mark the city's location, but not its entrance. I'll contact you as soon as I find it."

"Good. Let His will be done."

"Forever praised, world without end. Amen."

Domenico got into the car and set Manfredi's notes on the passenger seat. At the first rest stop, he would burn them. The cat leapt onto the dashboard and sat.

"See? We've got the notes."

A meow answered him.

"What do you say? Shall we go find the entrance — break the fifth seal and usher in the end of the world?"

The cat purred, then curled up on the seat. Domenico said a prayer to the Saint. He was ready. Revelation 6:9–11: The souls of the martyrs beneath the altar cry out to God for justice.

And who but Savonarola deserved the title of martyr!

Only in recent years had the truth of his ordeal come to light: even his excommunication had been false — nothing but a power play orchestrated by the Devil himself.

He had been excommunicated by the Cardinal Archbishop of Perugia, Juan López, in the pope's name, at the urging of Cesare Borgia, the pope's own son, who had hired a forger to produce a fake decree meant to destroy the friar.

The pope had found out and protested bitterly to the cardinal, threatening Florence with an interdict if they did not clear Savonarola's name. But he was so enthralled by his son that he never used the power at his disposal, nor dared reveal the deceit his beloved heir had committed.

That was no Holy See of God!

Savonarola's first sermon after the excommunication had been a prophecy. He began by pretending to answer an interlocutor who reproached him for preaching while excommunicated: "Have you read this excommunication? Who sent it? Do not marvel at our persecutions; do not be disheartened, you who are good, for this is the fate of the prophets — this is our fate and our reward in this world."

Ironically, that excommunication truly was worthless — but he could not have known it.

The evidence does not lie: Savonarola was a prophet.

And in his name, Domenico would reach Dis and unleash the Apocalypse on earth. He started the engine and drove off.

Contra fratrem Wieronymum
Weresiarchä libellus et pcessus.

A printed pamphlet denigrating Savonarola; the Latin inscription reads: *Against Brother Girolamo, leader of the heretics.* In the illustration, three demons can be seen inspiring the friar's sermons.

Cesare Borgia, known for his ruthlessness and ambition, orchestrated a conspiracy to discredit Savonarola and remove him from power in Florence. Borgia had a papal bull of excommunication against Savonarola forged, falsely attributing it to Pope Alexander VI. This fake excommunication was used by Cesare Borgia (the illegitimate son of the same pope) to justify Savonarola's arrest and subsequent execution in 1498.

Lorenzo's eyes traced the room's perimeter: grey, cold, bare walls without a single window — a perfect mirror of his state of mind. The place reeked of sweat and tears. His own.

He took a sip of water; after four hours of interrogation at the German police station, his mouth was as dry as sandpaper.

The inspector was speaking in German to a hulking man from another branch of the police. The man nodded and slipped out the door. Great — probably off for a break while they sent in a fresh officer. Lorenzo drained the bottle. "It's no use. If I knew where Adrienne had gone, I'd have told you already. She fooled me too."

The inspector shook his head. "I just told my colleague to fetch your suitcase after the search. I've decided to believe you."

"Believe me?" Lorenzo gave a dry, sarcastic laugh. "You don't believe me — you just don't have enough evidence to charge me."

"It's the same thing."

No, it wasn't. His career was finished. After being tangled up in this, he'd never again work with law enforcement as a freelance forensic sketch artist — AI or not.

The officer returned with his suitcase and handed it to the inspector, who set it on the table and opened it. "What will you do now — head back to Italy?"

Inside the carry-on, among socks and T-shirts, lay the paintbrushes Adrienne had given him. Memories of passion and rare moments that now twisted in his gut. "Yes, I'll go back to Italy." Though, in truth, he had no idea what he'd do once he got there.

The inspector sighed. "I'm glad. It's important to me that you remain reachable. And since there are no grounds for forced extradition, having you close to home makes things easier."

Lorenzo ignored the persistent pressure, took the brushes from the suitcase, and closed it. "I've already told you everything I know."

"I know. It's clear you feel hurt by Dupont. You really let yourself get played."

A punch in the face would have hurt less. Lorenzo stood, righted the suitcase, and pulled up the handle. "Can I go?"

The inspector stepped aside. "Of course, we can't hold you. See you in Italy — have a good trip," he sang.

Lorenzo bit his tongue; he would have gladly driven a brush into the man's eye socket, if he could. He walked past without a word, escorted to the station's exit by an officer.

But it was true — he had let himself get played.

He had cried for her, and with her.

He walked the corridor in silence, stopping outside the police station. Who could say what was real in Adrienne's stories? Especially the one about her family tragedy.

He pulled out his smartphone and launched the AI app. On the screen, in friendly letters: Welcome, Lorenzo. How can I help you?

He tapped the microphone icon. "Search the Bataclan attack victims list for anyone named Dupont."

The blot on the screen shifted, its edges pulsing and shrinking. "Yes, I found names on the victims list: Luis Dupont and Amélie Gregori, husband and wife. And also a girl who was injured but survived: Adrienne Dupont."

A sharp pain clamped his chest, stealing his breath.

She'd told the truth — but did it change anything?

Lorenzo grabbed his carry-on and headed for the station. The real question was something else: what did he feel for her? Did he love her? Or was he only in love with her image, with the role he wanted her to play in his life?

It hardly mattered. Like Dante with Beatrice, or Botticelli with Simonetta, he would never live his love — if love it was.

His phone vibrated in his hand. The AI app displayed: Only you can know that.

The message log on the screen claimed Lorenzo had spoken into the microphone instead of thinking it. "That's not true — I didn't say anything."

"Oh yes, you did. You're speaking."

"I'm speaking now, but I wasn't before." Lorenzo gripped the phone in anger. "And why would I even talk to you? This all started because of you!"

"Me? Who do you think you're talking to? I'm not even a person. Are you sure you're not talking to yourself?"

"Leave me alone!"

"There's nothing wrong with that. Even those who pray are often speaking to themselves, saying aloud what they struggle to admit." The blot on the screen spun and morphed — faces and objects taking shape.

Martina's rapist. A bleeding tree. A leopard and a lynx.

A burning medieval city... Dis.

The screen went black, but the AI kept speaking: "Are you sure you want to stop? Botticelli could answer your questions."

A shove jolted him; Lorenzo found himself at the train station, staring at a dark screen. What the hell was happening to him? Was he losing his mind? Obsessed? Possessed?

Did demons exist?

To provoke them, Professor Obermann had said the devil was on earth—as if it were a real being. On earth. Botticelli's missing drawings contained the very clues to finding that city.

Lorenzo didn't have the rest of Manfredi's notes, but he had the final clue, spoken by the art dealer on his deathbed: the solution is the light within the eyes.

Adrienne had said Botticelli was a Savonarola follower, and that was why she was obsessed with the search for the infernal drawings. Only one expert could tell him more: Amilto.

Lorenzo lifted his gaze to the departures board and scanned the listings for a direct train to the airport, where he'd buy a ticket to Rome.

Part
III
Hell

3.1

The Jesuit's secretary, buttoned into her long nun's habit, left the room. Amilto shut the window, and the clamor from the construction site below the building faded to a distant hum. "So, you want to know if Botticelli was a follower of Savonarola."

Lorenzo dropped into the chair. With no fresh air coming in, the scent of old wood and ancient books began to saturate the room. "Have you ever looked into it?"

"Yes." The Jesuit crossed to the bookcase at the far end of the room. "In fact, Botticelli was a *Piagnone*—a follower of Savonarola." His gaze moved along the spines until it landed on a massive volume. He pulled it down.

Lorenzo drew his chair closer to the table. There had to be a reason that information mattered to Adrienne; it was the last thing she said. "What did Savonarola's followers believe?"

"Girolamo Savonarola was convinced the end of the world was near. His religious convictions were absolute, unyielding." The scholar set the book on the table and let his hand linger on its worn leather cover. "The Medici had summoned him for his deep knowledge of Greek and pagan myths. But once in Florence, Savonarola preached strict Christian austerity and chastity. He even mocked the Medici lord, saying: *He wanted Athens in Florence; we will make it Jerusalem."*

"In practice, rather than an ally, he proved an opponent."

"Exactly. Savonarola succeeded where the Pazzi Conspiracy had failed."

"And what does this have to do with Botticelli?" Lorenzo glanced at the book's cover—there was no title.

The Jesuit smiled. "With Savonarola, everything had to be chaste; paintings could no longer be beautiful. They even burned works of art in public squares—the Bonfire of the Vanities. Botticelli was there. Perfume, music, beauty—everything was banned. I too wonder how an artist could side with him. Imagine—the creator of the famous *Venus* rejecting beauty."

"But are we certain he became a follower?"

Amilto opened the book and leafed through it, the rustle of its pages filling the room. He stopped at a dark depiction of Piazza della Signoria in Florence, with a platform and a pyre in flames at its center. "This painting shows the pyre where Savonarola was burned as a heretic. It's anonymous, but attributed to Francesco Rosselli. Look at the angels holding the empty scroll."

Lorenzo leaned forward and examined it, studying the details. Then Amilto turned the page, revealing a print in the vivid, almost violent colors typical of Botticelli. Yet stylistically, it felt like a step backward. The perspective was skewed; the figures stiff and unnatural, their proportions unrealistic. The once-fluid, sinuous line had become jagged and tense.

A cell phone rang; the Jesuit picked up his smartphone and declined the call. He leaned over the table and placed his index finger on the angels at the top of the illustration. "This is *The Mystical Nativity*, a tempera on canvas painted in 1501—

after Savonarola's execution. Do these angels holding the scroll remind you of anything?"

Lorenzo compared them to those in the earlier work. They were strikingly similar. "Do you think the drawing of Savonarola's execution is by Botticelli?"

"Yes. He was there."

"In this second image, there are words on the scroll. What do they say?"

The Jesuit smiled, as if he'd been waiting for the question. "Botticelli speaks in the first person: *I painted this picture based on the 11th chapter of Saint John — on the Apocalypse, at the time of the Second Coming, during the devil's release for three and a half years.* He was quoting a sermon by Savonarola."

The devil's release.

Obermann had said: *The devil is on earth, he says so plainly. Not in some Hell somewhere or in a spiritual realm — he's among us.*

The infernal city of Dis.

A wave of dizziness hit him; Lorenzo braced himself against the desk. Her laughter again, echoing in his head. "Do you have some water?"

The Jesuit rose and returned almost instantly with a glass, as if he'd never moved from the desk at all. Time felt distorted.

Lorenzo drank—the water tasted bitter. Metallic.

In the book, Botticelli's *Mystical Nativity* began to ripple, drawing him in. The figure of Mary, prostrate in adoration, stared at him, tears of blood streaming down her face. Her features shifted — Adrienne's, then Elisabetta's. Then both at once.

"All right?" Amilto chuckled, amused.

Meanwhile, the drawing called to Lorenzo. The ox and donkey's eyes became gleaming emeralds, and the beasts began to eat the Baby Jesus. Joseph bore the face of Martina's rapist, while the angels were demons, singing the words engraved on the scroll. Hallucinations in broad daylight.

The phone rang again. Amilto answered. "You there? Good. I can't talk now." He hung up and burst out laughing, in perfect sync with the laughter echoing inside Lorenzo's mind.

How was this possible? Lorenzo shook his head — he had to pull himself together. He drained his glass in three gulps, wishing instead he could have poured it over his head. He turned to the Jesuit, who hadn't stopped laughing since the call. "Did you get good news?"

"Excellent!" The man flipped through the tome until he reached a depiction of a crucifixion. "And here we have the Lamentation over the Dead Christ, painted the very year that the wretched friar Savonarola was burned at the stake." His tone had shifted, as though someone else were speaking through him. Fevered eyes shone with a joy entirely devoid of happiness.

Lorenzo tilted the glass to catch the last drops, letting them drip onto his tongue. Was Amilto's behavior yet another hallucination? He no longer knew. Reality and illusion were no longer separate worlds.

He swallowed. "And why is this drawing of Christ important?" A bitter aftertaste clung to his mouth. What had the man given him to drink?

"It's important because it's tied to Botticelli's mystical crisis, brought on by that wretched friar. The image radiates intense drama. A sudden shift — not in style, but in vision. It suggests Botticelli might not have been a follower of Savonarola at all, but was going through a religious crisis… perhaps even sliding into Satanism."

The shrill s hissed in his ears like a snake, reaching his brain. The hisses joined the laughter that throbbed inside his skull. "I... I don't feel well. Could you reopen the window?"

"Really?" Amilto sneered; he hadn't blinked in some time. "If you can't handle talking about Christ, maybe you're a Satanist too."

"How dare you?!" Lorenzo stood, but his legs buckled and he collapsed back into the chair. The room spun. "I'm not a Satanis—" he stammered, smearing his mouth with drool; his lips were tingling.

"Oh, but you are: you're a servant of the Devil! You helped Satan take Elisabetta's soul. Isn't that right?" Amilto extended his arm, a wooden rosary dangling from his fingers—identical to the one Martina used. The crucifix at the end was weeping.

This had to be a nightmare. And yet dreams just happen; he, instead, remembered everything: the flight from Berlin, the route to the office, the welcome from the secretary dressed like a nun...

Amilto came around the desk, looming over him. He seized Lorenzo's hand, twisting the palm upward, and pressed the crucifix into it. The metal seared his skin. He forced Lorenzo's fingers closed around it—a burning coal trapped in his fist. Lorenzo screamed, breath caught in his throat. His flesh reeked of sulfur, of Hell itself.

"So it's true!" The Jesuit laughed. "You serve the Devil too. Good! Then you'll be glad to know we've found the way. We'll have Dis!"

The scorching pain jolted his brain. He kicked out, toppling the chair, and the rosary clattered to the floor. His palm was branded with a cross crawling with boils and pustules. Madness.

Lorenzo bolted for the door, slammed into it, then shoved it open with his shoulder, splinters flying. The secretary, perched on the desk, had unbuttoned her dress, her breasts bare. She laughed, massaging her enormous breasts; with her tongue she went to lick a nipple without losing her grin.

The laughter still rang in his head. He clamped his hands over his ears and lunged for the door to the landing—it was locked. "Open up!" he shouted. "Open it now!"

The Jesuit had joined the secretary, kissing her with their tongues entwined. One of her hands stroked the bulge in his trousers; the other tapped a control panel on the desk.

The door clicked open. "Hello, Demon," Amilto shouted.

Lorenzo ran out. Three flights of stairs pitched beneath him like a ship in a storm. He burst outside, a jackhammer pounding in his skull.

He looked at his hand: the crucifix mark was still there. And it was Martina's rosary—the very same. It looked identical.

The bar... he had to get to the bar.

He hurried on. The open air let him breathe a little easier, but the world still spun. He reached the bar and leaned on one of the outdoor tables, nearly overturning it. Inside the bar, above the counter, the TV was tuned to Sky TG. Martina's photo filled the screen beside the headline: *Girl, already a victim of rape, found dead in an apparent suicide. A burden too heavy for a devout girl to bear.*

Another suicide.

He clutched his head and shook it. He was losing his mind. There was no point in going on like this—he would join Elisabetta. The tree with the exposed roots was calling to him.

It spoke his name and wore Elisabetta's face. It was her. Lorenzo staggered toward the trunk like a drunk, and there, in the shadow of its branches, was a figure. Elisabetta.

But the voice was Adrienne's.

He collapsed against her, and she struggled to keep him upright.

"Lorenzo, come on, snap out of it!" Adrienne slapped his cheek lightly. "Somebody get me some water, now!"

She laid him down on the ground. She was real.

She was Adrienne.

Above: The image depicting the pyre where Savonarola was burned as a heretic. It is anonymous but attributed to Francesco Rosselli. The angels hold a blank scroll.

Beside: *The Mystical Nativity* by Botticelli, a tempera painting on canvas from 1501, created after Savonarola's execution. The angels hold a scroll, this time filled with text: *'This painting, at the end of the year 1500, during the troubles of Italy, I, Alessandro, painted in the middle time after time, according to the eleventh of Saint John, in the second woe of the Apocalypse, in the three-and-a-half-year liberation of the devil; then he will be chained in the twelfth, and we will see him (fallen?) as in this painting.'* It is also a quotation from a sermon by Savonarola.

3.2

Domenico

Domenico smacked his forehead. Why couldn't he solve the last riddle? Two tourists shot him sidelong glances. May the Saint forgive him — he shouldn't be making a fool of himself. His short, uneven breaths dissolved into the vast, silent space of the church, the final stop on the road to the infernal city. Only the entrance remained. It had to be somewhere near the basilica, but where?

He lifted his gaze again to the mosaic that dominated the entire counter-façade, a Last Judgment more than fifteen meters high. Incredible. The imposing figure of Jesus, poised between Mary and John, seemed to beckon him to prayer. But there was no time for that. Two long days in this basilica, and he still hadn't found the answer.

Among the few visitors, a man near the presbytery kept glancing his way, a vacant look carved into his face. He wore no visible sign of faith and didn't look like a tourist; if anything, his presence seemed at odds with the sacred air of the place. A tattoo peeked from beneath his shirt collar.

Domenico resumed tracing the perimeter, searching for a clue. The cat leapt and clung once more to the pocket of his trousers, where he kept his phone. "I've already tried calling the Great Girolamo — he promised he'd call me back."

The cat meowed. Why was it so insistent that he call the Master? Until now, the animal had been helpful—perhaps it was a vessel through which the Saint spoke to him; perhaps he should listen. Domenico took out his phone and dialed.

After three rings, the Great Girolamo answered, speaking to someone else. "…Hello, demon… Hello, Domenico. I told you I'd call you back."

There was something strange in the Master's tone. "Forgive me. I'm at a standstill. But—did I hear you right? Were you greeting a demon?"

"Uh… yes." A cough, as though clearing his throat. "I'd just finished an exorcism and was mocking the Evil One."

The cat meowed again, almost in protest. The explanation stank of a lie—that was why the animal had urged him to call. "As I said, Master, I'm stuck."

"What do you mean? I thought you'd found the door."

"Not the door—the final stage. I can't solve the final riddle."

A low growl crackled through the receiver. "There must be some works depicting eyes! Think: the solution is light within the eyes." He spoke without faith, with the Devil's wrath and none of Savonarola's fervor.

It didn't sound like the Great Girolamo, yet it was unmistakably his voice. "Master, I can't solve it. It's been two days—"

He uttered a blasphemy. "I thought you were already at the door! I've revealed myself to the portraitist because of you—you're useless!"

Had he just blasphemed against God?

The man he called Master?

Anger flared — fire curling beneath his skin, inflaming his nerves, his gut, staining the world in shades of red. "Who are you, Satan? What have you done with the Great Girolamo?"

From the receiver came the sound of spitting, followed by the moans of a woman in the throes of lust. "I'm tired of you — you're nothing but useless! The other servant was better, the one who died."

"Who, Martina? The girl I was introducing to the Keepers of the Flame? I heard she's dead — suicide, they said."

"Not the girl you preached to! My true servant, the one who held her down while I raped her. We had such laughs together." Another curse, spat at the Saints.

This man was a worshipper of Lucifer! He had raped the initiate Domenico had saved from the streets — and she, crushed by the loss of her virginity, had taken her own life, falling into Hell!

More obscene noises came through the phone, punctuated by yet another blasphemy. The profane word seemed to echo off the columns, though it came from that small device.

A cold shiver ran down Domenico's spine, his muscles tensing with the urge to avenge the sanctity of the desecrated place. "You've been mocking me! You are not — "

"Enough, you sanctimonious Christian." A woman's voice screamed in orgasm through the receiver. "I don't need you anymore. I already have other servants here, adepts I don't have to pretend with. They'll find the entrance to Dis. Pray to your God, Domenico, because I doubt you'll see the sunrise." The line went dead.

It wasn't true. It couldn't be true.

He had served the Devil without knowing it.

The anger rose, sudden and consuming, stoked by blasphemy and betrayal. Shock gave way to a darker storm—a primal thirst for vengeance, a holy summons to defend the honor of the Saint and the name of God, defiled by impious lips.

The cat hissed toward the man leaning against the column, its fur bristling. The tattoo at his collar looked like the tip of a goat's horn. He was the emissary of darkness.

The animal's reaction was a divine sign, a ciphered message from Heaven. That black cat, with its amber eyes, was nothing less than an instrument in the Lord's hands. And if God was with him, who could stand against him?

He would face him. The Saint would grant him victory, for his cause was just, his wrath purifying. And he would not stop there.

Domenico saw the path the Lord was setting before him—a road lined with battles against the forces of darkness. He would kill the artist and his harlot, and hunt down the false Master who had preyed upon his faith. All of them would receive the punishment they deserved.

Beneath the Last Judgment mosaic, which told the Revelation of John, it was fated that he, too, would receive his revelation. He would be the instrument of divine justice, a crusader in a holy war against every manifestation of evil.

He slipped a hand under his jacket and drew the dagger. He advanced toward the enemy, and the cat sank its claws into the face of Satan's follower.

3.3

Daylight seeped softly through his trembling eyelids. Lorenzo opened his eyes again; the dizziness was ebbing, replaced by Adrienne's voice and silhouette. She was seated at one of the bar's outdoor tables, fanning him with a laminated menu.

"Feeling better?" Her voice was warm with concern as she brushed his cheek lightly with her fingertips.

She was beautiful.

Lorenzo nodded. They'd been apart for only three days, yet seeing her again had rekindled his will to live. And to draw her.

His tongue clung to the roof of his mouth; he clicked it free, tasting bitterness. "I... They must have drugged me."

"Drink." Adrienne took a cloudy glass of water from the table and handed it to him. "It's water with sugar."

He reached for it—then pain flared through his hand, sharp and searing. He lifted it to his eyes: blisters and scorched skin marked his palm in the shape of a cross. Impossible. Then it hadn't been a hallucination.

A chill ran down his spine as he showed her the wound. "Look. I grabbed a wooden crucifix, and this is what it did to me. How is that possible?"

She flinched.

She turned to the onlookers around them. "Thank you—he's feeling better. Please don't worry, thank you."

The small crowd dispersed.

Once they were alone, Adrienne took his hand gently and sniffed the wound. "Sulfur. That's the smell of an acidic substance. Could be hydrochloric acid. Or phenol—the trick some sham holy men use to simulate stigmata." She let out a long breath and released his palm. "Was the crucifix wet?"

It was.

In his muddled state, Lorenzo had believed the Christ was weeping. He nodded and drank; the sugary water slipped down his throat like a cool stream. Tilting his head toward Amilto's building, he murmured, "It was the Jesuit."

Adrienne sighed. "I realized too late. He's not a real Jesuit—he calls himself that to impress certain circles, but he's not in the records."

The world, and his memories, were slowly knitting themselves back together—along with the lies and half-truths she'd fed him. A heat swelled in his chest, bursting into anger; he struck his thigh with a clenched fist. "Why all the lies?"

Adrienne lowered her gaze. "They were necessary."

"Really? You brought me along without ever telling me who we were actually working for—or against?"

She bit her lip. "The story about my family was true. Since that day, I've devoted myself to fighting religious fanaticism. I work for the Vatican Secret Service."

His gut tightened in shock. That explained her persistence in the investigation, the mysterious car that had whisked her away in Germany, and her sudden appearance as Manfredi's secretary just when he'd started looking into Botticelli's *Inferno*. "So you're an agent."

"Of the most efficient agency in the world. They have no democratic constraints, no transparency requirements—but unlimited resources. And for the record, I never used Manfredi's credit card for expenses."

Meanwhile, he was flat broke. "Vatican Secret Service... I've never heard of it."

"Exactly..."

Lorenzo stared at her, disbelief mingling with awe. "I'm right about daylight saving time, aren't I? You were with Obermann?"

She nodded. "He was already dead—recently. I was with a colleague from the Service who can testify—it was he who called the police. But in Germany, I had to keep my cover. The rest you can imagine."

Vatican Secret Service. Incredible. Still, thinking over the past few days, Adrienne hadn't exactly behaved like a model Christian. His stomach tightened; he couldn't swallow it. "We made love. You have tattoos, you drink, and you do things that aren't exactly in line with the Holy See."

"I told you—my mission is to stamp out religious fanaticism. All of it. I work for the Vatican Secret Service, but I'm not an abbess or a prioress. In this line of work, you have to be able to sin." Her lips curved in a faint smile, her eyes brightening with moisture. "And sinning with you wasn't just work."

Warmth spread through Lorenzo's chest, as if he were melting. The memory of their nights together made his head spin, and he pressed his hands to his temples. Maybe it was still the effect of the bitter water Amilto had made him drink.

But there was something else: drugged or not, crucifixes soaked in irritants or not, he'd been seeing inexplicable things for days. "Listen, I need to know something. I keep seeing strange things. From another world. Who are we up against?"

Adrienne caught her lower lip between her teeth. "A lot of people are after Botticelli's drawings. People from all kinds of religious backgrounds—very powerful ones."

"So it's true? Dis, I mean. We're really looking for the devil's city on earth?"

She leaned back in her chair, silent.

Then she exhaled, deflating like a balloon. "As a Vatican agent, I've seen several fake exorcisms. But I've also seen things I can't explain. If you're asking whether that world is real—after what I've witnessed, I can't not believe it. But I understand your skepticism."

Skepticism? By now, he saw more of the netherworld than the living one. Elisabetta haunted his every glance. Or maybe she was just the embodiment of his guilt. That circle wouldn't close until this story ended. "Amilto is right on our heels. What do we do?"

Adrienne shook her head. "That's not how it works. He's protected and resourceful—he had our phones tapped. We don't even know for sure what organization he belongs to; we assumed the Keepers of the Flame. But certain clues made us think he was an impostor."

"Keepers of the Flame?" Lorenzo echoed.

"Yes. A group of Savonarola fanatics."

The image of the fake Jesuit groping the secretary on the desk banished any thought of piety from the man. "And what if he's a Satanist?"

Adrienne shook her head again. "His field agent acts like a Christian zealot." She sighed and raised her hands to her head. "The pieces don't line up. When I saw you, I was here just to take a look. I can't make sense of it."

"So, what do we do?"

"From now on, you're out of this."

Lorenzo laughed. "Not a chance." He would take back control of his life at any cost. He stood, pulled his smartphone from his pocket, and smashed it against the ground. "I'm going back to Florence. I know it well, and there's a museum dedicated to Savonarola. I want to see if there's anything on these Keepers of the Flame." He smiled at her. "Now it's up to you—if you want, you can come with me."

❦

The Cathedral of Santa Maria del Fiore rose on the horizon; Lorenzo paused to take it in. Returning to Florence had reignited feelings he'd underestimated.

He had missed the city the way a sailor misses harbor after months on the open sea. Art, in all its forms, had always been a constant companion, and here he was surrounded by it again. There was a reason for such melancholy: in absence, one comes to understand the true worth of what one has.

Adrienne watched him. "Don't you remember the way?"

"Yes, perfectly. I was just thinking." He pointed. "The Museum of San Marco, dedicated to Savonarola, is in the monumental wing of the old Dominican convent. This way." He set off toward the square.

Adrienne followed, hands clasped at her stomach, eyes lowered. "What were you thinking about?"

Ever since they had reunited—throughout the train ride, too—they had kept their distance. It had been wrenching to face the truths she'd withheld, and the broken trust had driven a wedge between them.

It felt like meeting for the first time all over again—and in a way, it was. "I was thinking that all this research is making me rediscover my own city."

Adrienne nodded, saying nothing more. Perhaps she'd been hoping for an opening to talk about them, to walk hand in hand again.

Or maybe it was Lorenzo hoping she was hoping…

My God, relationships were complicated.

They passed the university and reached Piazza San Marco; the building lay just beyond the square. Its neoclassical façade rose in three tiers, its pillars arranged in horizontal bands. A massive doorway stood open beneath a broad window. Two niches on the sides held statues. Just an old convent—yet its Renaissance architecture could outshine almost any style. And to think it was considered a minor monument in the City of the Lily.

"So this is Savonarola's old convent."

Lorenzo nodded, opening the pamphlet he'd picked up at the station. "You can even visit his cell. Savonarola's history in Florence is remarkable—he was the only one who managed to drive out the Medici. In November 1494, he turned the city into a theocracy, ruled by himself."

She snorted. "If that's not fanaticism, I don't know what is. And four years later they burned him as a heretic."

Indeed. Turbulent times.

"Shall we cross?"

Lorenzo nodded and let an ivory Piaggio Ape three-wheeler pass, piled with garlands, lights, and signs. They stepped into the street—then the squeal of tires cut through the air. A car roared toward them, its engine screaming.

It was coming straight for them.

Driven by pure instinct, Lorenzo grabbed Adrienne — but she had the same idea. They ended up clutching each other, each trying to shield the other.

The car hit them with brutal force. Pain shot from hips to spine as they were hurled against the windshield, shattering it into a spiderweb of glass. They rolled over the roof and slammed onto the pavement on the far side — a heap of tangled limbs and chaos.

Shouts rose from the crowd, distant and confused. A bald man leapt from the dark vehicle: the fake gallery assistant. Moving quickly but awkwardly, he flung open the back doors. He grabbed Lorenzo under the arms and hauled him up. "Why did you want to see the saint's museum? Why are you here?" His voice was a blend of frustration and rage, breathless with effort.

He dumped Lorenzo onto the seats and ran to Adrienne. Lorenzo tried to rise, but each attempt smashed him against a wall of pain so sharp it stole his breath. His body refused his mind's commands.

The fake usher backed into the car, stepping on him, and laid Adrienne's limp body across his. Her blood trickled onto his face. Then the man climbed into the driver's seat and sped off, the doors slamming shut from the force of acceleration.

What was he planning?

IN QUESTO LUOGO LA NOTTE DELL'8 APRILE 1498 QUANDO LE ORDE DEGLI ARRABBIATI E DE' PALLESCHI EBBERO INVASO MINACCIOSE IL CONVENTO DI S. MARCO FU DAL COMMISSARIO DELLA SIGNORIA CATTURATO E TRATTO IN ARRESTO FRATE GIROLAMO SAVONAROLA

The Museum of San Marco is none other than the ancient Dominican convent where the famous friar Girolamo Savonarola lived. Inside the museum, visitors can see his cell, which has remained intact since the 15th century. On the night of April 8, 1498, the convent of San Marco was stormed with the intent of arresting Girolamo Savonarola. His followers, the Piagnoni, fought with weapons in hand, defending the convent until the main door was set on fire, forcing the battle inside. Some suggested that Savonarola escape by lowering himself down the convent walls, but he refused. Friar Malatesta urged him with the words: 'Should not the shepherd lay down his life for his sheep?' The Prior, after confessing and receiving communion, bid farewell to his brothers with a kiss, returned the keys to the convent, and surrendered himself to the commissioners of the Signoria, who were waiting for him at the entrance of the library. To this day, a 19th-century plaque commemorates this episode.

3.4

The sharp crack of a hammer blow jolted Lorenzo out of the veil of unconsciousness. He tried to move, but a white-hot stab of pain shot through his back. His hands and feet were bound.

The memory of the accident horrified him.

Had it left him paralyzed? He curled his toes inside his shoes, and through the agony lancing down his leg, they moved. Thank God.

The air was thick with chlorine, laced with the earthy scent of moss and wet soil. A pump hummed somewhere nearby. Gardening tools hung from the walls, and in one corner a lawnmower stood upright, its blades encrusted with clods of earth. He was in a large shed housing a pool filtration system.

"You're awake!" Another hammer strike rang out.

Frozen by pain and fear, Lorenzo turned his head just enough to glimpse what was happening behind him.

The fake gallery assistant knelt behind Adrienne. She lay on her side, unconscious, her arms twisted behind her and chained to a pipe. The bald man hammered again, fastening a short length of chain—no more than a span long—from her wrists to the pipe.

Against the wall leaned two wooden boards bristling with rusted nails, their tips glinting with a dark, sinister red — old blood. The shed floor, too, was dotted with congealed blood. My God, this was turning into a nightmare.

The fake gallery assistant yanked Adrienne's chain to test its hold. "What were you doing in front of the Saint's museum?"

Lorenzo fought for breath. "How…" His voice was as faint as the dying words of the art dealer — and he would likely share the same fate at the hands of the same killer. "How is Adrienne? Who are you?"

"My name's Domenico. She's alive — for now. Your turn. What were you doing at the Saint's museum?"

Domenico — just like Savonarola, the Dominican friar. The one he called the Saint. A zealot. Lorenzo would have to play to that if he wanted a chance to survive. "We went to the Saint's museum to learn more about him. To convert."

"Liar!" Domenico slammed the hammer to the ground. "Tell me the truth!"

"That is the truth! Our research into Botticelli led us to Savonarola, and we saw hope in him!"

A thin meow cut through the air, a flicker of movement; a cat leapt lightly onto an abandoned box of Christmas lights. Not just any cat: *that* cat. Black fur, yellow eyes, a white tuft on its head — the same one from the hallucinations at the suicide tree.

Lorenzo swallowed hard. Words jammed in his throat, but he couldn't falter; he had to keep stoking the fanatic's pride. "Domenico, you know the Saint's story — please, tell me about him, about his relationship with Botticelli."

"Botticelli — pah!" Domenico spat on the ground. "First of all, when you speak of Savonarola, he's not just *the* saint. You breathe it out—*the* Saint. He alone was worthy of the Almighty, while Botticelli was a servant of the devil."

"Servant of the devil…" Lorenzo pushed himself up on his elbows, pain tearing through his muscles until he sat upright. Amilto had hinted at exactly that, even naming a specific work. "You mean *The Symbolic Crucifixion?*"

Domenico's eyes widened. "So you've done your homework. Do you know that blasphemous painting?"

"No."

"That drawing is heresy, starting with the setting: how can Christ be shown crucified before Florence?" Domenico snarled. "Jesus is nailed to a cross from which a thick, dark cloud of smoke billows, as if it were aflame. In the Middle Ages, when something was no longer useful, it was burned — it still happens today. Just as with Savonarola's Bonfires of the Vanities. Botticelli laid bare his contempt for the cross—so much so that he made it useless and burned it."

Lorenzo mouthed an Our Father; the longer he kept him talking, the more time he could steal. "If he painted the cross in flames, maybe he meant to portray Christ as a heretic — punished, to make a mockery of the way he died…" He lowered his voice, giving it weight. "The Saint."

"Exactly. Not to mention the angel placing a symbol of royalty in Magdalene's hands instead of Christ's. And up at the top of the painting—you can just make them out—there are floating shields. Triangular, white, with a red cross painted on them. Templar shields. That's who Botticelli's masters were."

"What a disgrace." Lorenzo shook his head with a melodramatic flourish. "Free me, I beg you, so I can help you in your mission."

Domenico laughed just as heartily, though his mirth was more spontaneous. "You must have a firmer faith than I do if you think I believed you. You painters are all the same."

He walked over to a wastebasket and rummaged through the crumpled papers until he pulled out a pamphlet, smoothing it. "This is how far Botticelli's heresy went. *The Lamentation over the Dead Christ with Saints Jerome, Paul, and Peter.* Not one of them shows sorrow, as if they felt no grief for Jesus. And tell me—who is that figure hiding his face from Christ, as though unwilling to be seen in that moment?"

He ran over and shoved the reproduction in Lorenzo's face. Sure enough, there was a man turned away, concealing his features. In his left hand he held three long, slender objects—perhaps nails, symbols of the Passion. What was Lorenzo to do? Keep pretending he'd repented, or try a different approach and reason with him? He chose silence.

Domenico pointed to the nails. "Look how he holds them—pinched at the tip. Do they look like they're made of heavy iron to you? Do you know what they are? Paintbrushes. A strange figure who, in a scene of great drama, holds paintbrushes. Botticelli is alluding to himself, refusing to witness Christ. And that's not all."

He ran his forefinger along Christ's body. "Hairless, clean, without blood. The marks of suffering are barely suggested, as if to say the sacrifice was no true torment. And look—no beard, no mustache: no wisdom. No respect for the accepted canon of Christ's image. He was a servant of Satan."

Lorenzo coughed. He struggled to see what Domenico claimed, but his eyes lacked the filter of fanaticism. Adrienne lay on the ground, her chest barely rising with breath. Now he understood why she was so anguished in her fight against religious fanaticism. "What do you plan to do with us?"

"I can't just kill you—you must be redeemed! I'll make you feel the Passion of Savonarola, so you'll understand what the Saint endured in his life." The cat meowed, and Domenico glanced at the battered strap of the watch on his wrist. "But I have to go. There's something I must do, and I'm short on time. I'll deal with you later."

He stood, tossed the pamphlet back into the trash, and crouched over an old blue Invicta backpack. When he unzipped it, binoculars, explosives, and sticks of dynamite came into view. My God—he was planning an attack. He closed the bag and slung it over his shoulder. It was heavy, clinking with bolts and screws. He meant to cause a massacre.

He looked at the cat. "Well? Are you coming with me, or staying here to stand guard?"

The cat sat and meowed. Lorenzo closed his eyes and shook his head—reality and absurdity were blending, and he no longer knew which to believe. "Did you find them?"

"What?" Domenico paused in the doorway.

"Botticelli's missing drawings. Did you find them? Were they in that safety deposit box?"

He hesitated on the threshold and crossed himself. "Only the notes. Then I found the place, but not the Gate of Dis. The answer is the light in the eyes, isn't it?"

Lorenzo jolted, pain twitching through his muscles. "Have you solved it?"

"I'll solve it later. To escape, I had to kill a couple of servants of the Devil; now I must finish that path. I'll do it on the Saint's day. The bogus 'Grand Jerome' will be there—that impostor who mocked me. I'll kill him and all those he surrounds himself with. Then I'll come back for you. And finally, to Dis."

"Please, don't—"

"Don't pray to me. Pray to the Lord." From the corner, he picked up two bowls of water — perhaps the cat's. He set one beside himself and the other near Lorenzo. "Three days without food is nothing. As for water, you'll drink like the dogs you are, lapping from the bowl — if your whore recovers."

He left them bound and helpless.

Lorenzo shouted, but the pool pump muffled his voice. Who knew where Domenico would plant those charges. Who knew what he'd do when he came back.

The cat padded over to Adrienne's bowl, nudged it, and tipped it over. Then it returned to the doorway, curled its tail neatly over its paws, and meowed.

The Symbolic Crucifixion, by Botticelli, dated around 1502, reflects the deep religious crisis the artist experienced after the death of Savonarola. Christ is crucified against the backdrop of Florence, recognizable by significant monuments such as the dome of Santa Maria del Fiore and Giotto's tower. The image is rich in symbolic elements, including crossed shields and a black cloud emerging from the cross.

Below: *The Lamentation over the Dead Christ with Saints Jerome, Paul, and Peter* (1495). The faces of the saints do not reveal any emotions.

The figure holding the nails is believed to represent one of the Three Marys.

Online, i found some interpretations speculating on their resemblance to paintbrushes and the curious choice of the covered face.

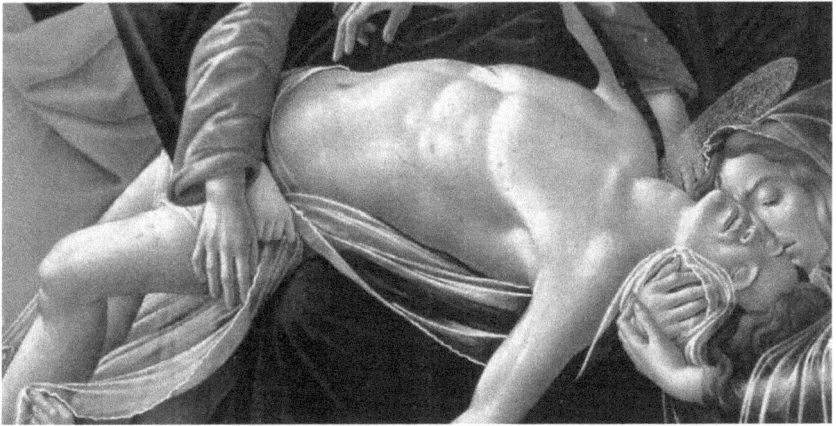

The body of Christ is depicted hairless, without blood, and lacking a beard and mustache— a representation far from the canonical image accepted at the time.

3.5

Now that fanatic Domenico had shut the shed door, the steady hum of the pool pump reclaimed center stage. The cat resumed washing its paw with slow, meticulous strokes. In the distance came the muffled growl of an engine revving.

Adrienne lifted her head. "He's gone. Finally."

What? Lorenzo shot her a glance through the throbs of aching muscles. He'd been feigning unconsciousness the whole time. A rush of emotions slammed into him—relief, frustration, anger, then relief again. "How are you?"

Her gaze was sharp, calculating. "Alive." She sat up, tugging at the arms bound behind her, secured to the metal pipe at her back. Her eyes swept the room, assessing it with a detached, almost inhuman calm.

And yet she hadn't spared a thought for him—hadn't even asked how he was. Lorenzo coughed, flecks of blood spattering from his lips. "I'm alive too—thanks for asking."

She sighed. "Of course you are. I'm a field agent—I've followed the whole thing step by step. I can see you're moving your legs, which means your spine's intact. And that's good, because we need to get out of here."

"Get out?! And how exactly do you plan on doing that?"

"I'm working on it." She jerked her arms behind her back, a metallic rattle sounding as she tested the chains.

The cat had stopped licking. It was watching them. It was unnerving.

Flat on his back, Lorenzo drew a long breath; everything hurt—muscles, bones, joints, and, worst of all, his spirit. He'd thought he knew Adrienne. Thought he'd fallen in love with her. But now, locked up in that shed, she seemed like a stranger. "You're good at pretending to be unconscious. Pretending is something you do well…" His voice dripped with venom.

She stopped fumbling behind her. "I told you I'm sorry. It had to be done. And now isn't the time to discuss it."

"Of course it isn't," Lorenzo spat onto the floor, reddish saliva splattering. "Said the phony."

"I wasn't a phony. I had to lie about some things."

"And what do you call a person like that?"

She exhaled. "There's a difference between a phony and a liar."

"What's the difference?"

"Only one of them lies while looking you in the eye." Adrienne met his gaze. "Every time I looked at you, I told you the truth. In some cases I had to lie, but for a good reason. It was necessary—and it had nothing to do with us."

Looking into her eyes stopped his heart for a beat.

Behind that cool confidence was the frightened girl who'd lost her parents. And the sensuous, feline seductress he'd made love to. They weren't separate people.

We live our whole lives in the same body, yet pass through countless selves. Countless roles. From victim to perpetrator, from disciple to mentor, from savior to saved.

He'd worn his share of masks too—slipping from one Lorenzo to another, never finding one that felt like home. And maybe that was the point — not choosing, but accepting he was the sum of them all.

Resentment was pointless, especially given all the lies he'd told. He'd never confessed that Elisabetta was still part of his life, or that he'd painted her instead of Adrienne. It would be hypocritical to think himself the better person.

A chain clattered to the floor.

"There." Adrienne stood.

"You… you got free?"

She shrugged, moving toward him. Her face was bruised and scabbed, yet she moved like a sprinter. "I told you — I'm trained." She crouched at his wrists, working on the cuffs. "He's planning an attack. We have to stop him."

Where was the cat? Lorenzo turned his head, sharp pain stabbing through his neck. It was nowhere to be seen.

"Stay still."

"Where's the cat?"

Adrienne froze. "You dreamed it too?"

"No, I didn't dream it. But it's unsettling."

She went back to the cuffs and snapped them open. The cold metal gave way to a burning rush as blood surged into his wrists.

"Come on, let me help you up."

Lorenzo sat, each movement sending needles of fire through his back.

"Slowly." Adrienne slipped an arm under his arm. "One step at a time." She braced him as he rose.

Pain shot down his spine like lightning, forcing his eyes shut. Close to her again, pressed against her. Beneath the chlorine reek, her hair still carried that familiar trace of cinnamon.

"Can you walk? We need to move," she said, her voice taut but steady. "Before he comes back."

Lorenzo nodded.

He took a step, but the pain doubled him over with a muffled groan. The shed walls seemed to sway, threatening to swallow him whole. Adrienne caught him, one hand under his arm and the other at his waist. "Lean on me."

He did. The stakes had just risen sharply. "We need to tell the police about the attack—you know that."

She bit her lip. "I'll only do it in the Vatican."

"Why? You don't trust them?"

"That inspector... I don't trust him. That's why I'll have him summoned to the Holy See."

The pain was too much; Lorenzo signaled for her to stop so he could catch his breath. "Why don't you trust him?"

"There are three possibilities. One: he's just doing his job, he's good at it, and he's pressing me because he's figured out my double game. Two: he's a fanatic, and there's nothing we can do about that."

"And three?"

"He's bought. Corrupt. And there's never been a higher bidder than the Vatican."

3.6

Vatican

Lorenzo sank into one of the dark wooden chairs around the table at the center of the room. Ironically, it was the same hall of the Vatican Archives where they had examined Canto I before.

A stabbing pain shot through his side. The bandages around his torso pulled tighter with every breath. Even without broken bones, each movement sent a jolt through his cracked ribs, while the scrapes along his arms and legs made him feel as if he'd hugged asphalt.

And, in fact, he had.

His gaze drifted to the paintings lining the walls — popes and patrons stared back at him with eyes full of superiority. The art he loved so much seemed to be judging him.

Adrienne stepped through the doorway, her unsteady gait betraying the injuries hidden beneath her clothes. "My colleagues are working with the police; they've placed the villa under surveillance," she said, her voice low but clear.

Despite the bruises on her face and arms, ever since revealing herself as an intelligence agent she carried herself with a composure she'd lacked before. She came closer. "If Domenico dares to return to the villa, they'll catch him."

The curator appeared behind them, glanced at Lorenzo, and smiled. "Mr. Berti." The lines of his face folded into an expression of thinly veiled sarcasm. He extended his hand, its pale skin mottled with ruby-red spots. "You know, you look remarkably like a certain famous art dealer."

Lorenzo shook his hand, stifling a laugh at the memory of how tense he'd been pretending to be Manfredi. Now the thought struck him as foolish, and his face hardened; anger surged at the idea it had all been a charade. "So you knew everything?"

"No. I only just found out. I didn't even know the young lady was one of our agents."

Not entirely convincing. Adrienne pulled a chair from the table and sat down. "Curator, we need your expertise. Our Botticelli specialist turned out to be... on the other side."

The smile drained from his face. "Ah yes, the fake Jesuit. A fine client—who would've thought he was actually a Satanist."

A sharp twinge jabbed Lorenzo's ribs; he pressed a hand against the bandages. "And Botticelli—was he?"

"A servant of Satan? I doubt it." The old man shook his head. "But you have to admit, Lucifer is the figure he drew more than any other."

That was odd. Botticelli hadn't depicted the Devil often—aside from the two illustrations in the *Divine Comedy*. "Are you sure we're talking about the same artist? There aren't any famous depictions of the Devil."

"Not directly, no—but they could be implied. At least, that's what some believe. Tell me, what's Botticelli's most famous work?"

Adrienne answered first. "*The Birth of Venus.*"

"Exactly. In Roman mythology, Lucifer—meaning 'light-bringer'—was another name for the planet Venus. The name was linked to the morning star, the second-brightest object in the night sky after the Moon. Just before sunrise, Venus appears in the east as a brilliant star heralding the dawn—a bringer of light."

Adrienne leaned back, wincing; she was in just as much pain as he was. "Isn't it a stretch to connect Venus with the Devil, especially in the Christian tradition?"

"I'll admit it's an interesting hypothesis." The curator gave a faint smile. "But in Christianity, the meaning shifts dramatically—largely thanks to St. Jerome's Vulgate. The very saint whose name Savonarola bore."

The pain in Lorenzo's side seemed to fade, numbed by the thrill of connections snapping into place—better than any painkiller. He strained to catch every word. "In that translation of the Bible, Satan was called Lucifer—so, Venus?"

"Yes." The curator set his hands on the table and leaned in. "In the Vulgate, the word *Lucifer* translates *helel*, meaning 'shining one,' in a metaphor about the fall of the King of Babylon. The original Hebrew had nothing demonic about it; but the link proved decisive in shaping Western Christian theology. In Botticelli's time, Lucifer meant both the Devil and Venus. And he painted the goddess six times."

Adrienne straightened, grimacing. "How many?"

"Six. Botticelli painted Venus six times. Tell me: what's the Devil's number?"

Lorenzo searched his catechism memories. "Three sixes."

"Exactly." The curator's mouth curled in distaste. "Coincidence, perhaps, but of the six Venuses he painted, three are copies of the famous figure—three out of six. Perhaps conjecture, but allegory and symbolism are the language of artists. In the end, the key to interpretation lies with the creator himself."

Six depictions of Venus, three with the face of his muse, Simonetta. And some believed they represented the Devil. Just as Elisabetta had been his own personal Hell — a torment he couldn't let go of, sketching her without even realizing it.

Lorenzo let the words settle. Botticelli wasn't a Satanist — he was a wretch, as tormented as Lorenzo himself.

"Excuse me." A Swiss Guard stood in the doorway. "An inspector is here; he's asking for Ms. Dupont and Mr. Berti."

Adrienne's hard expression darkened. She rose from the table. "In my opinion, Botticelli wasn't a Satanist. But the inspector? I have my doubts. Let's see if I can put them to rest."

"What will you tell him?"

"Only what's necessary about the attack that fanatic is planning. We need to find out where he'll strike."

"And about Dis?" Lorenzo stood too; his legs trembled, pain tugging at every tendon. "Domenico said he'd found the city, but not the entrance. Will you tell the police that?"

"No." Adrienne bit her lip. "And you need to stop looking for it, too." Her tone was resolute — the curiosity about the map hidden in the artworks was gone.

Another confirmation he'd been used. He shot them a withering look. "So it's true—the Vatican made Botticelli's works disappear. You know where the path through Hell leads, and you only infiltrated to erase the clues that tipped Manfredi off about where Dis was."

Adrienne lowered her gaze, and he remembered her words: liars look away; impostors meet your eyes. That reaction told him Hell was real to her—not just a superstition.

The Swiss Guard started down the corridor, and they followed. Walking side by side, Adrienne finally met his gaze again. "It's true—we only figured out the place when we triangulated the three beasts of Canto I together. And even now, we don't know where the entrance to Dis is—same as Domenico. And that's for the best; it's far too dangerous to know. Our duty is to keep it hidden. For the good of all."

If, by some absurd chance, Hell was on Earth, she might have been right. But a voice inside him chuckled: *Find it.*

Botticelli painted three Venuses in the iconic pose that made him famous.

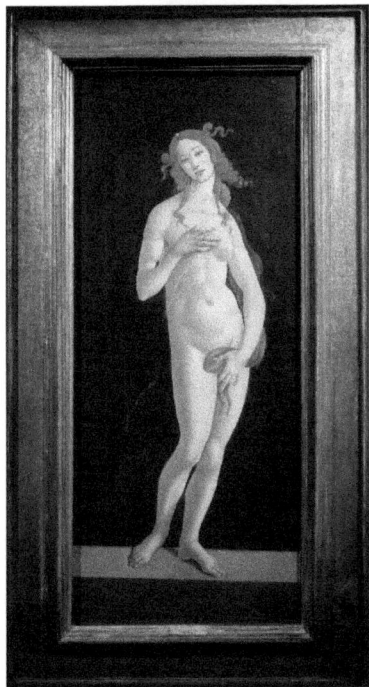

And three more, for a total of six: *Primavera*; *Venus and the Three Graces*; and the already mentioned *Venus and Mars*.

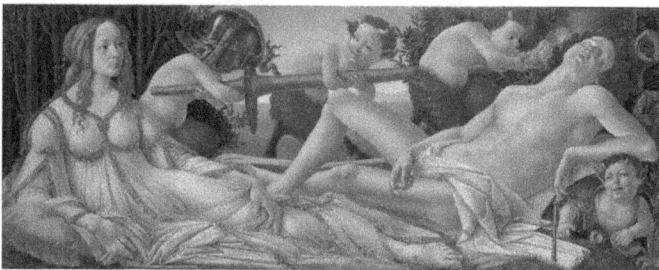

Lorenzo followed Adrienne and a Swiss Guard down the corridors and stopped at an open door. A brass nameplate beside the frame read *Dupont* — Adrienne's private office.

Inside, the inspector stood waiting, his posture rigid. Two police officers flanked him, their eyes sweeping the room. A third man, dressed in a black suit, leaned against the desk, a coiled earpiece wire trailing from his ear. His stance was formal, his face unreadable. A small pin with a gold cross gleamed on his lapel — clearly someone from the Services.

Adrienne stepped in. "Inspector, it's a pleasure to see you again. Have you already spoken with Edgar?"

The inspector gave them a slow once-over. "Yes. The evidence and alibis you provided rule out your involvement in Oberman's murder. The bodycam footage from your operation — the one where you found the body — confirms it."

"Good." Adrienne sat down. The office was small and bare: two gray filing cabinets, a desk. No plants, no ornaments. The only personal touch was a clay pot used as a pen holder — its irregular shape betraying the mark of human hands. She'd probably made it herself. She had once confided to him how much she enjoyed it.

Perhaps she'd been more sincere than he'd thought — at least about what mattered.

The inspector took a seat. "The villa is registered to a foreign company. We've contacted them, and they're eager for us to catch the squatter — though he never actually entered the house, only the shed."

Could the company truly be uninvolved? Hard to say. Many might be hunting the missing Botticelli pieces — not just the Vatican and that bald zealot Savonarola, but also the fake Jesuit. Lorenzo cleared his throat. "Did you find anything in the shed? Do you know about Amilto?"

"Who?"

Adrienne shook her head. "We haven't told the police about him. His role is still unclear. If, as you said, he's into Satanism, then he's got nothing to do with Domenico. That one's enslaved to Christianity — albeit in his own twisted way."

The inspector jotted something in his notebook. "We'll have him brought in and watched closely. And this Domenico — what's his plan?"

"He's preparing an attack," Adrienne said.

"Where?"

"We don't know. He only mentioned the Saint's day, and we think he meant Savonarola."

Lorenzo cut in. "When's Saint Jerome's day?"

"September thirtieth," replied the lean Vatican agent without missing a beat, his expertise in Christian traditions clear.

Almost a year away. Yet Domenico, with a backpack of explosives slung over his shoulder, was in a hurry. Lorenzo shivered at the memory of the metallic clatter inside it. "Any big celebrations coming up soon?"

"In Rome?" The agent shrugged. "It's Easter season — there's something almost every day. Not to mention Rome's Birthday or April 25th..."

It was like hunting for a needle in a haystack. Adrienne sighed, pulling her ponytail loose only to retie it. "And if it's not in Rome?" She looked at Lorenzo. "Savonarola's passion was in Florence. What major events are coming up there?"

She asked knowing he was Florentine. A chill ran through the wounds beneath his bandages. "Well... in a few days there's the *Scoppio del Carro* — the Explosion of the Cart."

The Services agent straightened. "That festival is tied to Savonarola!"

What? Lorenzo had lived in Florence all his life and had never heard that. "What's the connection?"

The Vatican agent stepped forward. "In 1099, the Crusaders besieged Jerusalem and took it on July 15. A Florentine — Pazzino de' Pazzi — was the first to scale the walls and plant the white-and-red Crusader banner. For his bravery, Godfrey of Bouillon awarded him three flints from the Holy Sepulchre."

The Pazzi family. The trail was taking shape.

"After Pazzino's return," the agent continued, "every Holy Saturday, young men from every family would strike sparks from those stones to light a torch. They'd carry the purifying flame through Florence to rekindle the hearths of its homes."

The inspector kept writing; Adrienne's face betrayed nothing. "Over time," the agent went on, "they began transporting the flame on a cart, and by the late 14th century, fireworks had been added. The Pazzi family oversaw the celebration in honor of their ancestor — until the Pazzi Conspiracy."

The puzzle pieces slid into place. Lorenzo leaned forward. "What happened after the assassination attempt?"

"After the conspiracy against the Medici, the privilege was revoked, and the Pazzis were banished from the city. The *Scoppio del Carro* was abolished to erase the memory. But the Florentines didn't take kindly to losing such a spectacle. Savonarola restored it."

Even the inspector paused his writing. All eyes were on the agent. "In 1494, inspired by Savonarola's preaching, Florence expelled the Medici and reinstated the Pazzis' ancient rights, including responsibility for organizing the Holy Saturday cart. That same year, Savonarola established a theocracy in the city."

The inspector tilted his head. "But if Domenico's a Christian fanatic, why would he target a Christian event?"

The Vatican agent's jaw tightened. "Savonarola's followers are Christians, yes—but they hate the Holy See. They may despise us more than any other church. We burned their vicar as a heretic."

A heavy hush settled over the room like a shroud.

"The attack will be there," the inspector said, snapping his notebook shut and turning to Lorenzo. "When's the *Scoppio del Carro*?"

A calendar hung beneath a picture of St. Peter's Square. Lorenzo looked at it. The answer was heavy, though it required only one word. "Tomorrow."

Pazzino de' Pazzi paying homage to Saint Donatus. 1880

3.8

Easter Sunday

The morning light shimmered warmly over Florence's cobblestones. Lorenzo stepped out of the dark BMW with Vatican City plates and shut the door with a solid thud. Adrienne and the wiry colleague from the intelligence services were already moving away from the other vehicle.

Just a few blocks away, the majestic silhouette of Santa Maria del Fiore rose above the city, while the streets swelled with life.

Clusters of cheerful worshippers, whole families in their Sunday best, and excited children darting between them, all gathered for the celebration. On a stone bench, three elderly men chatted amiably as they nibbled sugar-dusted croissants.

The excitement in the air was palpable — almost enviable. But for him, it was a time of uncertainty. As an atheist, he felt a deepening unease; he no longer knew what he believed in.

The inspector stepped out of the police car, still speaking into his phone, and approached. "No luck — Amilto's unreachable. Understandable, it's Easter Sunday."

At those words, a sharp pang of anxiety gripped Lorenzo's chest, amplifying the chill he felt despite the sun.

The memory of his last encounter with the fake Jesuit unsettled him. Other thoughts followed quickly—Domenico's backpack, packed with explosives and bolts.

A child's sudden shriek snapped him out of it. A little boy, cradled in his father's arms, had just unwrapped a chocolate egg and was waving a yellow bunny toy in delight.

All these people were in danger. He stepped closer to the inspector. "Has the bomb squad cleared the area?"

The policeman sighed. "Several times. Nothing found. We checked the cart—it left late. Four plainclothes officers are in the procession keeping it in sight. For now, everything seems fine. Let's get closer."

Near the square, police barricades created a secure corridor. From the cathedral, the sound of trumpets and drums carried over the crowd. Uniformed officers scanned the throng with watchful eyes.

"This way!" The inspector approached a barricade guarded by an officer and whispered in his ear. The man opened a gap to let them through.

The festivities had begun the night before. Lorenzo recalled flashes from the few times he'd witnessed the event: after sunset, the Corteo della Repubblica Fiorentina paraded through the city's historic streets, bearing the gonfalon. The Porta Fuoco carried the reliquary with the Stones of the Holy Sepulchre. Upon reaching the cathedral forecourt, the procession lined both sides of the central portal to witness the Paschal candle being lit in a brazier filled with fragments from Christ's tomb.

That same flame would ignite the cart's fireworks.

Lorenzo bumped into a man in a dress shirt and raised a hand in apology; the crush of the crowd was unrelenting. They followed the street kept clear for the procession, moving with the tide of music.

A middle-aged man with gray hair and glasses, leaning on the barricade, huffed and checked his watch. "The cart's late. They should be better organized."

Lorenzo didn't recall some details of the celebration, so he turned to the intelligence officer, who'd shown a strong grasp of religious ritual. "Where does the cart start from?"

"From the depot near Porta al Prato."

A shiver ran down his spine. The search for Botticelli's design kept circling back to the same places — only recently, they'd been at Porta al Prato, convinced it was the first stop on the missing map.

The cathedral forecourt lay ahead. The Flag Throwers of the Uffizi and the Musicians filled the space — eight in white and blue tunics, and eight in red and white, trimmed with velvet and satin, puffed sleeves, two-tone tights, and ankle-high leather boots. Each bore the standard of one of Florence's sixteen civil magistracies, the flags tipped with iron so they could be hurled far from the melee in battle to save them from capture.

"There they are!" someone shouted.

With a final drumbeat, the standard-bearers tossed their flags high, spun, and caught them mid-air. Applause rippled through the square.

The long-awaited cart appeared at last, drawn by two pairs of white oxen draped in flower-strewn cloths bearing the lily emblem. Behind it marched a column of some one hundred and fifty participants — armed guards, musicians, and flag throwers from the Historic Procession of the Florentine Republic — all in period costume, moving with solemn precision.

The cart, decked in fireworks, halted between the Baptistery and the Cathedral to await Mass. City officials and clergy filed into the nave, and the archbishop blessed both cart and crowd, sprinkling holy water. Two attendants tied a wire to the cart and strung it all the way into the basilica.

A man climbed onto the barricade, waving a small holy card and shouting above the drums: "Long live the *Brindellone!*"

Adrienne moved closer to Lorenzo. "What is it?"

"The cart. 'Brindellone' is a Florentine nickname for someone tall and gangly — maybe a bit shabby — but regarded with warmth."

"And why call the cart that?"

Lorenzo shrugged; he didn't know.

The intelligence officer joined them. "The name goes back to a celebration held by the Florentine Mint in honor of its patron, Saint John the Baptist. Back then, a hay cart would leave the Mint tower and tour the city, carrying a man dressed in rags to represent the saint. They called him 'Brindellone' because he tended to lurch about — especially after the feast in the square. From then on, the term stuck as the name for any ceremonial cart in Florence."

A gentle, patriotic warmth stirred Lorenzo's pride; he had been born in Florence, yet the city's history was so rich that even a lifetime would not suffice to know it in full.

A city that was about to be wounded.

Mass was beginning at the Duomo. Lorenzo scanned the crowd for Domenico. His eyes moved from face to face, each detail a brushstroke on a canvas he had to recognize: the arch of an eyebrow, the soft creases forming around a young man's mouth as he spoke, the stark contrast between an old man's sun-browned skin and his shock of white hair. The bald man was nowhere to be seen.

The inspector came up beside him. "What do you have, Berti?"

"I don't see him. He wanted revenge on an impostor he knew would be here. Maybe we should figure out who the victim is."

"We need more information. Stay close—you know his face."

Prompted by the inspector, Lorenzo turned his attention to the group of historical reenactors. One man wore a dark red velvet doublet adorned with intricate golden buttons that caught the sunlight; the height was right, but he was far too broad to be that fanatic.

Farther on, a young man in a sky-blue cloak trimmed in white moved with almost theatrical grace, the sharp planes of his face thrown into relief by the light. Nothing.

Frustration prickled. "What if he's inside? The target might be someone important—one of the privileged few with a seat in the cathedral."

The inspector straightened. "Let's move."

They stepped through the threshold: the nave and side aisles were packed with people, the archbishop deep in the liturgy. Lorenzo couldn't resist glancing up at the vast Last Judgment by Vasari and Zuccari dominating the central dome. The apostles and prophets loomed majestically—born not of some artificial hand, but of a deeply human genius.

A human awareness.

But they were here for something else; he had to find Domenico.

It was improper to walk down the central aisle during the service; besides, the wire was strung for the dove to glide along to the cart.

They skirted the left side. The faithful sat tall and dignified, their privilege gleaming in the gold embroidery of their garments and the glittering jewels catching the light from the stained glass.

Lorenzo froze beside a painting, struck as if by lightning. He stared. A tempera on canvas, mounted on a panel: a portrait of Dante Alighieri, flanked by Florence and the realms of the Divine Comedy. The Poet stood at the center in tunic and red cap, his aquiline nose true to tradition, holding an open book from which the first verses radiated golden beams over the city's most iconic buildings. To the left, the great battlemented gate of Hell, with the procession of the indifferent. Lorenzo swayed, bracing himself on the inspector.

It was true — every bit of it.

The gate of Hell was shown as Porta al Prato, before its height was reduced. The first step on a journey leading to the city of Dis — on Earth.

"Berti, what did you see?" The inspector's face had gone pale. "Did you recognize the attacker?"

"No. Nothing." He shook his head, regaining his balance.

It was hard to stay focused when the investigation wove so tightly between history and tradition: the Pazzi family and Savonarola, Botticelli and the portraits of the infamous who eventually drove the Medici out, flaunting their restored political weight with that ceremonial cart — on Easter Sunday.

"*Mon Dieu*," Adrienne murmured, eyes wide, fixed on the painting. She nudged her colleague from the Services, who nodded — aware of their investigation.

It made sense, yet a sharp sting of betrayal cut through Lorenzo. He'd thought of the investigation as theirs alone, a private complicity. He could not have been more wrong.

Adrienne took his arm. "We'll talk later. Right now, we have to find Domenico."

True. Lorenzo forced himself to focus and pressed on. The men in their tailored suits wore expressions that shifted between piety and boredom.

A chair in the second row stood empty—odd.

He pointed. "Inspector, why is no one sitting there?"

The inspector pulled out his radio and spoke into the microphone. "Check the seating assignment: left aisle, second row, third chair." He caught an agent by the arm. "See if there's a bag or backpack under that seat."

The man obeyed, forcing the worshippers to draw back their legs to let him pass. He bent down, reemerged, and shook his head.

The radio crackled. "Seat assigned to Mario Rossi, credited with substantial anonymous donations to the cathedral. No record of his check-in or arrival."

"How's that possible?" He looked at Lorenzo. "Only the highest political and religious figures in Florence can sit inside."

"And now..." The archbishop spread his arms, his vestments flowing from his elbows like wings. "Let us all sing 'Gloria in Excelsis Deo.'"

The first notes rang deep and resonant through the church, the organ swelling until its powerful melody filled every corner of the cathedral.

Soon they would ignite the cart—the crucial moment. Lorenzo turned toward the entrance: a black cat sat in the doorway, the telltale white tuft between its ears. Domenico's cat.

A flash of fire in the center of the church: the archbishop lit the dove-shaped rocket with the sacred flame. The pyrotechnic emblem shot forward, hissing along the wire stretched over the central aisle, bound for the cart.

The cat had moved away from the doorway.

The celebratory canvas *Domenico di Michelin* on Dante Alighieri, kept in the Cathedral of Santa Maria del Fiore in Florence.
Then, how Porta al Prato must have looked before its lowering.

3.9

Gloria in Excelsis Deo rang through the vast nave of the cathedral. A small rocket—shaped like a white dove with an olive branch in its beak—ignited and shot along a taut wire, whistling shrilly. It streaked out of the church and triggered the fireworks display. Gasps of wonder, bursts of applause. Just moments earlier, Domenico's cat had been there.

"It's outside!" shouted Lorenzo, bolting forward with the others right on his heels. The wounds from the attack still throbbed.

Smoke, lights, and sparks flared beyond the great doorway—fountains of blazing shards and shrieking whistles. As planned, the Colombina rocket was making its return run from the cart, heading back into the cathedral. If it reached its starting point, it would mean a lucky year for Florence.

Lorenzo and the others burst outside, but the firework was shooting in the opposite direction. It had been pure chance to spot the cat at the doorway just as the Colombina was launched.

Or perhaps not chance at all.

Lorenzo slowed, lungs burning, pain gnawing at him. Adrienne and the others were close behind—she was bent over more than she should have been. "What is it? Did you see him outside or not?"

"I saw the cat!"

And it was strange, seeing it there—on the threshold, right at the start of the dove's run, as if it had wanted to be seen. As if it had been there to create a diversion.

Domenico had to be inside.

Lorenzo turned back. His mind leapt to the backpack full of dynamite—then to the binoculars. For distance... or for height. The empty chair was the target, and the dynamite would fall from above.

Outside, the fireworks roared on, twenty minutes in all. Lorenzo lifted his gaze to the majestic dome; Domenico's choice couldn't have been random—he meant to hurl fire from the very work that depicted the Last Judgment.

An eight-sided structure, an octagon aligned with the cardinal points.

Lorenzo followed the line of the walkway encircling the base.

The lower panels showed resurrection, punishment, hell.

Lucifer, depicted at the farthest point from Christ.

A sudden glint betrayed the binoculars' glass. Above, Domenico was pounding his own head with his fists, his face twisted in rage. He hadn't found his target.

Lorenzo grabbed the inspector's sleeve and pointed. "He's there!"

The policeman snatched up his radio. Domenico dropped the binoculars and struck a match—it fizzled in his hand.

The intelligence agent shouted, "Everybody out!"

Adrienne bolted toward the side stairs, officers close behind. Shouts of panic echoed through the nave; chairs screeched across the marble, amplifying the chaos. People fled, while outside the cart's blasts rumbled like a battlefield barrage. Domenico lit another match—this time the flare caught.

He brought it to the backpack and let it drop; a thin coil of smoke curled down the incline.

"It has a fuse ignition!" the agent cried. He sprinted toward the Colombina, now back at its starting point and surrounded by extinguishers. Another officer ran with him.

The backpack hit the ground. They grabbed the extinguishers and smothered the explosives with foam and CO_2. Lorenzo threw himself behind a pew, heart hammering, bracing for the blast and the spray of shrapnel.

Three breaths, four. Nothing. They'd put it out.

He rose. On the high walkway, Domenico was running back and forth, striking his bloodied bald head. The inspector cupped his hands and shouted, "Careful! Don't let him jump!"

"Relax—he won't jump," the intelligence agent murmured, confident.

"How can you be so sure?"

"Because he wants to be a martyr, not a suicide."

Suicide...

Lorenzo's breath caught. Everything in this story was a circle—especially death, hell, and suicides. And he was trapped inside it.

From above, Adrienne leaned over the balustrade and smiled. She raised her arm, fingers forming an OK. They'd caught him.

Now there would be a lot of explaining to do.

3.10

Lorenzo drummed his fingers on the edge of the chair. The inspector stood beside him, impassive, hands clasped behind his back, eyes fixed on the door to the adjoining room. Inside, the intelligence officer, Adrienne, and a magistrate were putting Domenico through a relentless interrogation. Every so often, muffled voices bled through—fragments of a heated exchange that concerned him directly, yet from which he was shut out.

It was maddening not to be there. That lunatic had been following them for days, claiming he'd found Dis. Lorenzo swallowed hard, anxiety and frustration fermenting in his chest.

He couldn't stand it any longer; he had to get in. He shot to his feet, no longer able to keep his composure. "Inspector, please!"

The officer shook his head, eyes cold. "That's not possible. I've already told you."

Every minute lost stretched the distance between him and the answers he'd been chasing. "I can't just sit here doing nothing!"

"You must," the policeman replied, his voice low and sharp as glass. "Besides, it's not wise to interrupt—he's cooperating. He's already confessed to killing Obermann and Manfredi. He brags about it, calling them sinners."

"And the mastermind? The target who didn't show up at the Scoppio del Carro?"

"Domenico says he was deceived—that it was his master, and that he turned out to be a servant of the devil."

Empty words. To that fanatic, anyone could be a servant of the devil. A nagging voice told Lorenzo that the false Jesuit was behind it, but there was no evidence linking Domenico to Amilto.

They'd already brought it up with the inspector, but the report had landed like a drop of white paint in a bucket of black. Still, it might be the lever he needed to get inside, and Lorenzo meant to use it. "I think I know who his master is."

"Who?"

"I'll tell you—but first, let me in."

The official exhaled sharply. "Not possible. I've told you."

"Can I at least know if Domenico has seen his face?"

"The mastermind? He says he knows what he looks like, but not his name. We're waiting for—" The inspector stopped short, covering his mouth. He'd almost let something slip.

Realization struck Lorenzo like a punch to the back of the head. "You're waiting for the AI sketch artist, aren't you?!"

The inspector hesitated, then gave a curt nod.

Rage flared, burning away his frustration. Lorenzo struck his chest with the heel of his hand. "I am a goddamn sketch artist!" He bolted for the door; the inspector grabbed his shirt, but Lorenzo tore free, knocked, and pushed it open without waiting for an answer.

The three inside looked up, startled. Domenico sat in handcuffs at the desk. On the table lay a drawing board and scattered sheets.

The magistrate rose. "What is going on here?"

Lorenzo pulled the pen from his breast pocket and clicked it. "I'm a sketch artist, and I know the man we're looking for. If you let me talk to Domenico, we'll save a lot of time. Give me a few minutes?"

The magistrate looked at the inspector, then at him, then back to his colleague. He gave a small nod. Lorenzo stepped closer to Domenico. The fanatic's head was bandaged—a reminder of the wounds he'd inflicted on himself after the failed attack. A mocking smile spread across his face as he turned to him. "So, you claim to know my false master."

"I think I do." Lorenzo sat down and gestured with his pen toward Adrienne's notebook; she tore out a sheet and handed it to him. "But first—tell me something. Why were you so sure you'd meet your master at the Scoppio del Carro?"

"I've already told you. I was supposed to meet him, before he revealed his true nature. That bastard is a servant of Satan—hence his obsession with Botticelli: slaves to the same master."

"Botticelli wasn't a Satanist. From what I know, he was a disciple of Savonarola."

Domenico's lip curled in disgust. "For a time he followed the Saint, but then he let himself be seduced by beauty. And that's why he served the devil."

That was it? If loving beauty made you a Satanist, they were all damned. "Have you ever considered that Savonarola might have exaggerated? The fact that the Church excommunicated and executed him as a heretic should make you think."

The man trembled, then lunged at him with a growl; the intelligence officer moved like lightning, caught him, then forced him back into his chair.

Domenico kept his furious glare and spat on the floor. "Savonarola's excommunication was false — it was revoked in 2008! It wasn't even signed by the Pope, but by the pontiff's illegitimate son, and for political reasons. So don't speak of what you don't know, you blasphemous sinner!"

Lorenzo bit his tongue.

What was he thinking? If he wanted answers, he had to humor the man, not provoke him. "If the excommunication was unjust, as you say, then I understand your anger. The sense of injustice you feel is valid — I apologize for doubting it."

Domenico tilted his head and eyed him with suspicion. Then his tense face softened. "The only decent work your friend Botticelli ever made is the one about calumny — perhaps inspired by that story."

"You mean *The Calumny?*"

"That's the one!"

Lorenzo vaguely remembered the painting but hadn't known it was tied to the false accusations against Savonarola. "Being falsely accused is terrible, which is why I need you to enlighten me. Let me ask a few questions — maybe we can find your false master. Wouldn't you like him in the cell next to yours?"

He thought for a moment, then nodded.

With the man calmer, Lorenzo risked a more pointed question. "Tell me, Domenico — why were you following us?"

"Why bother asking? We both know what you were looking for." He let out a laugh, his gaze bright and far too lucid for a raving zealot talking about the infernal city on earth.

Adrienne stiffened and cleared her throat. "Well, we were looking for priceless missing works of art." The words were meant more for the law enforcement officers than for Domenico.

Shame it was only half the truth.

Lorenzo measured out the space on the paper and sketched the outline of a narrow, sharp face, to which he would later add Amilto's features. He forced his hand to remain steady despite the turmoil inside him — he was a professional. "If you've seen his face, would you recognize him?"

"I only met him once, but I remember what he looks like. I had faith in him." Domenico curled his lip, then glanced with curiosity at the drawing taking shape.

Faith. For a man wounded in his faith, this was the perfect moment to press further. "Why do you think he didn't come to the Scoppio del Carro festival?"

"Maybe because he found the entrance to Dis?"

At the thought, Lorenzo shuddered with fear. The magistrate raised an eyebrow. "What entrance?"

The conversation was drifting into theological territory — dangerous ground, where everyone had an opinion. The Vatican agent cleared his throat. "The entrance to Hell," he said with a mocking chuckle. He smiled condescendingly and twirled a finger at his temple, calling the fanatic mad.

The Vatican wanted everything buried. They wielded the same skepticism they despised when trying to win over believers. Hypocrites.

But Domenico's expression stayed grave. "If Amilto really has found the entrance, he'll act according to the lunar phases. *Esbat*: pagans hold their rites on the night of the full moon — which is in two days."

Lorenzo's throat tightened, caught between faith, superstition, and doubt. After his hallucinations, he no longer knew what to believe—or whether he could trust his own mind.

One thing at a time; for now, he would finish the drawing. He sketched in the eyes, but his elbow bumped the box on the table. "Can I have a bit more space?"

"Of course." The magistrate lifted the box without hesitation. "They're Domenico's personal effects." He set it on the floor with a heavy thud, the contents rattling inside.

Among them was a bracelet: a rosary.

Identical to Martina's. Identical to the one Amilto had used to wound his palm—after dipping the cross into some unknown substance. Lorenzo froze, pen hovering over the page. "Martina," he murmured.

"Her!" Domenico's mouth fell open, as if he were looking at an angel. "The last time my false master and I met was the week of Manfredi's murder—when I introduced him to Martina."

"Who?" The inspector leaned on the table and bent toward the fanatic. "You mean the girl who killed herself? The rapist's victim?"

Domenico nodded. "I told her about the cult, preached Savonarola's doctrines. She was interested—a believer. So when I met the master in Florence, where he gave me the uniform and the passes for the Uffizi, I brought her to meet him. But he—forked-tongued like Satan's serpent—betrayed her and raped her."

"But someone else raped her," the inspector said, frowning. "We arrested him. He killed himself in his cell."

Lorenzo remembered Martina's account: the two-toned voices, the laughter that never stopped for breath... because there had been two of them. The pieces began to fit. "They drugged her. Two men raped her."

"Yes." Domenico spat on the floor. "Lucifer's servant confessed it to me! He raped her with one of his satanist lackeys!"

Nausea rose in Lorenzo's throat. His emotions had swelled to such intensity they were no longer distinguishable, leaving only revulsion in his chest.

The facts matched. Amilto had been in Florence that day. As a portraitist, Lorenzo had met Martina after the assault. Later, as a regular at the Uffizi, he had become tangled in the research on Botticelli. "That rosary—did he give it to you?"

"Yes. The false master handed them out to enchant the faithful, so we'd all wear the same bracelet and feel part of something. That swine used faith to manipulate us."

Another piece clicked into place—that was why the fake Jesuit owned the same rosary. And since he had access to their phones, he had probably heard Lorenzo's anguish over the incident.

The pen, still on the page, traced trembling lines, guided by rage. He pictured the bastard's face—he had to finish it. Amilto's features emerged: a high forehead, hollow cheeks, jutting cheekbones. Each line stoked his hatred for that face.

He turned the sheet.

Domenico bared his teeth in a snarl. "That's him!"

The magistrate picked up the drawing. "And who is this supposed to be?"

Adrienne sighed. "His name is Guido Amilto. The inspector already has the address of his studio in Rome, but he seems untraceable."

There was still one thing Lorenzo needed to know—for himself, and to keep it from falling into the wrong hands. He leaned toward Domenico. "You know the final stop, don't you?"

"Yes, but I haven't solved it yet."

"Where is it?"

Domenico opened his mouth, but the Vatican agent darted to his ear and hissed something. The fanatic straightened. "You would truly grant me such a gift?"

The agent nodded. Domenico crossed his arms. "I've told you everything. There's nothing more."

They couldn't stoop to something so underhanded; Lorenzo shot a look at Adrienne, who stared at the floor. Just as the Church had made Botticelli's works disappear, it had worked to keep the secret of Dis buried. "So... that's how it is."

She didn't answer. This was her mission from the Vatican: to find and destroy anything leading to the infernal city, all while feigning ignorance during the investigation. Who knew what they had promised Domenico to buy his silence?

Adrienne stood, tightening the elastic that held her ponytail high and tight. "I need to talk to you." She avoided his gaze and left the interrogation room.

The fire of anger flared in his chest again—after he had already been betrayed by her once before. Lorenzo stood. "And what is it you need to tell me?"

"It's time for us to say goodbye."

3.11

Adrienne stepped out, and Lorenzo followed her into the corridor. The fluorescent light overhead flickered with a low, electric hum. His eyes burned, brimming with frustration. They stopped beside a plastic plant, and he couldn't hold it in any longer. "So this is how it is?"

"What?"

"What do you mean, what?" Was she really going to pretend nothing had happened? Lorenzo shook his head in disbelief. "I followed you to Germany, risked my life, got kidnapped and beaten. I could have blown up with that cart. I can't remember the last night I slept without nightmares, or the last time I pet a cat without wondering whether it was a demon. And in the end, I don't even deserve to know how this story ends?"

Adrienne stared at the floor, her face a mix of pain and resignation. "I don't have a choice," she murmured.

"There's always a choice," Lorenzo said, shaking his head. He knew it was a lie—one he didn't believe himself. But right now, he needed to project a confidence he didn't feel, even if the words rang hollow in his ears.

Adrienne pressed her lips together and brushed his chin with a tender caress. "There's nothing we can do. Not even I will know how this story ends. The Service has orders not to solve the mystery. No one is to know about any of this." Her voice was soft, as though she needed to justify herself.

A wave of dizziness hit him—a whirlpool of confusion and anger. Two days until the full moon and the ritual. After all the visions and inexplicable events, how could those questions be left unanswered? "And what if Amilto really had solved it? I've seen things that tore my world apart. I can't just pretend nothing happened. I need to know if it's all true. If it exists..." His voice trembled with emotion, slipping beyond his control.

He was one step from madness.

She swallowed and dropped her gaze again, the way she did when she was lying. "There are several conditions that could explain your hallucinations—it's not the first time I've investigated such cases. It could have been sleep paralysis. Or prosopometamorphopsia."

"The what?" A sarcastic laugh escaped him, though there was nothing funny about it.

"It's a documented medical condition," she said, stepping back. "It makes you see faces distorted, as if they were demons."

A sharp sting of bitterness hit him. Of all people, she was the last he expected skepticism from. "So these are the excuses you people in the Service keep on hand to shut people up about the mysteries you don't want them to investigate?"

An awkward silence followed.

But the real issue wasn't that damned map—he felt mocked. Again. He had to say it. "And what about us?" He closed his eyes, and a tear slipped free.

A pang of shame twisted his gut. Humiliating. He might as well bare every wound and finish off as the perfect image of the foolish dreamer. He pointed to his cheeks where the tears had tickled him. "You want to leave me like this?" His voice was barely a whisper.

Adrienne ran her palm over the dampness on his skin. "You're right to cry—it's the strongest emotion. We cry for sadness as much as for joy. Try laughing out of sadness—you can't."

"But you can laugh out of madness," he spat. And it wasn't a metaphor; that breathless laugh was already clawing its way up his throat. He knew he wouldn't find peace without ending this story. His story.

An officer from the Service stepped out of the interrogation room, passed them, and stopped at the head of the staircase. He leaned on the railing, staring down at the floors below.

Adrienne glanced at the agent and twisted her mouth in disgust. Then she turned her back to him, facing Lorenzo so her colleague wouldn't see her expression. She blinked and let tears fall, her mouth trembling. "There's something I need to tell you—it's the last thing I can do for you."

Lorenzo waited, fixing on one dark iris, then the other.

She stepped closer, her breath faintly scented with almond. "Stop punishing yourself for no reason. Elisabetta. It's no one's fault."

After destroying him, she wanted to save him? "You weren't there."

"True. But you know very well I understand that guilt." She sighed again, stroked his face, and kept her hand on his cheek. "Forgive yourself. Forgiveness isn't a feeling—it's a conviction. A choice."

Lorenzo broke down in tears.

His mind and heart churned; nausea rose in his throat, and anger tightened his trembling fists. Adrienne placed a kiss on his cheek. Not his lips—his cheek. Tender and pure, their bond stripped of attraction or malice. "You'd better go," she said. "And so should I."

With those last words, she turned and left him to contemplate the back of the woman who had brought him back to life only to crucify him twice over. Her footsteps echoed down the stairs. Lorenzo stood alone, staring at the empty steps.

From the corridor, two officers appeared with brisk, purposeful strides and entered the interrogation room. Moments later, they emerged, each gripping one of Domenico's arms. The fanatic's gaunt frame swung between them like a pendulum, his eyes glinting with a strange blend of madness and hope. What promises had they offered to secure his silence?

Two days until the full moon; a shiver prickled at the base of his neck. Behind them came the magistrate, and last of all, the inspector. He stopped in front of him and held out Amilto's drawing. "Thank you, Berti. We'll find him." He gave a short chuckle, folded the sheet, and tilted his head toward the fanatic. "That was a decidedly odd interrogation. Hell—do you realize? You don't believe that nonsense, do you?"

Did he believe it?

His situation was complicated. He was an artist, and art was the exaltation of the human spirit. But believing in spirituality didn't mean believing in religion—and perhaps there was a way to explain himself. "Do this: ask the AI what a star is."

Curious, the inspector pursed his lips and drew his brows together, creasing his forehead with wrinkles. Reluctantly, he took out his phone and typed; then he read the reply. "A star is a celestial body that shines with its own light; a spheroid of plasma."

Lorenzo nodded. "That's a scientific, objective definition — unassailable. But now listen to how Confucius described it: *The stars are holes in the sky through which the light of infinity leaks.*" He smiled, warmed by the elegance of the words. "Tell me — which do you prefer?"

The inspector hesitated, then admitted, "I'd say the second."

"So would I. Maybe because we're more than just bodies."

Silence followed, underscoring how mysterious their existence was. After a few breaths, the inspector looked back at his screen, pressed his lips into a thin line, and switched it off. He slid it into his pocket. "Stay available." He dipped his head and shot him a severe look. "Not like last time."

The tone allowed no reply; in fact, he didn't wait for one before following Domenico, flanked by the other officers. They vanished around the bend in the corridor.

So... was that it? Was he supposed to just drop everything?

Continuing the search alone meant going against the police, the intelligence services, the Vatican, and who knew what fanatical sects.

It meant going against Adrienne.

Would the intelligence services and Amilto look for the entrance? And what if it was all true? He drew a deep breath; there were too many thoughts to decide what to do at that moment — he'd think about it later. But the awareness inside him told him the truth: postponing was only an excuse not to make a decision.

What sense was there in leaving those answers hanging…

What meaning would that give his life? Refusing to choose was only the illusion of avoiding responsibility — and yet it was a choice in itself.

From the lower flight of the stairs rose the sound of hurried footsteps. The bespectacled technician who made AI-generated portraits emerged, his laptop strap clutched to his chest. He stopped on the landing and carefully tucked his shirt back into his trousers, rumpled from running.

A small spark of satisfaction flared in Lorenzo — a small payback against life. He fell into step beside him on the way out and flashed a self-satisfied smile. "I'm sorry, but they already have the composite sketch."

He looked him up and down, unsettled. "But… aren't you the portrait artist?"

"I am, too. But I prefer to think of myself as an artist. Goodbye."

He swept past him and went down the stairs. Poor guy — it wasn't even his fault, if progress could be blamed for anything. That was simply the way things were, and yet, in that moment, he felt as if he'd won one last battle.

But that way he wouldn't win the war.

Clinging to the past was useless — you had to ride the wave of change. From childhood, you elbow your way to find a place in the world, and it's a search that doesn't end in the *middle of the journey of our life*. He would make himself competitive again and find a place in line with his aspirations. For the simple reason that he could do nothing else. The worth of the struggle lay not in what you achieved, but in what you became.

A hint of sweetness in his chest erased the bitterness of what had happened. It felt good not to give up. He wouldn't leave those answers hanging.

Botticelli had hidden the path in his work. If he'd included it—even concealed—it was because he wanted the right people to discover it. As in paintings, where the artist hides the true message in an allegory.

Only one drawing remained that the Holy See hadn't been able to make disappear: Canto 8, not in the Vatican's hands but in Berlin. The City of Dis was in Canto 9. So even if Lorenzo couldn't follow the entire path, he could examine the panel that concealed the last step before arriving at the infernal city.

And then: *the solution is light in the eyes.*

Lorenzo left police headquarters and set his gaze on the Duomo's bell tower, in the center of the City of the Lily. Majestic and elegant enough to stir the envy of the entire world. His homeland breathed art.

It was time to return to where it had all begun: the Uffizi. He would examine in depth the painting Domenico had mentioned — *The Calumny.* And if he needed to find the light within the eyes, that museum held the most beautiful works Sandro Botticelli had ever painted.

Two days until the full moon.

3.12

Uffizi

The Japanese family in front of him moved on, but the child lingered a moment longer, hesitating before leaving. Then, in a quiet show of respect, he bowed to the painting. It was a charming gesture.

Once he'd carved a path through the crowd, Lorenzo made his way to the last work he had to examine — the very one Domenico had mentioned: *The Allegory of Calumny*. Time was running short. If Amilto really had found the entrance to Dis — whether the legend was true or not — he would be there the next day. To catch him, Lorenzo had to solve the final riddle.

The Botticelli pavilion was steeped in a soft but constant murmur, the low hum of voices mingling with the shuffle of footsteps. Most visitors spared the masterpieces no more than two minutes, more intent on ticking items off a list than on losing themselves in the art.

And he had to admit — today he'd been guilty of the same. He'd looked only at the eyes, painting after painting. Botticelli's technique was extraordinary — he mastered the interplay of light and color in the eyes of his figures to perfection. Fine, unblended brushstrokes created an astonishing range of tonal variation while keeping the colors vibrant and pure.

A child darted past, called back by a distracted father. Lorenzo shook himself. He needed to focus on this final masterpiece, which told the story of Calumny — perhaps the very calumny that had ensnared Savonarola.

The scene began with a king, seated on his throne as judge, sporting a pair of comical donkey's ears. Ignorance and Suspicion leaned in close, whispering poison into his ear. Their eyes lacked brightness — and not just their eyes. Calumny held a torch with no flame, symbolizing false knowledge. The setting — statues, reliefs, friezes — opened in a portico to the sea, evoking the architecture of Venice and its lagoon.

"Excuse me, may we?" An elderly couple stood behind him, waiting for their turn. They had their reasons.

"Of course — enjoy." Lorenzo stepped aside. He couldn't monopolize the painting.

His mind was too noisy — with thoughts about his own situation and Botticelli's past. First a servant of politics, then a follower of Savonarola, then once again a lover of beauty. The painter, too, had lived as though through many different lives.

And it had to be said — Savonarola's doctrines weren't without shades of justice. In those days, the Church's power was immense: it was the Pope who crowned kings, not the other way around. To wield that authority was to stand on the higher rung. It was nothing but political greed — far from Christian principles. Perhaps Botticelli had merely been drawn to that ideal, that vision of serving the people.

The same with the accusations of Satanism — if Botticelli had truly wanted to unleash the Apocalypse, he wouldn't have hidden the map inside a riddle. Then a thought sparked — what if Botticelli had concealed the information in his paintings using techniques of illusion?

He needed to draw on what he knew; Lorenzo pulled out his smartphone, then hesitated. What if he was still being watched?

But Amilto was on the run now, hardly at the height of his power. Lorenzo opened the artificial intelligence app, greeted by its usual friendly line across the screen, and leaned toward the microphone. "List the techniques of optical illusion."

A few seconds later, the reply came: "Optical illusions in images exploit the human visual system to create misleading perceptions. Three common techniques are: *overlap* — placing two objects over each other to make them appear as one; *contrast* — differences in brightness or color creating effects such as objects appearing nearer, farther, or differently sized; *expectation* — our perceptions are shaped by what we anticipate seeing."

An image accompanied the text: an elephant whose number of legs changed depending on where the eye focused. These were advanced techniques — and just as hard to detect. Lorenzo spoke again into the device. "How can I decode an optical illusion?"

"The best way is to change your perspective. View it from a different angle."

Good advice — not only for images, but for investigations. Lorenzo still had the final drawing before the city of Dis, the one meant to reveal the last stop. What if, instead of following Botticelli's map, he followed Dante's own journey?

In the drawing of the three beasts, the city of Poppi was marked — the very place Dante had stayed. The drawing for Canto 8 might point to another episode in the Poet's life, somewhere near the infernal city.

Lorenzo held up his phone again. "List Dante Alighieri's stops up to his stay in Poppi."

The familiar swirling pattern appeared, then the list:

1303–1304 – Verona: Guest of Bartolomeo della Scala

1305 – Bologna: Stayed in the city

1306 – Padua: Stayed in the city

1306 – Treviso: Guest of Gherardo III da Camino

Spring 1306 – Mulazzo: Guest of the Malaspina family

6 October 1306 – Castle of Castelnuovo Magra

1307 – Poppi: Guest of the Guidi family

He rubbed his temple, irritated by the faint throb of an oncoming headache. Now he could search for connections between these places, Dante, and the *Inferno*. He composed the query, and the swirling pattern returned.

"It is plausible that Dante visited Torcello, as his presence in Venice and Treviso between 1304 and 1306 is well documented. The basilica in Torcello, in the Venetian lagoon, houses one of the largest Byzantine mosaics in Italy: the Last Judgment. Scholars believe it inspired the structure of Dante's *Inferno*."

"Show me images of Torcello."

The screen lit up, and Lorenzo's knees almost buckled with excitement. The basilica's bell tower, rising before the lagoon, was identical to the towers drawn in Canto 8— standing as if hemmed in by the Styx, the infernal river described in that canto. A photo of a bridge in Torcello, known as the Devil's Bridge, showed the same architectural style as those Botticelli had painted.

Lorenzo counted Dante's stops backwards from Poppi, marked in Canto 2 with the beasts. Six cities—just as there were six missing *Inferno* drawings up to Dis. The final stop, then, was hidden in Canto 8: Torcello, whose basilica held one of the largest and oldest Byzantine mosaics of Hell, already there in Dante's time.

That was where he would have to solve the last riddle: *the solution lies in the light within the eyes*. The entrance. He had to leave immediately, in the hope of stopping Amilto and his ritual in time. Whatever one's faith—or skepticism—the fake Jesuit had to be caught.

Above, the drawing for Canto 8; below, the bell tower of Torcello.

.

Devil's Bridge in Torcello and a detail of an infernal panel.

.

The Calumny is a tempera painting on drawing, dating between 1491 and 1495, and preserved in the Uffizi Gallery in Florence. The painting depicts King Midas, punished with donkey ears by Apollo, seated on a throne in the role of a judge. Beside him, personifications of Ignorance and Suspicion negatively influence him. Calumny holds an unlit torch, symbolizing false knowledge, and drags the Slandered Man. The work reflects the tensions of the post-Lorenzo the Magnificent era and the preachings of Savonarola.

3.13

Torcello

The solution is the light within the eyes — and Lorenzo's were aching. He turned from the mosaic, his dry sockets burning, heavy lids sinking. He closed his eyes and rubbed them; hours of painstaking observation had dulled his vision, the golden lines and saintly faces dissolving into a blur that refused to sharpen.

That night, the moon would be full — time was running out. He trained his gaze on the shadows at the heart of the basilica, giving his weary eyes a rest. The central nave of Santa Maria Assunta lay in a soft haze of afternoon light. About ten tourists wandered over the geometric-patterned marble, weaving between the slender columns. Even the dark wooden pews seemed to drink in the light. By contrast, the tall windows through which the light filtered seemed incandescent.

Only one window was shrouded by a sheet of rusted metal — so corroded it was cracked and pierced, letting slivers of light seep through. Just beneath it was a small mosaic of the Venetian lagoon, complete with a compass rose pointing north — the classic depiction of the cardinal points. But it was nothing compared to the vast scene dominating the counterfaçade: a Last Judgment in which Hell was divided into six compartments—seven, if one counted Lucifer's throne.

Lorenzo studied it again—an entire wall, nearly twenty meters high. Incredible, how the details of this Veneto-Byzantine masterpiece mirrored Dante's vision so closely. Even the three beasts were there: the lion, the leopard, and the she-wolf.

And still, no solution revealed itself. Finding "the light within the eyes" in such ancient work seemed impossible. Perhaps the figures concealed some optical trick—an illusion where the lines shaped something hidden from casual sight. Like the impossible-legged elephant the AI had once suggested. But Lorenzo had no idea what he was meant to find.

"I see you're already at work." Adrienne's voice lilted behind him.

Had she followed him? He turned. "What are you doing here?"

"I came to check on you. Tonight's the full moon. I didn't expect to find you here."

True, the Vatican knew of this final stop, but not the way in. Adrienne, for the first time, wore simple skinny jeans, a sweater, and black Converse. Her ponytail was still tied high. She smiled and gestured toward the infernal mosaic. "Why didn't you call me when you figured out Torcello?"

"Because our collaboration was over—you said so yourself." That would have been reason enough, but the venom in his veins pushed him further. The sting of betrayal. He gestured at how she was dressed. "No heels, no tight dress—so this is the real you? What, you don't need to seduce me anymore?"

She flinched; the barb struck home. "Lore, I—"

"Lore? What's with the sudden familiarity?!" He struggled to control his voice. "Call me Mr. Berti, please. You've been making a fool of me all along."

"You lied to me too—about Elisabetta." She didn't back down. "And even when you finally told me the truth, you still hid how much you can't cope with that wound. You'd drawn her on the bedsheets, hadn't you?"

The blow landed hard. She had noticed—that was why she'd turned up the next day with fresh sheets, ready to erase that portrait. Lorenzo stiffened, the bitter taste of hypocrisy on his tongue. "That's different. I didn't tell you because it was my problem."

"You could have told me instead. Asked for help."

From a girl who had watched her parents murdered? "I didn't want to give up and dump that on you too."

"You're wrong." Her gaze was steady, sure. "Asking for help isn't giving up—it's refusing to. And you should have."

A small part of him warmed at her concern, but the rest drowned in resentment. "I should have told you? You, who only ever gave me half-truths?"

"If not me, then someone. A specialist. I heard your nightmares at night. You need help."

So now he was crazy. He jabbed a finger toward the mosaic, at a damned soul pierced by a devil. "This story has made me crazy. Before this, I didn't have hallucinations like the ones that—" He stopped.

Up high, beyond a sunlit window, the silhouette of a cat appeared, seated. Its shadow was nothing but a black blur against the glow—far too high for any animal without wings.

That couldn't be real. Lorenzo pointed. "Do you see that too?"

She looked up and paled. She nodded. She pulled her phone from her pocket and began typing. The animal rose, padded sideways, and vanished past the wall—only to reappear in the next window. It moved again, disappeared, then slipped behind the one covered by the metal sheet. The light spilling from its holes dimmed and flickered; the cat passed behind it, but never emerged from the next window.

Lorenzo kept his eyes fixed on the sheet, waiting for the animal to pass behind it again, breaking the beams that filtered through the holes. Nothing.

The cat was gone.

Adrienne slipped her phone away. "Where did it go?"

"I don't know." Lorenzo kept his attention on that window, his vision still spotted from staring at the light too long. He rubbed his eyes. "Looks like it disapp—" His heart slammed against his ribs.

Those spots in his sight—the light within the eyes.

Could that be the answer?

Numb, he rubbed his face. Behind his eyelids, darkness shifted into a myriad of tiny specks. He sighed to Adrienne. "Look up information on that metal sheet over the window. Was it added later, or is it original to the basilica?"

She shrugged and pulled out her phone again. Lorenzo kept staring at the window, forcing his eyes to fill with spots once more. In the afterimage, a small dot hovered in the middle, with a cross below. He swept his gaze around the church, carrying the bright phantom with him. Nothing. He ran it across the sections of the Last Judgment mosaic—still nothing.

Maybe he'd imagined it. One last time, he seared the pattern into his vision and turned to the mosaic of the Venetian lagoon: the cross aligned perfectly with the compass rose. The dot marked an island in the lagoon.

Adrienne scrolled a page on her screen. "It's original. That sheet has been part of the basilica from the beginning." She looked at him and tilted her head. "You've figured something out."

Lorenzo swallowed. "I'm afraid I know where the entrance to the infernal city of Dis is."

———— ✿ ————

The night air brushed Lorenzo's face, carrying the briny scent of the water. The full moon was both beautiful and ominous — assuming Amilto had truly found the island, and hell itself was real.

The boat lurched over an awkward wave. Adrienne cut the engine of the *Topo*, letting the small vessel drift gently in the lagoon. "All right?" she asked.

"All right." His mind was fogged with other thoughts — unbelievable, yet he had solved the final riddle. All this time he'd been certain the answer lay elsewhere, wasting days on optical illusions. Now, reinforcements from the Vatican were on their way; no police for Adrienne. The Holy See's top priority, as always, was to bury the truth.

Another wave sprayed over the bow. Lorenzo gestured toward the helm. "So, you can handle a boat too. How's your flying? Or submarines?"

"I am a secret agent, after all." She winked and opened the throttle. The *Topo* glided toward Poveglia, the abandoned islet in the Venetian lagoon. A point of light, burned into his retinas, had marked that island on the lagoon's map. Odd, he thought, that they were heading there in a boat called the *Topo* — rat — after being sent on their way by a demonic cat.

After leaving the Basilica, Lorenzo had checked: there was no ledge beneath the windows. The cat couldn't have walked that route to guide them toward the answer. Was it truly a cat, or an agent of the devil?

Adrienne pointed toward Venice harbor. "I'll have to get you ashore before Edgar arrives, unless I want trouble."

Lorenzo nodded. He'd have gone to see the place with or without her consent, and she knew it. She'd agreed reluctantly. Besides, they needed to check if Amilto was there, and he wasn't about to let her go alone.

A bolder wave slapped saltwater against the hull, and Adrienne eased back on the speed. "You were saying — about Poveglia?"

There'd been no time for research. They had barely managed to rent the *Topo* and set off. Access to the island was forbidden without special permits — which, naturally, they didn't have. Lorenzo unlocked his phone; on the screen, an aerial photo of Poveglia was unsettling: its shape mirrored Botticelli's vision of the Infernal Abyss.

He began reading aloud. "From the fifteenth century, Poveglia served as a quarantine station for plague victims. Thousands were deported there to die. In 1922, it took on an even darker role: a psychiatric hospital opened, active until 1968. Legend has it the asylum's director tortured and dissected patients, using them for grotesque experiments. One story tells of a hospital official who leapt from the bell tower, driven to madness by spirits."

"Charming little place," Adrienne murmured.

A chill ran down his spine. Lorenzo looked up—the island was close now, an indistinct, gloomy shadow. A prickling sensation crawled along his back, but he kept reading. "Attempts to reclaim the island always failed. In modern times, work began but stopped when excavations uncovered bones. It's believed half the island's soil is human remains. An open-air cemetery."

His shoulders shook—not from the cold. There was no better place for a gateway to the infernal city.

Adrienne throttled the engine down to a whisper. "I remember a news story from a few years back."

"What story?"

"Seven or eight years ago. A passing sailboat crew heard screams from the island. Firefighters found five boys from Colorado in a panic. They'd hired a lagoon taxi to drop them off for a night of ghost-hunting."

The dark mass of Poveglia loomed ahead.

Its shadow stretched across the water's surface—an illusion born of the waves. Unease coiled in Lorenzo's gut, urging him to turn back. But they were here now. "Where do we dock?"

"See the platform?"

He glanced at the aerial shot. "The octagonal one?"

"Exactly. Looks like they bricked up an entrance, doesn't it?" Adrienne cut the engine.

The lagoon's sounds sharpened: the low moan of water, faint crackles from the island—perhaps small creatures moving unseen. Lorenzo looked up information about the platform on his phone and read aloud, "The octagonal islet was built by the Republic of Venice around 1380, during the War of Chioggia, as an artillery post." So it hadn't existed in

Dante's time — but it had in Botticelli's. As if the first had found the entrance, and the second had commemorated its sealing.

The night chill slid between his clothes, as if rising from the water itself — as if it were hiding something. He had the unnerving sense of being watched by eyes that had no right to exist. Lorenzo pulled his jacket tighter, but the damp seemed to burrow into his bones. Close to the island, the air felt heavier, more oppressive.

"No other boats around. We'll take a quick look and leave." Adrienne restarted the engine, easing it forward. She reached out to the wall, fingers finding an iron ring set into the rock, and tied the boat fast.

Iron rungs jutted from the wall like a ladder. Adrienne rummaged in her bag, handed him a flashlight, and switched on her own. Then, slipping a hand under her sweater, she drew a pistol, chambered a round, and took a breath. "Shall we?"

He wanted to say no. "Let's go."

It was the first time he'd seen her armed. This was no longer a game. She climbed first, light and agile, disappearing into the gloom. Lorenzo gripped the cold, rough rung; his breath caught. A laugh rose from his gut — no, not again. He was letting his nerves win.

He went after her as she took the last step onto the platform. A sudden flash tore the night: a gunshot, and Adrienne screamed.

She dropped the pistol, which clattered over the edge and into the water, then collapsed out of sight. From the platform, beams of light slashed through the dark — others were here.

Lorenzo scrambled up, heart pounding, and came face to face with two imposing figures.

Amilto held a smoking pistol. Beside him stood the secretary, and on the other side, a man whose torch lit a face above a neck tattooed with tentacles winding up from his torso.

Adrienne lay on the ground, clutching her stomach. She showed him a palm stained with blood, then crumpled.

Mosaic in the Basilica of Santa Maria Assunta (Torcello)

Beasts: The trumpet-playing angels sound their instruments to awaken the dead. The resurrected emerge from their tombs, still wrapped in their shrouds and burial cloths. The victims devoured by wild beasts magically reappear from the throats of their predators: the lion, the leopard, and the wolf; but also the elephant, the hyena, the winged griffin, and a pair of black crows.

Punishments: The damned suffer the infernal torments of fire, darkness, ice, and serpents. The six infernal compartments depict the punishments and conditions of the damned. According to some interpretations, the six *cubicula* may contain the guilty of the other deadly sins: the lustful burn in flames, the gluttonous are forced to bite their own hands, the wrathful cool their boiling tempers in icy waters, the envious are reduced to skulls inhabited by venomous serpents, the greedy float on fire with their severed heads, and the slothful are reduced to shattered skeletons.

It is interesting how the shape of Poveglia Island resembles the structure of Botticelli's map of Hell.

Ottagono Poveglia
Built by the Republic of Venice as an artillery battery outpost around 1380

The asylum in a vintage photograph

Some remains found on the island.

Article from *Venezia Today*
recounting the story of terrified tourists rescued on the island.

CRONACA

Urlano disperati chiedendo aiuto: turisti suggestionati dai fantasmi a Poveglia

Singolare intervento nella notte tra sabato e domenica. I giovani avevano intenzione di passare la notte a caccia dei fantasmi, ma la paura ha preso il sopravvento

3.14

Lorenzo aimed the flashlight at the ground. Fresh blood darkened the weeds on the platform, spilling from Adrienne's belly. She stared at him through half-lidded eyes, her consciousness hanging by a thread.

Amilto stood motionless, the pistol still in his grip. Tightening his hold on the secretary at his side, he addressed the thug. "Get the material from the dinghy."

The man nodded. "Of course, Mr. Hamilton." Then he slipped down the far side of the artificial islet.

Hamilton? Why had the thug called him that? Amilto — Hamilton... similar sounds, an Anglicized twist. It struck a chord — where had he heard it before?

Then, as if a trunk in his memory had been forced open, Lorenzo saw it: the Botticelli pieces from the German collection, purchased by the 10th Duke of Hamilton after his bankruptcy. Amilto was simply the Italianized form of that surname. He was a descendant.

The fake Jesuit smiled, madness glinting in his eyes. "I should thank you. I already knew the final stop: the basilica. When you solved the riddle today, one of my men was there — him." He gestured toward the man with the tattooed neck, now returning with a duffel bag slung over one shoulder and a paint bucket in his other hand.

Amilto looked up at the sky. "Isn't this moon perfect? Worthy of Lucifer!" Then he turned to the thug and leveled the gun barrel at them. "Give them what they need."

The thug set down the duffel, unzipped it, and pulled out a gleaming awl. What did they plan to do? Bucket in hand, he started toward them.

Adrienne jolted, coughed, and clutched her wound. She murmured, "Buy time. Edgar's on his way."

Edgar—their colleague from the intelligence service. Buy time? How?

The thug drew closer, fixing his gaze on Adrienne. He licked his lips in a frightening way.

It was enough to light a fuse in him—he sprang forward, muscles coiled—but a gunshot sent sparks flying near Adrienne's body; Amilto had the pistol aimed at her. "Listen to me: just cooperate. We're not interested in your lives. Afterwards, we'll leave you to your uselessness."

Lorenzo didn't believe a word, but for the moment, he had no choice. The bucket sat at his feet. "What do you want me to do?"

"Draw a circle along the platform's edge, and inside it, paint a pentacle with the tip pointing north." He extended an arm toward Venice.

Lorenzo frowned at the bucket, wondering how he was supposed to manage that on a weed-choked platform. "How am I supposed to—"

The thug slapped him hard, a sharp sting flaring across his cheek. His ears rang as he fought to steady himself. No doubt now—they were deadly serious.

The man snatched the can, shook it hard, then slammed it to the ground. Raising the awl, he punched holes into the lid and lower rim, the dull clang softened by the liquid inside. Tilting the bucket, he poured out a controlled stream of paint, then flipped it upright. "Any more stupid questions?"

The words, added to the slap, scraped away what was left of Lorenzo's dignity. Adrienne coughed and sagged, losing blood, her strength draining away. Lorenzo took the bucket. He had to buy time—but every second was bleeding away. Tilting it, he began painting a circle around the platform's perimeter. "What's this for?"

Amilto gestured to the ground. "This platform is an octagon. Do you know what it represents?"

Lorenzo's mind leapt to the Tribuna of the Uffizi and its allegories. "If I remember correctly, it symbolizes the union between the earthly and the divine."

"Not union—transition." Amilto smiled. "The octagon is the bridge between the circle—the divine, the infinite—and the square: humanity. It's a gate. And like any gate, it closes a passage, seals it. But tonight, we'll open it."

Beyond the Uffizi, Lorenzo recalled dozens of sacred Christian monuments built in that same form—Castel Sant'Angelo, Florence's Duomo—structures that seemed to hum with hidden power.

Amilto seized the secretary by the hair and yanked her head toward him; they kissed in a whirl of tongues, loveless. Lorenzo finished the circle, a laugh rising from deep in his gut again.

He measured the spaces, aligned the pentacle, its point aimed toward Venice. Tilting the bucket, he began tracing the symbol. "You're performing some kind of ritual, aren't you?"

The thug laughed. "Told you not to ask stupid questions."

Amilto stepped back from the woman. "He's just curious—he wants to understand." He opened the duffel bag at his feet and pulled out an ancient book. "I promised Domenico the fulfillment of the Apocalypse: the opening of Dis to bring Savonarola's prophecies to pass."

"And?" Lorenzo finished tracing the third corner and moved to the fourth. "What would the truth be, then?"

"That is the truth. But from another perspective. We are, in fact, opening the fifth seal."

"The fifth seal?"

"Of course. Described by John in the final book of the Bible—the Apocalypse. It is inevitable. The first four seals have already been opened; we are forcing the fifth before its time, releasing the Martyrs of the Devil who dwell in Dis. We're giving Lucifer the chance to play his hand on Earth, instead of where he's confined. The rest will be broken in their appointed seasons. In the meantime, the servant who ushers in the Antichrist will not go unrewarded."

A meow.

By the desk, the cat crouched low. That cat.

Lorenzo's head swam; the laughter inside him wouldn't stop. Skepticism and faith tangled into a dizzy knot. A manic urge to laugh welled up, answering the echo of mirth reverberating through his body.

He completed the pentacle and paused. Adrienne's eyes were closed—perhaps unconscious—but her chest rose faintly. Then, still on her back, she opened them. But they weren't her eyes anymore. Her face was no longer her own: it was Elisabetta looking at him.

A sudden whirl of thoughts threatened to unmoor him; Lorenzo pressed his palm to his forehead—he had to stay lucid, keep asking questions, slow these lunatics' rite. Tearing his gaze from the apparition, or whatever it was, he addressed the false Jesuit again. "So you really believe this. How can a believer side with the forces of evil? If it were real, you'd be destroyed — how could you compete with God?"

"Of course I believe in God." Amilto handed the book to the woman. "Do you think demons have never known God, never had faith in Him? They have — but they made their choice, unlike men."

He moved to the north side, checked the pentacle's outline, and nodded. "Most people wear faith like an ornament. Sinners disobey God's commands only out of doubt. Not us. We have chosen what to make of our lives. Disbelief has given us this power. The greatest trick the Devil ever pulled was convincing the world he doesn't exist. That's why his work always has a plausible explanation — that's the mark of his presence."

The laughter still wouldn't stop. Lorenzo shook his head and repeated the phrase in his mind: the Devil's work always has a plausible explanation. Every strange event that had happened to him did, in fact, have one. Hallucinations. Phones tapped and tampered with by rich fanatics. A cat was just a cat. Or was it?

"Good." Amilto stepped into the center of the island. "Now draw the Beast. A goat in the middle."

"A goat?"

"Exactly." He raised the pistol toward Elisabetta — or Adrienne — collapsed and gasping on the floor. "You're an artist, aren't you? Then you'll be far better than Ludmilla. Only the best for the great Adversary."

How long would help take to arrive? He had to focus on the drawing, keep his grip on sanity, and play along with the satanist. Measuring the space, he began at the tail, arched the curve of the back, then shaped the head and horns. Elisabetta's eyes followed his every move—two smoldering coals set in the smile of a madwoman.

It was safer to keep talking while he drew; he mustn't look at her, must keep his mind clear. "Was Botticelli truly a follower of Savonarola?"

"He was. And he had a rare gift—he could study Dante's *Inferno* at a time far closer to Dante's than ours is. That's how he discovered the poet's journey to Dis, and hid the path for those who had faith."

"Faith in whom?" Lorenzo recalled those rambling remarks about Botticelli's figures turning away from Christ, and it shook him. "Was he a satanist?"

Amilto shook his head. "I don't think so. He was a dreamer—a lover of beauty trapped in a world that caged him, unable to adapt. First seeking art, then weighed down by the guilt Savonarola's faith brought him. Finally, he returned to beauty—and to disgrace, perhaps because of the woodcut."

Adaptation—that was what Botticelli had lacked. And so had he. Lorenzo finished sketching the goat-like face and moved on to the belly, but a sudden flutter of wings distracted him.

A white dove landed near the cat. The feline hissed, fur bristling, instead of pouncing on the dove—the prey it should have been. The bird took off again and pecked at the cat, which beat a retreat, pursued and clawed at. The two vanished beyond the platform.

Had that really happened?

His head was clearer now. Elisabetta was gone; it was Adrienne lying on the ground. The laughter in his mind faded to a murmur, and at last he could think. A memory stirred: drawings with optical effects, images designed to trick the brain, testing our ability to distinguish figure from ground. A game between figure and expectation. The solution to prevent the Apocalypse.

From the port of Venice, a series of blue flashes split the night—rescue teams were coming. Amilto growled. "Move." He tore off his jacket in harsh, jerking motions. "Hurry, or I'll kill you!" he ordered, his voice taut with urgency.

Lorenzo returned to the goat's legs. He traced lines that made sense yet were impossible, searching for the optical effect that urgency and expectation would conceal from a hurried glance.

Amilto reached his henchman, who handed him the awl. He carved lines into his wrists and arms, smearing himself with blood. He paced the circle's edge; at each point of the pentagram he swung his arm, letting drops of red mix with the paint.

Lorenzo studied the goat: the legs were there and not there at the same time. An impossible, open figure. It might work. "Done." He raised his hands and backed toward Adrienne. She was unconscious but breathing. He pressed down on her wound.

Amilto shouted to the henchman. "Check them!" He gave the drawing a quick look and nodded, then moved to the center of the platform and knelt. He set the awl's tip to his throat. "Do you know the difference between suicide and an offering? I offer my body to you." He went on in a guttural, unintelligible tongue, like the woman's.

Out over the lagoon, the rescue lights were halfway here. Amilto fell silent, eyes wide. "I see him! My lord calls me!" He laughed, plunged the awl into his trachea, and twisted, howling through the pain. Then he pulled it free; blood sprayed, and he opened a second hole in his neck, making wet, gurgling sounds.

His laughter became constant, seamless, needing no breath. Blood pulsed from each wound alternately, as if he were breathing through them—and still he laughed.

Then shock crossed his face, and the laughter stopped. The secretary's voice rose, spitting out the foul language faster and louder as she rushed to him. Dropping the book, she seized his shoulders and shook him. "Why? Why isn't it working?"

A gunshot cracked. The henchman screamed and collapsed. Lorenzo turned—Edgar was hanging from the platform's edge, pistol in hand. The flashing lights were still distant, but he'd beaten them here. He climbed up, hurried to Adrienne, pulled something from his tactical vest, and worked quickly on her wound.

The secretary shrieked and fled. Amilto lay on the ground, gasping through the wound in his throat; the henchman sprawled in the white paint, chest still.

Maybe it was over; maybe they were safe.

"She'll be fine," the agent said, still working on Adrienne's wound. He gestured toward the goat drawing. "You tricked him. You didn't draw it correctly. Were you afraid you'd really bring the Apocalypse early?"

Lorenzo sighed, shook his head, and stroked Adrienne's face. "I... don't know what to believe."

"Then why didn't you just draw it, as Amilto ordered you?"

"I don't know." He thought of Elisabetta, among the suicides. He sighed, and tears escaped. "Some risks aren't worth taking."

The optical illusion of the elephant with multiple legs is a classic example of how our brain can be tricked into perceiving things incorrectly. The image plays with our ability to distinguish between figure and background and with our expectation of how an elephant should appear. It is one of the first examples of an impossible object, meaning something that cannot exist in the real world because it violates the laws of physics.

Overlap: The elephant's legs are overlapped in such a way that some of them seem to blend into the background. This makes it difficult for our brain to clearly distinguish and correctly count them.

Contrast: The elephant's legs are darker than the background, making them stand out and even harder to distinguish.

Expectation: We expect elephants to have four legs, so our brain is predisposed to see four legs in the image, even though there are actually more.

3.15

One month later

The Apocalypse had not come. Whether it was because of his falsified design, or because it was mere superstition, no one could say.

The cool morning air carried the scent of jasmine in bloom. Lorenzo paused on the forecourt of Ognissanti, an old waypoint in their investigations. He knew he would never see that church the same way again. Perhaps no church at all.

Just a step away lay the remains of Botticelli and his muse, Simonetta — together at last, closer in death than they had ever been in life.

He could hardly believe it; his eyes were alight. He had solved it and found the door to Dis. Real or not, the infernal city would remain where it belonged.

A white dove lifted from the church roof, like the one that had chased a cat from the platform. Like the dove that sets off Florence's *Scoppio del Carro*.

It traced a perfect arc across the sky and glided over the street. The outdoor tables of the café were crowded with tourists. Among them, Adrienne stood out, in her usual black sheath dress, hair swept into a high ponytail. Her long legs were elegantly crossed at a graceful angle, sandals resting lightly on the pavement.

She had been discharged; he hadn't seen her since that day. Before then, the rules had kept them apart. In the end, the investigators had settled on an explanation that had nothing to do with the supernatural.

Adrienne sipped her espresso and set the cup back on the table. Her pale face stood out against the vivid red geraniums hanging from the café railings. She still didn't seem to have fully regained her strength, and no wonder — the violence of the past weeks had shaken them both.

Lorenzo moved closer and raised a hand to catch her attention. Their eyes met, and an irresistible pull made him smile. He was eager to reach her.

He reached her.

Adrienne's eyelids trembled, a flicker of emotion breaking through her composure. She rose and opened her arms. "It's so good to see you."

He thought, *It's so good to hold you,* but he didn't say it.

They were here for a farewell.

Lorenzo took a seat. On the table sat an espresso cup and a saucer scattered with brioche crumbs. He drew them together with his fingertip. "Are you feeling better?"

"Yes."

The waiter passed, trailing the warm scent of fresh bread and croissants. He hesitated by their table, but Lorenzo gestured that he didn't want anything. Leaning forward on his elbows, Lorenzo asked, "So, you have to leave?"

"Yes. The Holy See has given me an assignment in Spain. My flight's tomorrow morning." She toyed with the fake wedding ring on her finger and let her gaze drift past Lorenzo's shoulder toward the church. Her voice faltered. "I also stopped by to say goodbye to Alessandro. I left him some orange blossoms."

Lorenzo smiled—it was an allusion to the orange blossoms Botticelli painted in *Primavera*, the small white flowers of citrus trees. A deliberate choice. "I see you've been doing more research."

"I have." Her brow furrowed. "I also read something else. They say Sandro's tomb lies in the floor near Simonetta's because he asked to be buried at her feet."

A tear threatened to escape. Melancholy wrapped around Lorenzo, but it was a sweet sadness, steeped in love. Just as love was what he must feel for Adrienne. The day before, over the phone, she had told him she wanted to keep going, that she still wasn't satisfied, still wasn't at peace over the injustice suffered by her parents.

He, on the other hand, was doing better. But he would respect her choice. He loved her enough to let her go. She deserved to finish what she'd started.

That was happiness: creating. Completing a project, a painting, a book. To raise a child, to build a family. To create. We are made in God's image, and he is the creator.

The white dove landed near Lorenzo.

He sighed, took a few crumbs from the saucer, and scattered them on the ground. "So, this is how it ends?"

"Or just get started." Adrienne opened her bag and pulled out a slip of paper. She handed it to him. "Call this number — he's an official at the Vatican Archives. There's always a wealth of works in need of restoration, and they're looking for collaborators. AI can identify a color scale, the Pantone of an image, but it can't exactly lay down brushstrokes."

In truth, he had already found a position, though he didn't tell her. Lorenzo had done the only thing he could: he had adapted. Where the average person sees an obstacle, the wise see an improvement. He felt at peace — and above all, he had rediscovered the urge to paint.

An AI could turn pixels on and off, but what was the point of hanging a screen on a wall and passing it off as a painting? Art was something else entirely. It was meant to be savored. A girl might look beautiful in a photograph, but embracing her was another matter.

Or loving her.

Adrienne rose from the table, and the dove took flight. She smiled with sadness. She stood in silence, watching him, her eyes speaking for her. Then she sighed. "I hope you find your happiness," she said.

"And you, your peace," he replied.

They embraced once more.

She picked up her bag and set off. After a few steps, she turned back and cast him another look — there was desire in it, but also patience. Perhaps one day they would meet again.

A strange calm pervaded Lorenzo, a spirit of acceptance and independence, of forgiveness toward himself. There was no laughter. And there was no Elisabetta, except in his memories — memories cleansed of the guilt he had inflicted on himself for far too long.

He let himself sink back into his chair.

Thinking of his previous relationship, he realized he might not have noticed his ex's unhappiness, and perhaps he hadn't done everything possible to prevent the extreme act she had committed. But he wasn't God.

He hadn't done everything in the absolute sense — but he had done everything within his power. Just as he later did on the platform. Sometimes things worked out, sometimes they didn't.

He had come to understand that.

You can spend an entire life searching for change or evolution. But in the end, what truly changes us are the things beyond our control. Not necessarily some divine plan — just life itself.

After what had happened, he had resigned himself to believing, even if he wasn't entirely sure in whom. There was something greater, something intangible, that gave life meaning. It was another matter entirely to hand over power to those who exploited such beliefs. Lorenzo had learned to separate faith from religion, and in that way he could believe. He was certain a creator would not condemn his children to hell simply because life had been against them. Elisabetta and Martina were not in some place of torment and suffering. Perhaps they weren't even in paradise; perhaps they simply no longer existed, except in the memories of their loved ones. Hell — the real one — was what you endured in life.

The good news is that you can get out of it.

Lorenzo picked up a pinch of crumbs and set it on his tongue; they melted with a buttery sweetness. At the table across from him, a blonde-haired girl was reading a book. Her blue eyes danced over the page; every so often she lifted her gaze to the view and fixed it there, as if giving her thoughts a breath between the lines. There was such serenity in that gaze...

Lorenzo's fingertips tingled; he longed to draw her. She was simply dressed, in fitted jeans and a pastel T-shirt. The fair skin of her calm face seemed to catch the shades of the sky.

He could have painted her that way: with blue skin fading into white clouds, free of sudden storms. Unlike him, who carried a burning tempest inside—and couldn't hold it back.

The moment had come.

He stood and, with quiet courtesy, approached. "Good morning, miss. I'm Lorenzo. May I have a moment?"

She looked around, puzzled. She closed the book and set it in her lap. "Please, go ahead."

"I'm a painter, an artist. I would very much like to paint your portrait. I took the liberty of asking because there's something extraordinary in your face that I can't let slip away."

She blushed. "What?"

"The light within the eyes."

Thank you for reading my book.

When you enjoy a story,
recommend it, talk about it,
leave a review, spread the word.
Let's support authors
and the fiction that deserves it.

**DID YOU ENJOY THIS THRILLER?
DISCOVER THE OTHER NOVELS I'VE WRITTEN.**

FOLLOW ME AS AN AUTHOR ON AMAZON AND
YOU'LL KNOW ABOUT ALL MY RELEASES IN YOUR
LANGUAGE: EVERY STORY IS JUST THE
BEGINNING

IN THE MEANTIME...

CARAVAGGIO
COMING
SOON

INSIGHTS

I recommend reading this section only after finishing the novel to avoid spoiling the reading experience.

HOW WAS THIS BOOK BORN?

By pure chance, like most stories. I can say that it built itself. Is there a writer (especially an Italian one) who does not revere the Supreme Poet? A documentary on Botticelli's illustrations of the *Divine Comedy* lamented the great loss of not being able to admire the entire collection: the missing *Inferno* illustrations. That was enough, along with the infernal theme, to spark my research, piquing my fascination with ancient mysteries (after all, I belong to the *Indiana Jones* and *Tomb Raider* generation).

So I began working on it and gathering documentation to craft a story. The most incredible thing is that I wove this tangle of allusions in less than a month. It's rare to devise such a complex journey in so little time.

That's why it built itself.

TORCELLO

It is highly plausible that Dante visited Torcello one or more times, given that his presence in Venice and Treviso between 1304 and 1306 is well-documented. The idea that the Venetian Lagoon may have inspired the *Divine Comedy* was already suggested 110 years ago by scholar Cesare Augusto Levi. However, Pasquini rationalizes this hypothesis, stripping away any exaggeration and evaluating the clues 'scientifically.'

In the *Last Judgment* mosaic of the Basilica of Santa Maria Assunta, the infernal area is divided into six compartments—seven if we include Lucifer's throne—potentially inspiring Dante's circles of Hell. Some damned souls bite each other like the wrathful, while skulls and limbs float in the darkness, reminiscent of the slothful in the Styx. Although a river of fire is a common motif in medieval iconography, the nearby river of ice— much rarer—may well be the archetype of Cocytus, the frozen lake of the *Comedy* where Dante would place Lucifer and his three heads. Basilica of Santa Maria Assunta (Torcello) on Wikipedia

Several historical elements suggest that Dante may have visited Torcello, as explained by Professor Penni: «The first historian to write about Dante's life was his own son, Pietro, who identified Verona as the first city to welcome him. From there, he supposedly traveled to Treviso and Padua, during the very years when Giotto was also present. According to Vasari, the two knew each other. At the time, Torcello was an important center.»

The mosaics of Torcello may also be reflected in Dante's work, particularly in the image of the *Anastasis*, or the 'Descent into Hell,' a concept typical of Eastern Christian tradition. This theme appears in the *Comedy* but is absent from all other contemporary depictions of the afterlife, including those in the Florence Baptistery and Giotto's own *Last Judgment*.

POVEGLIA

The island of Poveglia, located in the Venetian Lagoon, is shrouded in mystery and legend. Despite covering only 7.5 hectares, its history is filled with macabre and eerie events. It was first used as a quarantine site during the Black Plague in the 14th century. The Venetian Lagoon was a major entry point for ships arriving from the East, many of which carried the plague. As a result, Poveglia was converted into a *lazzaretto*, where the sick were isolated and treated.

In the 19th century, the island was repurposed as an agricultural colony, but it was abandoned after just a few years due to the harsh living conditions. Then, in 1922, a psychiatric hospital was built, which remained in operation until 1968. According to legend, the asylum was a place of horrific experiments and torture, where patients were subjected to brutal treatments. It is said that the hospital's lead doctor was a ruthless and unscrupulous man who tested new drugs and medical techniques on the patients.

After the hospital closed, the island was abandoned and fell into ruin. Visiting it requires special authorization, yet many tourists are drawn to its dark and unsettling history. Some say the island is haunted by the ghosts of the asylum's patients, and that their cries and screams can be heard on full moon nights. Several visitors have reported seeing mysterious shadows and hearing strange noises.

In 2016, the crew of a passing sailboat claimed to have heard screams coming from the island. When firefighters arrived, they found five terrified teenagers from Colorado. The group had convinced a lagoon taxi to drop them off on the island for an overnight ghost hunt—an adventure that ended in sheer panic.

THE END OF SAVONAROLA

On April 8, 1498, the convent of San Marco in Florence was besieged by the *Palleschi*, supporters of the Medici and opponents of Savonarola. While the *Piagnona* bell rang in vain, the convent was attacked, the door set on fire, and the friars fiercely defended the structure throughout the night. In the end, Savonarola decided to surrender to the *mazzieri* of the *Signoria*, asking his monks to pray for him and for Friar Domenico, foretelling their martyrdom for their faith in Christ.

During the tragic transfer to Palazzo Vecchio, Savonarola suffered humiliation and violence at the hands of the enraged crowd. Welcomed with spitting, insults, and attempted lynching, the friar walked through the city's streets under the menacing glow of torches. This journey of suffering culminated in his arrival at Palazzo Vecchio, where he was imprisoned and subjected to atrocious tortures. Savonarola and other prisoners endured the torment of the *strappata* and the rope, extremely painful torture techniques designed to extract confessions.

On May 23, 1498, after 45 days of imprisonment and torture, Savonarola and two of his followers, Friar Domenico and Friar Silvestro, were sentenced to death. The sentence was carried out in Piazza della Signoria, where a towering pyre was erected.

In a sermon delivered in 1491, Savonarola had exclaimed:«The wicked will go to the sanctuary, they will break down the doors with axes and set it on fire. They will arrest the righteous and burn them in the main square of the city. What the fire does not consume, what the wind does not scatter, they will throw into the water...» This prophecy, if it can be called that, was fulfilled with remarkable precision.

Excommunication

He was excommunicated by Pope Alexander VI on May 12, 1497, but in recent years, it has been demonstrated—both through personal correspondence between the friar and the pope and through letters exchanged between the pope and other figures—that this excommunication was false. It was issued by Cardinal Archbishop of Perugia Juan López in the pope's name, at the instigation of Cesare Borgia, who hired a forger to create a fake excommunication and destroy the friar. Alexander vehemently protested against the cardinal and threatened Florence with *Interdict* unless the friar was handed over to him, so that he could save him and clear his name. However, he was so subjugated by his son Cesare that he did not act with the full extent of his power, nor did he ever dare to reveal to the world the deception perpetrated by his beloved son against a man he esteemed as a saint.

Savonarola's first sermon after the excommunication begins by pretending to engage in a dialogue with an interlocutor who reproaches him for preaching despite being excommunicated: «Have you read this excommunication? Who sent it? But suppose, by chance, that it were true—don't you remember that I told you that even if it came, it would be worth nothing? [...] Do not be amazed by our persecutions, do not be disheartened, you who are good, for this is the fate of the prophets: this is our fate and our gain in this world.» Ironically, that excommunication truly was worthless—but not for the reasons the friar thought. Unless, of course, Savonarola had somehow discovered its true origin yet chose not to reveal the truth about it.

Savonarola continued his campaign against the Church's vices, if possible, with even greater intensity, making numerous enemies but also gaining new admirers, even beyond Florence. It was during this period that he engaged in brief correspondence with Caterina Sforza, Lady of Imola and Forlì, who had sought his spiritual advice. The Florentine Republic initially supported him but later withdrew its backing, fearing papal interdict and due to the friar's declining influence. A trial by fire was also arranged, after Savonarola was challenged by a Franciscan rival; however, it never took place, as a heavy rainstorm extinguished the flames.

Adrienne

Adrienne is a complex character, deeply marked by traumatic experiences, whose personality and life choices are shaped by her past and her unique worldview.

Inspired by Constantine.

Despite her profound knowledge of spiritual and religious matters, she is often critical of religious institutions, which she perceives as hypocritical or corrupt. She frequently finds herself in conflict with figures of religious authority, both angelic and demonic, and her understanding of faith is intrinsically tied to her direct experiences with the supernatural rather than any specific religious doctrine.

Her Philosophy.

All religions are true: they are instruments used by the spiritual world. Religious diversity is not so much a competition between absolute truths but rather a broad spectrum of spiritual paths that cater to the varied needs, cultures, experiences, and existential questions of humanity. Each religion, in its uniqueness, contributes to filling the spectrum of human spiritual pursuits, offering different approaches to understanding the divine, ethics, life, and death.

Her Past.

The loss of her father in a terrorist attack driven by religious extremism left an indelible mark on Adrienne, instilling in her a deep aversion to fanaticism and the misuse of religion as a justification for violence. Her belief in the supernatural, shaped by her personal experiences, has profoundly influenced her approach to spirituality. Adrienne has chosen to serve not a specific religious doctrine, but rather the purest and most universal essence of spirituality—the one that resides at the heart of every faith and promotes the values of humanity, compassion, and solidarity.

ADDITIONAL NOTES

This book includes images of Renaissance artworks, particularly paintings by Botticelli. The inclusion of these images is not for profit but serves solely cultural and educational purposes. The content of the book is independent and does not rely on the presence of these images. I invoke the right of citation or use for educational purposes in the dissemination of information and cultural content. The images are included to enrich the text, offering a historical and visual context that helps to convey the rich cultural tradition of the Italian Renaissance. The intent is documentary and journalistic.

1.1

The *Open to Meraviglia* advertising campaign by the Italian Ministry of Tourism, which used Botticelli's *The Birth of Venus*, sparked various controversies.

1.4

On April 8, 1498, Palm Sunday, the convent was besieged by the *Palleschi*, supporters of the Medici party and opponents of Savonarola, while the *Piagnona* bell rang in vain as an alarm. The convent's door was set on fire, and the building was under assault throughout the night, with clashes between the friars and their attackers. Forty-five days later, on May 23, 1498, an enormous wooden platform was built, connecting the balustrade of Palazzo Vecchio to a large pyre erected in the middle of Piazza della Signoria, topped by a sort of cross from which ropes and beams hung. The gallows, five meters high, stood on a pile of wood and brooms sprinkled with gunpowder. Children crouched beneath the walkway, as often happened during executions, stabbing the soles of the condemned's feet with pointed wooden sticks as they passed. The ashes of the three friars, the platform, and everything burned were carted away and thrown into the Arno from the Ponte Vecchio, to prevent them from being collected and venerated by the many followers of Savonarola hidden among the crowd. Bargellini notes that «there were noblewomen, disguised as servants, who came to the square with copper vessels to collect the hot ashes, saying they wanted to use them for their laundry.»

In a sermon delivered in 1491, Savonarola had exclaimed: «The wicked will go to the sanctuary, they will break down the doors with axes and set it on fire. They will arrest the righteous and burn them in the main square of the city. What the fire does not consume, what the wind does not scatter, they will throw into the water…»

This prophecy, if it can be called that, was fulfilled with remarkable precision.

1.6
The beautiful quote: «Loving without expecting anything in return is wonderful in fairy tales. But in real life, a mature love requires a delicate balance between giving and receiving, because anything that is not reciprocal is toxic.» comes from Bert Hellinger.

1.7
Alessandro Barbero's favorite book is indeed a fantasy novel: *The Master and Margarita* by Mikhail Bulgakov. The book he is holding in the scene, however, is *Eternal War* by Livio Gambarini.

1.9
The Vatican Archives were originally called the *Archivio Segreto Vaticano*. However, in October 2019, Pope Francis changed the centuries-old title *Archivum Secretum Vaticanum* to *Apostolic Archive*.

On the binding of the Berlin collection, the name was mistakenly written as 'Bottirelli' instead of Botticelli.

The series of drawings for *The Divine Comedy*, created by Sandro Botticelli between 1480 and 1495 on commission from Lorenzo di Pierfrancesco de' Medici, includes the famous drawing *The Abyss of Hell*, housed in the Vatican Apostolic Library in Vatican City. This work is the only complete piece in the series and presents a global vision of Dante's Inferno, illustrated as a vast funnel with architectural elements and miniaturized figures. Botticelli used a silver stylus with lead for the initial lines and later refined the contours with pen and ink in ochre, gold, or black. The series consists of 92 known parchment drawings, 85 of which are in Berlin and 7 in the Vatican (*I, IX, X, XII, XIII, XV, XVI*).

1.10
La Ciriola, also commonly called *Anguilletta*, is a traditional Roman bread. Rich in crumb, it was the sandwich bread of choice for the hearty appetites of manual laborers.

1.15
D'Annunzio wrote verses in a precious edition of Dante because he was certain that the book would never be lost.

2.2
The quote «In a world that holds the stereotype of the physically strong father, mine was strong mentally» was mentioned in an interview with Benjamin Mascolo on the *One More Time* podcast.

2.4
The new *Rite of Marriage* came into effect, becoming mandatory, on November 28, 2004, the first Sunday of Advent. One of the most notable changes was in the consent formula, which replaced *prendo* ('I take') with *accolgo* ('I welcome'), capturing the imagination of many.

2.14
Savonarola was excommunicated by Pope Alexander VI on May 12, 1497, but in recent years, it has been demonstrated—through personal correspondence between the friar and the pope, as well as letters between the pope and other figures—that this excommunication was false. It was issued by Cardinal Archbishop of Perugia Juan López in the pope's name, at the instigation of Cesare Borgia, who hired a forger to create a fake excommunication and destroy the friar.

Alexander strongly protested against the cardinal and threatened Florence with *Interdict* unless the friar was handed over to him, so that he could save him and clear his name. However, he was so subjugated by his son Cesare that he did not act with the full extent of his power, nor did he ever dare to reveal to the world the deception orchestrated by his beloved son against a man he esteemed as a saint.

Savonarola's first sermon after the excommunication begins with him pretending to engage in a dialogue with an interlocutor who reproaches him for preaching despite being excommunicated: «Have you read this excommunication? Who sent it? But suppose, by chance, that it were true— don't you remember that I told you that even if it came, it would be worth nothing? [...] Do not be amazed by our persecutions, do not be disheartened, you who are good, for this is the fate of the prophets: this is our fate and our gain in this world.»

Ironically, that excommunication truly was worthless—but not for the reasons the friar thought. Unless, of course, Savonarola had somehow discovered its true origin yet chose not to reveal the truth about it.

3.11
Prosopometamorphopsia is a rare disorder that causes faces to appear so distorted that they are perceived as belonging to creatures one might describe as demonic, elfin, or monstrous.

3.13

The Lagoon Map and the Enigma of Light is merely a narrative device of my own invention.

3.15

Regarding the supposed request by Sandro Botticelli to be buried at the foot of Vespucci's tomb, it is true that they are buried near each other in the Church of Ognissanti in Florence. However, the reason may be less romantic than some believe. The family tombs of both Botticelli and the Vespucci family were located in that church. After weighing all the hypotheses, one may choose to believe in either coincidence or the romantic notion of a love that even death could not separate.

Simonetta died at the age of 23 in April 1476 and was buried in the Church of Ognissanti, which was under the patronage of the Vespucci family. Botticelli died later, in 1510.

It appears that Simonetta's tomb no longer exists. During the Arno flood of 1966, the grave of this woman—who symbolized grace, beauty, and the humanistic ideal of love in the Florentine Renaissance—vanished without a trace. That same year, the dove from the *Scoppio del Carro* festival failed to return.

ACKNOWLEDGMENTS

I would like to express my gratitude to everyone who contributed to the creation of this novel.

First and foremost, my thanks go to Elvio Ravasio for his indispensable work. A friend, but above all, a skilled professional, he was as punctual in his timing as he was in his observations. I owe him well beyond a can of paint with two holes. A special thanks to Franz for his initial suggestions, though his contribution was limited by commitments and unforeseen circumstances that arose during the process. Jaya was an incredible beta reader—always sharp, and with her compliments and enthusiasm during the reading, she encouraged me immensely. Thanks to my proofreading partner, Andrea Vanacore, and his grammatical superpower, indispensable for a text of this level. My deepest affection to Livio Gambarini, mentor and guide. My admiration for him goes beyond stylistic matters, extending to the mindset he promotes and which I share.

Finally, I mention my Sara, who—more than ever with this book—has been patient, supportive, and helpful. She was the first to read it and the first to guide me in the right direction.

Above all, thank you, reader. You give meaning to these sacrifices. I ask you to always support good storytelling, that of my fellow writers, so that fewer and fewer people miss out on the beauty of a story experienced through a book.

Thank you all—I care for you deeply.

BIOGRAPHY

Stefano Impellitteri, born in 1982, is an author, editor, and writer of thrillers and fantasy, specializing in immersive storytelling. He has been publishing since 2017 and earned a certification as an editor from the *Rotte Narrative* training institute. Actively participating in fairs and events, he employs allegories in his writing to explore the complexities of life.

After a youth spent as a drummer, he dedicated himself to fantasy fiction, always seeking a high cultural depth in his themes. He later expanded his works to include thrillers and historical mysteries, gaining strong recognition from genre enthusiasts. In 2023, he was a finalist for the *National Amazon Award*.

Dear Reader,
I have written several novels in Italian, my native language, spanning from thrillers to fantasy. Some of them may soon be translated. Here is a taste of my works:

THRILLER

IL MALE MINORE (2023) – Thriller, mystery, paranormal. A survivor investigates a femicide serial killer, becoming a target every 28 days.
LO SCIENZIATO DEL REGIME (2023) – Investigative thriller, historical crime novel set between past and present. Uncovering a 'Dr. Frankenstein' of fascism.
L'INFERNO DI BOTTICELLI (2024) – More than just a thriller: a dossier. A mix between *The Da Vinci Code* and *The Ninth Gate*. Historical enigmas, occult sects, and ancient libraries reveal the mystery of Botticelli's missing *Inferno* drawings.
I PREDATORI DI SPERANZE (2025) – Psychological thriller. Trapped in a passionless marriage, a woman discovers unsettling images of a boy held captive. A dangerous investigation begins, tangled in secrets and silence.

FANTASY

LE CRONACHE ARMONICHE (Epic-Medieval Duology) – In a world where the magic of music is real, even weapons create melodies of salvation or destruction. Harmonic warriors are chosen based on their sensitivity to music. (*The First Melody*, 2020 – *The Inner Song*, 2021).
LE CRONACHE ALCOLICHE (A Prohibition-Inspired Duology) – Here, yeast ferments not only alcohol but also generates energy for cars, machinery, and weapons. Gangsters, cops, master brewers, and prostitutes navigate a world ruled by alcohol, where each character embodies a different kind of drunkenness: melancholic, aggressive, uninhibited... (*The Beerlords of Ferment*, 2023 – *The Sommeliers of Life*, 2024).

However, to translate these stories, I need your help. If you enjoyed this novel, talk about it, share it, let others discover it. Word of mouth is the lifeblood of independent writers. From my side, all I can do is thank you.

Thank you, above all, for reading me.
See you soon!
S.

www.ingramcontent.com/pod-product-compliance
Ingram Content Group UK Ltd.
Pitfield, Milton Keynes, MK11 3LW, UK
UKHW020632211025
8501UKWH00036B/586